I0565140

The Bloody Princess

By

Al Hagan

Hexen Volume 3

he grabbed the teller by the arm and dragged her over to where they could both duck down behind a desk.

Frustrated, the robber pounded the pistol grip of his AR against the Plexiglas. "Get back here!" he demanded. It didn't do any good. The pair stayed where they were, but a young woman stepped up from the side and walked directly towards him.

"Finally," he said, and took a good look at the girl for the first time.

His breath caught in his throat. She was *gorgeous*. Blonde hair, very light-colored, framed her face and fell down past her shoulders. Her features were perfectly symmetrical, with dark eyebrows, high, delicate cheekbones, and big green eyes emphasized with a bit of eyeliner. It looked like she had a stripper's body under that light sweater, tight and toned and not an ounce of fat. Her boobs weren't huge, but that was no biggee. Anything over a mouthful was a waste.

"Holy shit," he muttered under his breath.

She looked young, maybe sixteen, but that was more than old enough as far as he was concerned. He definitely liked the low-mileage ones better. He seriously began to consider taking her with him. They were either going to get caught or they weren't, and if they weren't, then he could do anything he wanted to, couldn't he? And he could think of all kinds of things he wanted to do to that blonde. Repeatedly. He wondered if she'd scream and fight or if she was experienced and would just give in and take it. Maybe she'd even like it, once she had a real man and not the high school boys she'd been giving it up to.

He was mesmerized for a second when he saw the tip of her tongue come out and lick her lips, just a quick gesture, nothing slow and sensual, but interesting nonetheless. Abruptly, he realized that he needed to get back to business.

"Open the door," he ordered, with another head jerk, when the hottie got to the window.

"Okay," she replied. "I have to hit the release." She pointed down under the counter.

"Hurry up!" he demanded.

A little smile quirked up on one side and she kept her eyes locked on his for a second as she leaned down to open the door. He was slightly disappointed she wasn't wearing something that would show some cleavage as she bent down, but he figured he'd see it all soon enough. And have his hands on it. Yeah, she was definitely coming with him. He was already imagining her naked and sweaty, with-

Suddenly, his world exploded. It felt like he'd been hit with a baseball bat, if the bat was as big as a telephone pole and was swung by a giant trying to knock a ball out of the park. Pain blasted through his body, enough to bring tears to his eyes, and then it dulled down some to where it felt like he was only mildly on fire rather than under a blowtorch. He found himself on the floor, staring at the ceiling. People were screaming and there was shooting and movement and chaos and he was staring at his hands, which were somehow slick with blood.

This heist had obviously gone bad and they needed to get out. He tried to sit up but for some reason he couldn't, and something slid away from his body when he tried. He instinctively knew it was a part of him, and his hand shot out, grabbing the wet, slimy thing and clutching it against his stomach so more things wouldn't fall out. This was bad. This was very, very bad.

The noise dropped off, most of it, and then the little hottie walked up and squatted beside him, her long blonde hair hanging down, her big green eyes staring into his. She didn't do or say anything, just looked at him. He wasn't sure what was happening, and he just lay there, confused, mesmerized by her, until things grew dimmer and dimmer and then turned completely black.

***

Taylor kept a journal most days, writing entries when she wanted to record an event or her experiences or feelings.

I killed my first man yesterday. And my second man, and my first woman. It was probably thirty seconds for the whole thing from start to finish. Maybe less. It's hard to tell when the adrenaline is pumping through your body like it's coming from a firehose.

Three men and a woman tried to rob our bank. Texas is the only state with its own gold depository and the state started issuing gold and silver coins as currency. With everything digital crashed and everything electrical fried from the EMP, there are no bank accounts, stock markets, anything like that.

The old currency, dollar bills, is worthless, not even much good for toilet paper. Too small and stiff and non-absorbent. Don't ask me how I know. Fortunately, we, MCC, Marten Cattle Company, had a couple of battles and some smaller ambushes with a gang called Los Pistoleros de Oro, *The Golden Gunmen. The* Pistoleros *lost, badly.*

We ended them with an artillery strike that slammed down on them while they were asleep in their cozy little beds and machine-gunned the ones that tried to run away from that hell on earth. Then we executed the ones that surrendered. There's not a lot of mercy for criminals in this world right now.

Nor should there be.

The fortunate thing I mentioned about fighting the Pistoleros *is that they were making a major effort to clean out all of the jewelry stores in Dallas and Tyler and maybe some other cities. Guess who ended up with their stockpile? They certainly didn't need it any longer.*

It was actually a hassle until we expanded our warehouse space. We had pallets of ammunition cans that were stuffed with gold chains, diamond rings and bracelets, Rolex watches, you name it. And I don't mean two or three pallets. I mean dozens and dozens. Multiple 18-wheeler loads of pallets. Tens of millions of dollars' worth of stuff. Hell, I wouldn't be surprised if the retail price of all of that topped a hundred million or more. We had to keep moving it around the warehouse to get to other things so we had a good laugh that all of that gold and those diamonds were in the way.

Sounds like a nice problem to have, right?

When Texas started minting money, we swapped a few truckloads of that stuff for gold and silver coins. At the same time, we were working with our new best friend, the acting governor, to start a bank. Two banks, actually. One in Austin and one in Marshall, Texas, which is close to Louisiana, which does not have a gold depository. That means Louisiana money is paper money that is not backed by gold and not worth the full face value. Everybody wants Texas gold coin and we are happy to sell it to them. Of course, we make them pay a premium for it.

The risk we take is whether we will get anything for that Louisiana paper that we pay two-thirds of face value to get. The good news is that the governor wants to buy the leases to Louisiana's oil and gas, so the state pays us for the paper money. It's not the full face value, but it's more than we pay for it, so we make a profit and Texas makes a profit. Plus, they make another profit when they sell the leases to someone else.

Anyway, I just happened to be at the Marshall bank, running some paperwork on what should have been a quiet day, when the attempted robbery took place. Three men came in, wearing coats, which was not unusual for the weather this time of year. Then they pulled AR pistols from under their coats.

***

She had been behind the counter, behind the bulletproof Plexiglas, talking to the manager, when the robbers came in. But was it really bulletproof? Especially against rifle rounds?

None of them were sure. The teller backed up, hands up, stunned into silence. The manager screamed and they both ducked down behind his desk. Taylor stood there and evaluated the situation.

She felt the adrenaline dump into her system and the world seemed to slow down. The robbers had one guy at the counter, now raising his voice and telling the teller to get back there to her station. A second robber was at the front door, controlling access. He and a third one, off to the side, were yelling at the customers to get down on the floor.

They could have just told the robbers to get lost and they may have been safe. Maybe the Plexiglas really was bulletproof. Or maybe the robbers would have used the customers as hostages to force them to open up. But the situation just infuriated Taylor. She'd spent a couple of weeks being terrified, running and hiding from dangerous men, and she didn't have to take that any more. Now she trained multiple times every week on fighting and firearms and other weapons and she was damned good at it.

On paper targets, and sparring, that is. She'd never actually shot at anyone before, or been in a real fight. The rubber was about to meet the road this morning.

She walked up to the teller station in front of the robber. The counter under the Plexiglas was covered in steel plate and she was confident it was bulletproof. They had tested some steel sheets just like it before they put it up. Plus, there was a little surprise for would-be robbers located there, a shelf with a double barrel 12-gauge shotgun propped up on a sandbag. The barrels had been sawed off to about eight inches long and the stock cut down to a pistol grip. A small section of the steel right in front of those gaping barrels had a hole cut in it, so there was only about a quarter inch of wood veneer that the 00 buckshot would go right through.

It did. Taylor reached down like she was going to open the door, curled her fingers around both triggers, and squeezed. There was a huge explosion and she thought for a second that the weapon had blown up. It felt like a horse kicked her in the hand. She either dropped the shotgun or it flew out of her hand, leaving her holding her wrist with the other hand and cursing.

Then all hell really broke loose.

The shotgun had been positioned at waist height on a normal person. The robber took everything from both barrels from less than two feet away. It blew a considerable quantity of... stuff... from inside his body and deposited it across the bank floor in a bloody fan behind him. He hit the floor immediately afterwards, and as soon as he could take a breath he started screaming and kept it up. Scream — gasp — scream — gasp, continuously, while he poured what seemed to be quarts of blood and other wet stuff out on the floor.

All of that commotion woke up the balcony guard. Plus, the teller and bank manager and most of the customers started screaming.

The bank building had nice tall ceilings, maybe eighteen or twenty feet tall. When the Martens took the building over, they had built a runway around the walls like a second story, just wide enough for one person to walk, and shielded the side and bottom of it with sheet steel. A guard was stationed up there so he could look down on the bank floor and shoot down on any robbers.

When the robbers first came in, the guard had waited to see how they would position themselves, so he had been quiet and motionless up there, not attracting their attention. He was smart to not just start blasting away and hit customers, too. And since there were three of them, maybe he was hoping for a distraction. Taylor provided that in spades, and he was on them once she fired.

Now he whipped his own shotgun over the steel siding and blew the robber near the door straight to his maker with one shot. The load of double-aught buckshot caught him full in the chest and he hit the marble floor hard. He drew one leg up as far as it would go, and then it fell over to the side and gravity caused it to stretch back out. He never moved again. Hunters call that DRT, Dead Right There.

The next would-be robber was more of an issue.

That one was under the guard. He tried to lean over and get a bead on him, unsuccessfully. The robber tried to shoot the guard, unsuccessfully. They did a little dance for a couple of seconds, back and forth, peek-a-boo, trying to get the other in their sights without exposing themselves. Frustrated with that, the robber next tried to shoot up through the steel sheeting. The bullets didn't go through but it made the guard dance away from that section.

The customers had enough when the ricochets started bouncing around from steel plate to marble floors and walls, and with the robber at the door out of commission, the way out was open. A couple fled towards the offices, but the smart ones made a break for the door.

Taylor never could say afterwards, but maybe she thought she'd end that little standoff between the guard and the robber. There was always the chance that the guard would lose, and the robber was distracted at the moment. It was probably the perfect time to strike.

She went through the doors and little hallway to get out from behind the teller's area and onto the floor. That gave her a great shot at the robber, who had his back to her at the time.

If he had been smart, he'd have run at the first shot, she thought. *Too late now, asshole.*

She had her Glock 19 in her hands and brought it up, good stance, good position, sights on target, and stroked the trigger, just like all of those days on the pistol range. Two 9mm hollow point rounds slammed right into the zone, the middle of his torso, and she went up to put the third bullet into the back of his head in case he was wearing body armor. That's called the Mozambique Drill because it was invented there in one of those African wars, mainly to take down someone who's hopped up on drugs. It works equally well for Kevlar or chest plates. She intended to Mozambique Drill that bastard until he went down. She got two more shots into his back and he collapsed down to the floor, dropping out of her sight picture, before she could get off the next head shot.

Dropping the sights until they were back on him, she took a long look, a few seconds, and the guy was just slowly curling his legs up to his chest and twitching his head. He looked like he was head banging to some good music, but it was a sharper, more spastic movement. After a couple of seconds, it lessened and his head sunk to the floor.

Meanwhile, the guard peek-a-booed over the railing again, a quick look and then a longer one, first at the guy below him, and then at the other two men sprawled out on the floor, all of them leaking blood. Then he looked at Taylor. It was his first gunfight, too. His eyes were wide and his mouth was hanging open. He'd been a computer tech less than a year ago and he'd killed untold thousands of people and creatures on video games and in Dungeons & Dragons, but this was real freakin' life and he had dumped everything in his bladder into his pants. He probably hadn't even noticed it yet, though.

"Keep it secure here!" she yelled at him over the screaming of the wounded guy and ran for the door.

She realized that they likely had a getaway driver and she wanted him, too. There was no reason to let him get away, free as a bird. She dodged around a couple of customers who hadn't run when the shooting started and the blood puddle forming under the DRT guy and burst out the door.

Since the getaway vehicle wasn't directly in front of the bank, logically it would be to the right, and there it was, an old pickup with the tailgate down and engine running. It even had a couple of ropes tied to cargo hooks, for a guy to jump up into the bed and grab onto while the truck sped off. They'd look pretty stupid if they went sliding right out of the truck when it accelerated.

There was a woman with short dark hair looking back, intensely focused on the door of the bank.

Taylor ran up towards the passenger side, pistol up, and yelled at her "Hands up! Let me see your hands!"

The stupidity was strong in this bunch. She brought a revolver up from the seat and swung it in her direction.

Okay, maybe that wasn't such a great idea on my part, went through Taylor's mind. *I was trying to be nice. Fuck her, now.*

She danced back away from the window, stopping slightly behind the cab of the truck. The truck body was now blocking the getaway driver's shot but it wasn't blocking hers. The driver tried to turn and get her weapon pointed through the rear window but she was in an awkward position.

Taylor punched the first shot in under her cheekbone, not where she intended but they were both moving at the time. That wouldn't have been a fatal shot but the woman would have wanted it to be. It hit her upper jaw about at the gum line and came out her other cheek, really tearing the lower half of her face to shreds. Teeth sprayed out from the shot, hitting the windshield and scattering across the dashboard like bloody little dice. She turned her head away with the impact of that shot and caught three hollow points in the back of her skull. The second and third of those shots sent blood and brains squirting back out of the previous bullet holes in the skull and splashed across what remained of the shattered back window and into the bed of the truck.

There was no reason to pay any more attention to the driver at that point. Nobody was going to shoot or drive off with that much lead bouncing around inside of their skull.

She didn't know if that was their whole crew so she crouched behind the truck, scanning in all directions. No one who looked hostile was around. A couple of people were running and some others were standing there in openmouthed amazement. None of them looked like an immediate threat, so she dropped the partial magazine and slapped a new one in. She even felt safe enough to pick up the partial and put it in the carrier. Still no threats showed up, so she went back to the bank, still keeping an eye out.

Coming through the door, she holstered her weapon, raised her empty hands and called out "Don't shoot! Don't shoot!"

The guard was at ground level now and he started babbling at her, shaken up by the encounter. She wasn't much better. She was humming like a guitar string, just vibrating, like every nerve cell in her body was twitching in sync. If someone had touched her, she'd have jumped ten feet straight up.

But she did have the presence of mind to be concerned about safety. She pointed at his shotgun.

"Is that on safe? And don't point the damn thing at me when you check it!" He stopped talking long enough to make sure it was safe, and did it without endangering anyone.

"Stand outside the door. Tell people we're closed for an hour or so. But get those people out of here first." She swung a finger around the room to indicate the remaining customers, a couple that were crouched behind tables and the morons who had fled to inner offices.

"Yes, ma'am." He scurried off across the room to herd the remaining customers out, slipped in blood, and got back on track. Good thing he had the shotgun on safe.

Meanwhile, she pulled her pistol again and checked the robbers. She couldn't kick their weapons away because they had slung them and then put their coats on so it would take a bit of work to get them away from the bodies. But that's what they were, bodies. The one by the door and the one she'd shot in the back, anyway. She knew because she kicked them both hard in the side, low down in the floating ribs where it really hurts, and gotten no reaction.

The guy she'd shotgunned was still alive. He had run down on the screaming thing and was making little "ah — ah — ah" noises while he tried to hold his intestines in. They looked wet and slimy and kept trying to slide out. Blood and something else leaked through his trembling fingers, an almost clear fluid. Taylor wasn't sure what that was. She could smell shit, too, either from ripped intestines or he soiled himself. Maybe both.

She squatted down beside him. That way, only the soles of her boots got blood on them from the puddle that was flooding out of his body. He looked at her in wide-eyed amazement. She looked back at him in curiosity. They stared into each other's eyes like that until he died. It wasn't long; less than thirty seconds. She saw him go. There was light in his eyes and then over a long second or two it went out, like if you slowly said "one thousand one". His eyes went dull. It was like watching a time lapse video of water freezing over.

As soon as that happened his whole body just seemed to melt. All of the tension in his muscles went out. His hands fell to his sides and the intestines slid around a little. She watched for a few more seconds and got up when it seemed nothing else was going to happen.

I just watched a man die, she thought. *I saw the lights go out. And I was the one that turned them off. He's mine. He will be mine forever.*

She looked around. The guard was at the door, on the outside. The manager and the teller were still hiding. The customers were gone. Effectively, she was alone. The morning sun streamed in the door and the glass all around it, but otherwise the building was fairly dimly lit. She felt like a goddess in a temple. Three people had come before her, criminals, and she had chosen their fate. Death to all, the sentence to be carried out immediately. The whole thing seemed so surreal.

***

Six months ago, I couldn't have done that, Taylor wrote the next day. *I couldn't have just looked at the guy and his horrific wound like that. Eric knew that was one thing that affected people in combat, though, so he made sure that we gutted, skinned, and butchered a few hogs and cows. Once*

15

you've had your bare hands in animal guts, with blood up past the elbows and smeared on your face a few times it's not so bad to look at a human's blood and guts. Sure, there's a difference because it is a human, but blood and guts pretty much look like blood and guts no matter the animal.

By the way, as soon as your hands are thoroughly bloody, your nose will itch. It happens every single time. I think it's a law of nature or something.

Anyway, I was still buzzing from the adrenaline. That does some weird things to you. This wasn't that bullshit little riding-a-roller-coaster adrenaline, either. This was people-are-shooting-and-bodies-are-hitting-the-floor adrenaline. The real stuff. The two hundred proof. The genuine, pure and unadulterated life-and-death stuff. People have tried to tell me what it's like but words fail to describe it. I don't think anyone can adequately portray the experience. You have to go through it yourself. Otherwise, it's someone attempting to describe color to the blind.

I'm fifteen and I feel very adult. Eric and Dani had to fight their way up here from Houston, to get to his house. They were just trying to travel and they kept getting attacked by people. Bandits. I've heard the stories over the past seven or eight months, and of course there was the fight with the Pistoleros. *I guess I have kind of thought it was a rite of passage, a requirement for adulthood or something, to kill a bad guy.*

Nine months ago, I was a spoiled little rich brat. If Hexen hadn't hit I might have been in beauty pageants, maybe done some modelling, Miss Teen USA, who knows what absolutely worthless shit I might have done? I'd have gotten a BMW or something like that just for turning sixteen. There's no telling what I would have gotten for graduating high school. Maybe a condo wherever I would attend university. I'd have been a stuck up, frivolous little rich bitch, a useless scab on the ass of society, fit only to consume in excess.

And post selfies on social media about it all. Don't forget that shit.

The post-Hexen Me, Me right now, I'd have kicked that little bitch's ass. Not that that would have taken much. One slap and the Me-That-Would-Have-Been would have run, afraid to get her precious face marred in any way. I have to say that Hexen did do that one thing for me: saved me from becoming that worthless bitch. God, I hate that I was ever even on that path!

No, I'm something different now. I've trained hard, and I'm going to continue to train.

And I've killed bad guys.

Welcome to the new reality. You'd better be ready for the new Me.

Chapter 2

Taylor guessed that she was in charge for the moment. No one else was coherent enough. The manager was still hiding under his desk and the teller had joined him there. She rapped on the Plexiglas and called the woman's name until she cautiously poked her head up from behind the desk.

"Gimme twenty dollars from petty cash. Two tens." Taylor instructed. Coins in hand, she walked outside to where a crowd was gathering to see what all of the action was about.

She held up the coins in one hand and two fingers with the other.

"I need two big, strong men. Ten dollars each for a half hour of work."

Three men and one woman stepped forward. She pointed at one pair of guys, turned, and walked back into the bank.

"I need these bodies in that truck out there. And the bitch in the driver's seat goes in the bed of the truck, too."

One of the big, strong men looked at the guy with his guts sliding out, spun on his heel, and ran out, a hand clamped over his mouth. She looked at the other to see if he was going to blow his lunch all over the floor. He didn't look like it. He looked embarrassed.

"Can you give him a moment, Miss? He'll be all right once he's, you know, empty."

"He better not throw up on my fucking floor." She didn't mean to come off loud and bitchy like that, and she realized it sounded that way, so she blamed it on the adrenaline.

"No, Ma'am. We'll mop it up if he does. We really could use the money."

She paused long enough to actually look at the guy and evaluate him. He was making an effort to look presentable, dressed in decent work clothes, shaved except for a neat beard, and bathed adequately not too long ago. She appreciated that. Too many people thought that the end of civilization meant that they could just let their looks go all to hell. She made a decision.

"I'll tell you what. I'll make you the best deal you'll get all year. You can have that truck out there, plus the ten bucks each I promised you. But I want this place clean enough to eat off of this floor. I want the bodies gone. I don't care what you do with them. Just get them out of here and out of the parking lot."

The expression on the man's face was priceless. It lit up like he'd gotten the best Christmas present ever. Tears might have even come to his eyes. He took her hand in both of his and shook it, thanking her profusely. The wrist was starting to hurt again but she endured.

"You're looking for work?" she asked. "Do a good job here and maybe the bank manager will talk to you about a guard position. I think we need one or two. Although I'm not too sure about your friend."

That's something she'd learned from Eric. Offer someone a possibility of moving up. Pay someone a fair wage for what they're doing now, but show them a potential route to get into a better position. You might be surprised at the results.

***

The one guy gagged a few times but the other one took him aside and talked to him. Taylor couldn't hear what he said but he was using steady eye contact and a raised index finger. That toned him down some. Maybe he threatened to beat the living shit out of him if he so much as coughed again.

Whatever he did, it worked. They did a truly excellent job on the floor. They'd have polished the floor with the buffer if there had been electricity in the building. They threw buckets of water on the blood outside on the sidewalk, from where they carried the bodies to the truck, and scrubbed it with a broom, too. And the manager hired them both for guard positions. He was still in a daze and she was still hyped, so maybe she ordered him to hire them. Maybe he wasn't going to argue with a girl that had just shot and killed three people.

In the middle of the cleanup work, somebody flagged down a passing cop and told him there was trouble at the bank, so there was another issue to address.

When the police officer drove up, the guys were loading dead bodies into the bed of the truck. That didn't look suspicious at all, of course. He drew down on them, cuffed them, the whole works, and came into the bank to see if their story checked out.

Everybody pointed at Taylor to tell him what happened, so she did. She was still hyped and dropped a couple f-bombs or something because he interrupted her with "Lord, girl, you have a dirty mouth. Do you kiss your —"

He stopped abruptly and looked embarrassed. That's a Texas saying, or maybe it has a wider reach. The full thing is 'do you kiss your mother with that mouth?' It implies that profanities make your mouth physically dirty, and it would be wrong to kiss one's mother with a contaminated mouth. It's on the same order as washing a person's mouth out with soap for cursing.

What the cop had done, though, was violate one of the new customs, and that was to not remind someone of their dead friends and relatives. The Hexen pandemic had killed ninety percent of the world's population, so it's likely that a survivor's family is all dead. You don't ask who someone is related to, or do they know so-and-so who worked at the wherever, or where they are from, or pretty much anything about their background. Really the only acceptable questions are those relating to what skills a person may have. Anything else is almost always an extremely touchy subject.

Taylor thought the cop was being kind of an officious asshole so she pounced on his breach of etiquette to bring him down a few notches. She looked shocked, spun around, and hunched over with a hand to her face and mouth like she was crying. He apologized, called her "Miss", and offered a handkerchief. She reached a hand back blindly. He pressed it into her hand and she used it to rub her eyes to make them red, since she wasn't really crying.

She did cry about her parents sometimes, but they were both pretty distant. Her father had been a CEO and was always working, and her mother had been more interested in her tennis and bridge and committees for the whatever and fundraisers for the whomever. Her husband had wanted a kid, she had produced a kid, done.

Still, she didn't need to be reminded of their deaths. She turned back to the cop, giving him a sad and mad face combined, and he wrapped up his investigation. There wasn't a whole lot to it. Four people tried to rob a bank and got taken down. Screw them. End of story. Uncuff the guys so they can mop the floor and let the bank reopen for business.

Not that there weren't any laws now. It's just that ninety percent of the bullshit was gone. In a pre-Hexen world, the CSI team would have taken photos and made measurements, run ballistics, et cetera. If Marshall, Texas even had a CSI team pre-Hexen that is, but it certainly doesn't now; and the only cameras that may function are fifty-year old antiques and it may be next to impossible to even find film for them.

Next, the family and/or a scumbag lawyer might have brought a lawsuit for violating their civil rights or some ridiculous claim like that. Now, there is no family, and the lawyers are keeping a lower profile. It seems that people are a lot less offended by things when they are more concerned where their next meal is coming from, or if it is coming at all.

To cap it all off, if those guys had come in and simply asked for a job, they might have gotten one. The bank did have two guard positions open. They made a bad choice. No, that's wrong. It wasn't a bad choice. That would be like investing in the wrong company based on poor information. This was a conscious decision to commit a number of felonies, potentially including murder. They deserved every single bullet and shotgun pellet that the guard and Taylor fired into their bodies.

There was absolutely no sympathy and no regret coming from her.

And the cop knew not to push things too far. The bank was a money machine, a goose that was starting to lay golden eggs. The mayor and plenty of other people were delighted to have it in town. People were starting to come in from all around to get the gold and silver coins in return for the paper money that they didn't trust. One motel had reopened to handle the visitors, with another one being set up, plus restaurants and mechanics and other businesses were anticipating getting some of the bank customers into their establishments.

Once that money hit town, it turned over multiple times. Say someone gets a hotel room for the night. That cash goes to the hotel owner, who buys groceries and pays a maid. The maid also buys groceries. Now you have money going to a grocer, who hires people and buys produce from farmers, and so on. Every purchase causes a ripple effect. Little to none of that would happen without the bank.

When Eric and Dani first approached the mayor about opening the bank, he had jumped on it with both feet. He'd held some community meetings where he claimed it was his idea all along to open a bank, that he'd been the one to approach them, and that he'd fought stiff competition from other communities to bring the bank to his town. All of that was complete BS.

Whatever, they didn't care who took credit for it. The point is, if that cop had been a real problem, then a word to the mayor would have resulted in the police chief advising the officer that he should carry on with his other duties, with strong emphasis on 'other'.

***

Everything settled down with the cop gone and the floor clean. The bank reopened and got back to business, although the employees were still shaken up, and then Taylor's ride came.

The ranch was about sixty-something miles away, past Henderson. She could have driven herself but it wasn't a good idea to send a female out alone. That was just a fact of life now, so she had gone with an escort of two guys in full battle rattle. Since they were geared up, she'd only carried her EDC, Every Day Carry pistol and spare mags and knife. They had a shopping list — there was always a shopping list of things they needed — so they dropped her at the bank to do her work while they went on their errands.

They had both been flirting with her pretty heavily on the trip in but they were awfully quiet on the trip back. That amused her. She figured she was intimidating their manhood or something by shooting people. Encroaching on male territory. But she didn't flaunt it, and with no one talking, soon the events of the day were replaying in her head, and then the horrors that had been the fall of civilization.

Chapter 3

Civilization had ended about eight months ago. Taylor tried to look on the bright side, though.

A bird flu came out of China, like many of them do. No one knew if this one was an engineered bioweapon that got out of the lab or just a natural mutation. It didn't really matter. Either way, it worked. It worked incredibly well. It infected everyone, as in the population of the entire earth. This flu spread easily and it was fatal ninety percent of the time. You were either naturally immune, through some quirk of your genes or whatever, or you weren't. If you weren't, you died. It was that simple. About ten percent had that quirk, which meant that ninety percent of the world's population died over the space of a matter of weeks.

We called the flu 'Hexen' because the temporary designation for it was HXN2. Get it? Hexen is German for 'witch' or 'witchcraft' or something like that. It was like humanity had a curse put on it. The scientists never got around to an official designation for the flu. They probably all died first. And it was a curse for sure, but it wasn't the finale. No, that came when someone got the bright idea to EMP bomb the world. Electro Magnetic Pulse. It sounds like something you'd pay money for in a spa. Yeah, put that mud on my face and the cucumbers on my eyes and gimme a long session of that Electro Magnetic Pulse. That sounds good.

It wasn't. Not at all. What EMP does is knock out electronic equipment. All of the theories about what equipment would be shielded, through design or just chance, were wrong, or enough so it didn't matter. Did your phone survive? Well, that's nice if it did, but the towers it connects to, and the computers that route your calls, didn't, so your phone is less useful than a brick, now. We lost everything that had a circuit card, and that was almost everything. We lived in a digital society, didn't we? Well, the digits went away.

If you get through that, now you can try to feed yourself. With the reduced population, the grocery stores have maybe a month's worth of food. Are you willing to kill for it? Because plenty of people are. Or maybe you can farm? Ranch? Hunt? Fish? What's your plan for when the grocery store food runs out?

Hexen and the EMP took all the survivors down to nothing, down to a 'where do I get my next meal from?' level. Taylor thought she had a harder time than most. She figured if people were living near the bottom before Hexen, they didn't have that far to fall. They were probably raising chickens in their yards and hunting and getting by with very little and they were accustomed to it.

She wasn't, not by a long shot. She was living in the lap of luxury, had anything she wanted at her beck and call, until suddenly one night she didn't, and she was literally running for her life. Hiding to keep away from kidnappers who would rape her for the rest of her short, miserable life.

That's a damned hard fall, she thought. *Awfully hard. I don't want that to happen to any fourteen-year-old girl, no matter who she is.*

Liz Mitchell was the neighbor that took her in, along with two other kids. Orphans, although people didn't use that term any more. When ninety percent of the world dies, kids are orphans. It's a given. To call them orphans is redundant. Things were okay for a little while, meaning that they were eating, but then there was a lot of gunfire and columns of smoke, and the little group ran.

Ms. Mitchell led them east out of the Dallas-Fort Worth metroplex, that word "metroplex" apparently being a name for endless subdivisions that looked the same. They found houses to stay in, abandoned houses. The owner's bodies were out there by the side of a highway somewhere, rotting. Or maybe they survived. The odds were against it, but it was a possibility.

They ate their food, slept in their beds, took their canned food and bottled water, and kept moving. Taylor never asked Ms. Mitchell where they were heading. It was probably just 'away'. That was a pretty common destination. Lots of people headed there.

They picked up another kid along the way, and left a dead body. In one subdivision there was a man that had stayed in his house, and he invited them in. He cooked supper and heated water on the grill for baths and things seemed to be not so bad until later, after he'd been drinking.

She'd thought the man was a creep, but she'd been brought up to be courteous and so she'd put up with him. He'd sat beside her on the couch, putting his arm on the back, almost around her shoulders. He'd asked her age, and if she had a boyfriend, and some other things. If she wore a bikini at the pool. If she slept in pajamas or just panties and a t-shirt. Ms. Mitchell had come back into the room in time to hear that one.

"What kind of question is that to ask a fourteen-year-old girl?" she'd demanded.

"I was just going to offer some of my son's clothing if she needed a t-shirt or anything," he'd answered.

There was a tense silence for a couple of seconds before Taylor said she was tired and wanted to go to sleep. What she really wanted to do was to get out of the situation.

Later on that night, Taylor woke up. She had a moment of confusion before she remembered where she was. The room had apparently belonged to a teenaged boy from the looks of it. And by the scent. The sheets hadn't been laundered and she could smell him. A week ago, she'd have put her foot down and absolutely refused to sleep in that bed, but she was quickly learning that this world didn't quite work that way. She turned her nose up at a lot fewer things than she had previously.

What woke her up was Ms. Mitchell fumbling around with a candle. It didn't provide much light, and she was digging in the closet for something while trying to keep from setting the clothes hanging there on fire.

"What? What's going on?" Taylor asked, coming fully awake, afraid that there was some new disaster happening.

The older woman stepped back from the closet with a baseball bat in her hand. "It's okay. Go back to sleep," she whispered, walking out of the room. She left the door open since she had both hands full.

Taylor rolled over and pulled the covers up, caught the boy's smell, and pulled them back down, away from her face. Then she heard the thumping sounds coming from the master bedroom.

Her mouth dropped open, thinking that Ms. Mitchell was having sex with the man, and the sound was the headboard hitting the wall. Then she realized she'd heard that sound before, at school. The baseball diamond. An aluminum bat, getting a good, solid hit in on a baseball. *Tink.* A metallic sound, not the thump of a wooden bat.

And it repeated: *Tink. Tink. Tink. Tink.* The sound grew progressively less metallic and more like it might if you hit the mattress. She concentrated hard, trying to figure out what was going on, and it all came to her in a flash, the whole evening replaying in her head at high speed. And the conclusion: the man had raped Ms. Mitchell.

Maybe it wasn't even technically rape because she wasn't fighting him, but it was rape. It wasn't romance. Maybe he gave her the choice, her or me. Or maybe that's just me being snobbish. I don't know. I tried to ask her about it once, a few weeks afterwards, and she put me off. I've never tried again. We all have things in our recent past that make us cry, our painful, open wounds, and I didn't want to remind her of that whole situation.

So, he'd raped her and then, after he'd fallen asleep, Ms. Mitchell had found his son's baseball bat and hit a few home runs on that bastard's skull. I can still hear that sound. And how it changed. I guess you could say the integrity of the target was degrading. That means once his skull was crushed it didn't make as loud a sound when she kept hitting it.

Fuck him. He deserved it.

After that they were even more afraid of people, so the group tried to stay away from any houses. The problem was that's where the food was.

They made it out into the countryside and watched one isolated house for a while. Nobody moved around it so they holed up there until the food ran out. Travelling once again, they ran into a roadblock. Not a roadblock like a red and white bar across the road and guards asking for papers in a bad German accent or anything, just a couple guys on the side of the road. They watched them through binoculars and the guys were talking to people travelling by. They were being friendly and some of the people went off with them down a side road.

I had a bike and I was the oldest kid, so Ms. Mitchell asked me to go up and ask them for food. We were getting a little desperate by that time.

I was scared. Hell, I was fucking terrified. I mean, these were exactly the people we were hiding from, dangerous looking men. My whole body was shaking so badly I couldn't keep the bike going in a straight line. But I did it. I cried a little at first and got it out of my system and did it. I rode up and U-turned so I was facing away from him so I could get a head start if he came after me.

It was Eric, and he scared me shitless. He's a handsome guy but when he's in camouflage and battle gear and all those tattoos showing he's just intimidating as hell. But he sat down to be less scary and said he would put some food out and then go home and I could pick it up after he left. He wanted me to come back the next day and talk to his girlfriend. He didn't have much food to give me but it was more than we had, which was zero.

The next morning, I went back and met Dani. She's awesome. She had a shopping bag with probably five pounds of pork chops in it. I think that was the best meal I'd even eaten in my life. Tears were running down my face when I ate it. Dani also put a note in the bag. They wanted us to come in.

Said they'd protect us. Ms. Mitchell asked me to go spend the night with them to check them out. Later on, she told me she cried when I rode off but she held her tears until after I was gone. She didn't want to scare me. I was already scared enough. For all I knew they were just luring me in so they could kill me or turn me into a sex slave or whatever. But I went.

Eric says that is the definition of bravery — not being unafraid, but being afraid and doing it anyway.

It was good, though. I rode back and spent the night. Dani and Emily kicked Eric and Phillip out of the house and we had a girls-only sleepover. It was the first time I'd laughed since Hexen. And I cried in relief. Relief, and grief for my parents, and for everything, just deep boo-hoos for a while. Dani and Emily took turns holding me while I cried. Then we all had a couple of glasses of wine while we talked and I felt very adult. The next day they sent me back with more food and we all came in that afternoon.

That's when the real work began, a whirlwind of it. Dani and Eric were working to get the local farms and ranches up and running so they were bringing people in to work. And it was work, seven days a week, from before dawn to after sundown at minimum. They were starting from scratch and had to get everything up and running. Just look at water for an example. Pre-Hexen, you turned the tap to hot or cold and got whatever you wanted, as much as you wanted. Plus, it was safe to drink.

Post-Hexen, you had to chop and split wood to start a fire to boil pots of water to sterilize it so it wouldn't kill you. And you had to move that wood from the source to the fire manually, like carry it or push a wheelbarrow. In other words, getting hot, safe water no longer took two seconds. It took hours. Without that electricity, every little thing just seemed to be excruciatingly painful to accomplish. But it had to be done. They had to set up everything to get these people to work, to keep them safe from man and beast, feed them, house them, and keep the water and latrines from killing them.

Yes, latrines. Outhouses. Remember I mentioned how far some people had to fall? Can you just imagine me, this spoiled little bitch, in a fucking outhouse? It wasn't pretty, the first few times. Not at all.

I'm a different person now, and I like myself a whole lot better.

Chapter 4

When the attempted bank robbery took place, Eric and Dani were both sticking around the ranch for a change. They had gone to so many meetings in the last few months they were sick to death of them. That was why Taylor was able to go to the bank on a brief errand. If there were meetings taking place, she was present. They weren't doing anything earthshaking, just some details that their subordinates thought they needed to sign off on. They also didn't want to be strangers to their people. They walked around, asked after people and things, pressed the flesh, and showed an interest in what was going on. That night they planned on a nice steak dinner for two, some drinks, and then some serious alone time.

Taylor knew that but also figured they would make it back in plenty of time to not disturb that alone time. They had to ride around a little to find them but not much. They were on an ATV, one with a double seat that put Dani behind Eric, like on a motorcycle. It was a powerful one and he liked to gun it and hear Dani scream just a little and clutch him tighter. They looked like they were having a good time. Dani had a cowboy hat on and she waved it when she saw Taylor. It was easy to spot that corn-silk blonde hair, even with most of it under the black baseball cap that Taylor wore backwards.

She jumped out of the truck and stood there beaming as they motored up. She had a look on her face. Something was different. Even Eric, a typical numb and clueless male, picked up on it. Something was up.

"Everything's good," she started, which Eric appreciated. He liked to hear the bottom line first, then the detail. "There was a bank robbery. Well, attempted robbery. I took one out with the double barrel under the counter. Then the guard got one. I put the Mozambique Drill on the third one, and then I ran outside to get the getaway driver. A woman. She brought a revolver up and I put four into her head and face. It was awesome!" She bounced up and down as she talked.

"Are you okay?" from Dani, concerned.

"Yeah, I'm great!" She looked at Eric. "All those shooting drills you have us do? I totally understand now. People are screaming and shooting. You don't have hearing protection, so the shots are loud. My ears are still ringing. There are lots of distractions. It's not like golf where everybody has to be quiet for the shot." She shivered as a chill ran down her back. "God, I'm still wired and that was like two and a half hours ago!" She pulled up her sleeve to show the goosebumps on her forearm.

"Maybe you'd better stay with us tonight," Dani suggested. "You probably need a few beers to calm down. And you can tell us all of the details."

"Really? I'd love to but I don't want to mess up your.... you know, alone time." She parted her lips slightly, looked at Dani sideways, and made a gesture that Eric didn't know she knew. He'd only ever seen guys from Louisiana make that gesture. She snapped the fingers of both hands, made an open fist with one hand, and then slapped the other hand flat against the hole formed by the thumb and fingers. It means to have sex.

He was kind of shocked. Not by that gesture so much, but by the transformation in Taylor. He clearly remembered the first time he saw her. He had thought of her as a scared little bunny, terrified to be out in the open and ready to bolt at the first hint of danger. Now, mere months later, she was a totally different person. She'd aged eight or ten years since that afternoon a few months ago.

And he completely agreed with Dani that they needed to sit on her tonight. He was almost certain that she was a virgin but the way she was all hyped up, he thought she might jump some guy and bang his brains out in the middle of the road tonight. He didn't want her to make a bad decision when she was aroused by the gunfight. There were waves of energy coming off of her right now, mainly sexual.

Gunfights and combat do weird things to people. The survivors usually get a huge rush of euphoria afterwards, a relief that they are still alive after people have been trying to kill them. It is not uncommon to laugh after a gunfight. And frequently that sense of being so fully alive morphs into an intense desire for sex.

He wasn't too happy with the idea of giving young girls alcohol, but he was pretty sure Dani had sneaked her drinks before. Her tolerance shouldn't be too high so Taylor may head to bed early and give them some semi-alone time later on. Bringing her back to the house was probably the best course of action for everyone.

***

They sat around the kitchen table and had some beer while Taylor filled them in on every detail. Again, Eric was struck by how much Taylor had changed. She had examined the dead bodies in detail, fascinated at the effects of the shots and apparently not a bit squeamish. She laughed as she told how the guys mopping the floor had asked her to sit down for a minute while they knelt in front of her and scrubbed the blood off of her boot soles. Apparently, she kept tracking blood around where they had already mopped and they wanted to put a stop to it.

They ate their steak, Dani sharing her plate with Taylor, and then Eric retired to the couch to read. Taylor was still hyped, talking at a hundred miles an hour, now about boys. He didn't want to hear all that. An hour or so later, Dani took a brief bathroom break and came back to find Taylor with her head on her arm on the table, finally crashed. She got Eric's attention and they worked on getting Taylor up and to bed.

She was unsteady on her feet so Eric figured it would be easier to carry her. It wouldn't be the first time he'd had to carry a drunken girl. He put one arm behind her back and slowly but inexorably swung his other arm against the backs of her knees to sweep her up into his arms. She gave a little gasp when she fell but then put her arms around his neck and snuggled her head into his chest.

"You're so strong," she murmured, eyes closed contentedly.

Dani heard that and her temper flared. As soon as it did, she tried to tone it down but she felt a spike of jealousy. She gritted her teeth and tried to take deep breaths. Eric laid his sleepy burden on her bed and stepped back. Dani pushed him towards the door, saying "I got this."

Eric figured he was in trouble and there was probably nothing he could do about it. He sat on the couch and waited. Not for long. Dani sat on the couch with a space between them and crossed her arms.

He assumed Dani had taken Taylor's boots off and tucked her under the covers but he had to ask: "You didn't smother her with a pillow, did you?"

"It's not funny!"

"Look, there's nothing between us. She's like a kid sister to me. She had a big day and she's three fourths asleep and been drinking. She didn't even know who she was talking to."

Silence.

"I love you. I want to marry you. I've already given you an engagement ring."

Silence. Then "Are you sure?"

"Yes. I am."

"She looks like your late wife. Her photos were on the dresser when I first came here."

Eric's wife had died of cancer two years before Hexen and it had almost been the death of him. Thinking of her still cut him to the core and he had to pause for a moment before he could respond.

"Well, blonde hair, green eyes. That's like saying all Latinas look alike because you have dark hair and brown eyes. Okay, so you have unusually light amber eyes, but still."

Silence, but she was thinking, not just fuming.

"How about we get married now. By a Justice of the Peace?" he asked.

Those amber eyes flicked over to look at him. "I want a Catholic ceremony... but priests do seem to be few and far between," she pondered.

"We can do both. The JP now and the Catholic one if and when we ever find a priest."

Dani slid over closer. "Really?"

He slid closer and took her in his arms. "Really."

The rest of the night went much better. And with Taylor passed out, they didn't have to worry about keeping quiet.

Chapter 5

"Rise and shine!" Dani cried enthusiastically the next morning as she threw Taylor's bedroom door open. "Let's go, *chica*!"

The *chica's* eyes fluttered but never really opened. She closed her mouth, groaned, and turned over, away from the doorway and the annoying loud girl, pulling the covers up over her head.

The annoying loud girl sat on the bed. "Yeah, I know. I had a little to drink last night, too, so we're just doing a short two-mile run this morning. And then the pistol range!" She tugged at the covers.

There was nothing but a long groan in reply.

Dani pulled the covers all the way down and slapped her lightly on the butt.

"Noooooooooooooooooooo," Taylor murmured.

Her tormenter bounced up and down on the mattress, rocking the bed.

***

It took a few minutes but she was finally up, teeth brushed, dressed in running gear, and hydrated. Definitely not happy about it, but ready for a run.

They made about a quarter mile before she stopped at the side of the road and threw up. Dani walked ahead about thirty feet to get away from the smell and turned her back because she didn't want to watch. The sound of her retching was bad enough. Eric stayed closer and kept an eye on her. If it had been Dani, he'd have stood beside her and placed a hand on her back, for support and sympathy.

He wasn't going to do that for Taylor, not after the little flare of jealousy last night. Not with Dani right there. He had to look out for himself on this one.

Taylor finished and stood, hands on hips, taking deep breaths.

"You okay?" Eric asked.

She didn't reply, just cleared her throat, spat, then turned and started running again.

A smile crept across his face, becoming a full-on grin. He was filled with pride. He remembered doing that himself when he was in the Marine Corps, puking and then carrying on with the run.

She's tough, he thought. *She'd have probably never known just how tough she is if the whole end-of-the-world thing had never happened.*

Dani turned when she heard footsteps and started running herself, but the blonde was up to speed. She blew past, her long legs going faster than she could match.

They ended the run with Taylor dry-heaving a bit at the finish line, Eric and Dani coming up a full minute behind.

"Good job," he praised. "Let's get breakfast and then hit the pistol range. I'm ashamed I'm so out of practice."

Taylor speared him with a look as she wiped the back of a hand across her mouth.

"Just target practice," he promised. "I'm not going to be throwing water on y'all or yelling just when you're about to take a shot or anything like that. I think I might be risking my life to do that to you today."

"Even with hearing protection, the noise of the gunshots is going to be bad enough," she muttered, half under her breath, as she headed in to wash up and change clothes.

That wasn't just for the amusement value, throwing water on the shooters and making noise to interfere with their shooting. Eric wanted them to be able to handle situations, not just punch holes in paper targets. If you can hit the target when you're panting from a run and someone is throwing water on you as a distraction, then you can hit the target in nicer conditions, too. It's called "embracing the suck". It means you are in a bad situation of some type but you just accept it and carry on with your mission. Just put all of the shitty physical things out of your mind and go for your goal.

And Taylor used the term a little while later, as they made their way to the range, when a light rain started up. She looked at Eric like it was his fault.

"I didn't make it rain," he protested. "I didn't know it was going to rain. Honest."

She dug her baseball cap out of her little pack, the one carrying a first aid kit, extra boxes of ammo, and a stapler to attach the targets to the wooden frames. As she put it on, she sighed dramatically and announced "I am embracing the suck."

He laughed, but with a hand over his mouth as he tried to keep it quiet. He really wasn't trying to torment the poor girl.

***

They were making progress. Eight months in and they were beginning to hammer out something that might last.

Eric had been caught in Katy, Texas, in the Houston metro region, by Hexen. The friends he'd been visiting had died and he had to make his way back home on foot and bicycle, some 200 miles or so to his property in the Piney Woods of East Texas.

Dani, born Daniela Angelina Ruiz Vasquez, had grown up in Houston, in a not-so-good neighborhood. Her parents were from Colombia, having fled the corruption and drug violence in their native country. Her father was a doctor, but he could not get a license to practice without a residency, and he had not been able to find one. So, he sold cars, and the family did the best they could.

She headed out of Houston after her parents and siblings died, going north with no destination, just away, like so many others. Four men chased her and caught her when she tried to hide in an abandoned SUV. She was holding them off with her mother's butcher knife when Eric came upon the scene.

He'd already been in a couple of gunfights just trying to travel down the road, and he knew he wasn't going to be able to warn the men off with stern words. No, it was going to take blood, and his preference was that they would be the ones spilling it. When they all lay dead, he'd gotten his first look at Dani and his mouth had dropped open.

She was *hot*.

She was tiny, standing only five foot two and maybe a hundred pounds, with waist-length raven hair and eyes an almost golden brown. He'd immediately told her he was heading north to his house and asked her if she'd like to come with him.

She'd been distraught and confused, with the ordeal she'd just been through, but it sounded like a good idea to her. After all, he had just risked his life to save her. And he was a big, strong, handsome guy. And he did know how to shoot, which was something she had just decided she needed to become an expert on. She even scooped up one of the pistols that the thugs didn't need any more.

They started training that evening, when they stopped to sleep in an office building, which was a good thing because they were attacked that night. Dani was able to finish off the men by herself, and they got into several other gunfights after that. She got to be real good at it real fast.

Despite that random first meeting they matched perfectly. Dani tended to be more big picture, which works because Eric could hammer out the details. Then they switched when it came to military things. Eric spent four years in the Marine Corps and read military history for fun, so he could plan and manage a battle. Dani can't stand criminals and she was more than happy to shoot them.

Dani was the driving force behind them hiring more people and expanding their operations bigger and bigger. Where most people saw an apocalypse, she saw an opportunity to build an empire. If ninety percent of the population was gone, that meant that ninety percent of everything was out there, just waiting for someone to take it, or take it over.

But that's not entirely selfish. Her philosophy was that if they have more, they can do more for people.

Starting out, Eric knew they needed to farm and ranch but he didn't know how to do either. He did see the possibilities of a large population of refugees, a few surviving farmers and ranchers that knew what they were doing, and numerous abandoned farms and ranches available for the taking. He simply had to put them all together and provide security for them. He did, although there was nothing simple about it.

They were managing almost twenty-thousand acres of land, mainly farmland and ranches. There were plenty of wooded acres, pine tree farms, too, but they didn't actively take those over. They just happened to be between two agricultural properties that they wanted. They were growing as much on the farmland as possible, plus had cattle, chickens, and some goats and rabbits, plus a number of ponds stocked with bass and catfish. Feral hogs were plentiful and the Security Force shot them frequently for food.

They had a smokehouse for preserving meat and making jerky and a solar-powered complex of offices and warehouses that also included a large room with rows of refrigerators and freezers. One of the warehouses was nothing but rows of shelving that they were filling up with food in mason jars, cans and boxes from stores and houses, MREs, and anything else they managed to find. A separate building held a shower on one side, with posted times for male and female use, and a laundry facility. All of the appliances were older models that were either running until they stopped or newer models that they had gotten running again.

As much as Eric hated to create a bureaucracy, some of it was a necessary evil. As operations outgrew his little house and when they received solar panels in trade, they built the headquarters. It was right down the road from Eric's place and enabled him to have his house back, mostly. Taylor took over the small bedroom downstairs and he and Dani had the upstairs master.

Taylor was kind of like a little sister, but not an annoying, evil one. She was very mature for her age. She also spent frequent nights in the HQ building on duty as the person in charge. People were up 24x365 doing something. Security was always manning checkpoints and roving patrols to keep predators away, both the coyote and the two-legged type. Others may be up late or early tending the smokehouse, running the laundry, hunting hogs, tending heifers giving birth, or getting equipment repaired that had to be running at first light.

Using the military as a model, they always had a duty officer in the HQ. That individual had two or three runners, teen boys and girls who could ride a dirt bike or ATV, to run messages or summon people as needed. In addition, the warehouse part of the complex was surrounded by tall chain link fencing with barbed wire on top. A guard manned a station inside and guard dogs roamed the area at night.

Their fire station was also in the complex and some firemen slept there every night. It was a heavy price to pay to have all of those people doing something other than producing food, but it was necessary. Without that security, a gang could descend on them without warning and take everything they had worked so hard to create. It should go without saying that all of the guards were in full battle gear, weapons and ten magazines fully loaded. The HQ building had a rack across one wall with twenty loaded AR rifles and one hundred loaded mags ready to go. Nothing was locked up. Proper training made it safe.

Another vitally important thing in rebuilding civilization was in making the connections and agreements and alliances with other groups. The existing organizations and frameworks were all gone or radically changed, by reduction in numbers if nothing else. New organizations were formed and had to be fitted into the mix.

Instead of something simple like one sheriff agreeing to work with a neighboring sheriff, for example, all of the new organizations had to be included. Take just one section of one county for example. There were State Troopers, constables, sheriff's deputies, and Texas Rangers that had jurisdiction there pre-Hexen. Post-Hexen, those were all still valid but rare. In their place might be a citizen's militia or two, who may be proficient hunters but lacking any military experience. There may also be a few private compounds, farms and/or ranches that were populated by small groups who just wanted to be left alone and tended to shoot at trespassers. Then there would be a number of people who were just off by themselves. It was highly likely that there would be a peace-loving religious commune. All of these would be spread over an area that used to contain ten times their population, so there would be a large number of abandoned properties.

Marten Cattle Company, MCC, was different. They were the biggest operation in the state as far as anyone knew, including the acting governor. It was truly a company, not an organization of landowners or partners; not a co-op or an association. Eric and Dani owned it and ran it, no questions about that. Their word was law, literally. If they tried and hanged someone, then that was the end of the story, and they had done it more than once. They were recognized as having the full authority to do so by the state of Texas.

When they had defeated the *Pistoleros* they had captured about a hundred prisoners. The next day, following the governor's declaration that the gang were terrorists, Eric pronounced the penalty of death. Dani, personally, shot them. Again, end of story. No review, no investigation, nothing.

But the intent of MCC was to help people. The best way Eric knew to do that was to grow food. Without food you had nothing. With food, you could turn people to other tasks that would bring civilization back. With that simple philosophy, they took over abandoned properties and grew food, crops and animals.

The governor, Trey Marsh, loved Eric. Eric was a man of few words and he did what he said he would do. He was too heavy-handed to be mistaken for a diplomat but he made an excellent hatchet man. He was already a feared weapon that Marsh had wielded a couple of times, and threatened to on other occasions. Eric resisted such use except where it came to assisting the rebuilding of the country. Then he was enthusiastic and jumped in with both feet. No one who had dealt with him once and survived wanted him to jump on them again. Eric wasn't a bully but if he said something was going to be done by the deadline, it had damned sure better be done.

Marsh had encouraged Eric and Dani to grow their operation and was actively providing assistance for them to do so. He had introduced them to Dave Newberry, an oil and gas man, and they were expanding into that field. After food, they all figured that oil and gas, abbreviated O&G, was the next thing civilization needed. Actually, electricity was very high on the list but there were other people working on that. Pre-Hexen, Texas produced more than one third of the crude oil for the U.S., one quarter of the natural gas, and contained 30 percent of the refining capacity. They had to get that back online.

MCC was working in two directions regarding O&G. One was to send their own Real Estate Acquisition Team out to take over East Texas oilfields for the company. All they had to do was to 'post' the properties with a painted 4x4 painted wooden post and record the property with the county clerk. If they worked and maintained the property for a year and no one came along who could prove their ownership of the property, it became MCC deeded land.

The second direction was directly supporting Newberry's operation to get the wells flowing again, the crude refined, and the product out to the customers. In return for shares in his company, MCC provided food and a security force for the oilfield workers.

That was not as simple as it may sound. The food had to be grown and then prepared — canned, jerked, salted, smoked, or whatever. Then the transportation had to be planned to use routes that were not blocked by abandoned cars, or routes had to be cleared in advance. Once the truck was loaded, other gun trucks with armed guards had to escort it to prevent it from being ambushed and robbed. Fuel had to be available.

And before any of the trucks could be used, they had to be rebuilt. Vehicles built after about 1990 contained too many electronic components that were fried by the EMP. They had to find older vehicles and bring them up to running condition. Fortunately, they could clean out almost any tire shop, auto parts store, car dealership, quick oil change, or other similar outlet that they desired. They had written authorization from the state of Texas to requisition supplies of any nature for this specific project.

Eric had no desire to ruin any small business owner so he would trade with them if needed, but there were plenty of other sources. For one, the Texas Army National Guard had provided a limited number of trucks.

They were also working with the railroad experts at Fort Cavazos to bring train engines back online. Since Cavazos is tanks and armored personnel carriers, they have their own engines and extensive railroad experience to move heavy equipment to a port for overseas deployment. Eric didn't want to take over any rail operations but he could use the cargo carrying ability for cattle and O&G and he did see the possibility of passenger rail service until the roads were cleared and new fleets of trucks and passenger cars made available.

Most cities were digging out from under the rubble of the abandoned cars, so to speak. The highest priority was generally to clear at least one lane through the major thoroughfares and expand from there. Eric imagined if you plotted the clogged roads, the cities would look like doughnut holes. Streets were being cleared inside the city but interstates and highways were not, so there was travel inside a city but not long distance. No one was really taking responsibility for the long-distance routes.

Normally the state or the federal government would handle that, but the state governments were still limited to their own cities. Austin, for example, was still too busy with Austin to work on the rest of the state to any real extent.

The federal government was missing in action. The counties didn't have enough people left to do anything with the smaller county roads. And so, the cities remained islands surrounded by ribbons of dead cars.

Chapter 6

It was just a random run into Henderson to try to find something on their list when they stopped by the Walmart/Kroger/Tractor Supply area. There were always some people there looking for work. Apparently, they were eating something since they hadn't starved but they were trying to supplement their diet or move up. The MCC trucks attracted a crowd every time. Dani tried to have a supply of food of some type to hand out for free to anyone who asked. Today it was sausage links from a feral hog.

Once that was done, Taylor adjusted her holster and magazine carrier to put them more behind her than on her hips so she didn't look armed.

She looked at Dani and said, "I want to walk around behind the buildings to the campground. Take a look at who is *not* interested in looking for a job. Want to go?"

"Sure!" Dani grabbed her rifle. She had a long sling on it so she could hang it around her shoulder and neck yet have it ride in front at waist level. That way she could bring it up to fire without having to unsling it. Or she could just let go of it and it would still stay with her. It was a new thing she was trying out. She let Taylor get fifteen or twenty yards in front of her and then followed. She gave Eric a head bob to follow her. He motioned for their other guys to stay with the trucks.

Eric had decided on the AR rifle and the Glock 19 pistol as the MCC standards. He didn't really prefer the AR. In fact, he carried a Springfield Armory M1A Scout Squad. Basically, this was the civilian version of the M14 rifle with the barrel cut down from twenty-two to eighteen inches. It fired the 7.62x51mm or .308 round. There were two reasons he couldn't standardize on it for everyone, one being that they were relatively rare. They only had a half-dozen. The other is that it was a big, heavy rifle with stout recoil. Smaller-framed people like Dani, Taylor, and other girls and smaller guys had a hard time carrying and firing it.

The better option, much as Eric hated to admit it, was the AR. This was based on the M16, again in a civilian version that did not allow full-auto or three-round burst fire. It weighed in at six and a half pounds instead of almost nine, and fired the smaller 5.56x45mm or .223 cartridge. Eric thought the .223 was fine for shooting coyotes but not much else, but the AR was everywhere. It seemed everyone in Texas owned a half-dozen of them, and ammunition, spare parts, and accessories were common. The last couple of gun shows Eric went to pre-Hexen, he thought they should be renamed 'AR shows'. It was like Microsoft taking over the overwhelming majority of the computer operating system market with a product that was actually inferior.

True, the AR platform was offered in many different calibers, and they did use those in some cases, but as for one standard service rifle, it was the AR in 5.56. In the case of Dani, Taylor, and a few others, they had found full-auto and three-round burst weapons. The uppers were flat tops with 10.5-inch barrels and suppressors. This made the weapon the same length as a standard AR with sixteen-inch barrel, if a little muzzle-heavy, and made them quieter and easier to control.

The Glock was also common. It was easily found in every gun shop and the 19 was a little smaller and easier to handle and carry than the full-sized model 17. It still offered fifteen rounds of 9mm and magazines were available up to thirty-three rounds, although that made for a clumsy weapon with that much magazine sticking out of the grip. The 9mm was, again, a compromise. Eric would have preferred the .45 but that was also more difficult to carry and fire.

The usual carry method was a hip holster balanced by a dual magazine carrier on the other hip, for forty-five rounds or more depending on the magazines carried. Eric went with all fifteen-rounders while the girls carried a fifteen in the weapon and two nineteen-rounders in the carrier.

They went around the building into the field, walking the pathway that had been trodden down between the tents. Two thirds of the way, Taylor spotted exactly what she was looking for. He had short blond hair, a teardrop tattoo under his right eye, and other tattoos on his neck, throat, and hands. There were probably more but that was all of his exposed skin.

They had no objections to tattoos. In fact, Eric and Dani both had quite a few tattoos, but this was prison ink. It was crudely done with makeshift tools and only in black ink, no color. Plus, if he wasn't interested in even trying to hire on with someone or get a free bite to eat then he had some other source of income.

The former con was sitting on a ragged director's chair. Taylor slowed her pace and made as if to walk on by him. He stood when he spotted her and called out to her.

"Hey, girl. You're looking mighty fine."

She turned as if she was just now noticing him, gave him a wide smile to show off her perfect teeth that had cost her father a small fortune, and turned to walk towards him. When she did that, she also went into her sexy walk, feet placed one in front of the other, like walking a tightrope, which caused her hips to sway seductively.

He liked that. He started to sway his hips, too, like he was dancing with her, although they were a distance apart. His eyes went down below her belt and remained there while she sashayed closer. Things were looking up. Here was a beautiful young blonde coming towards him, no force necessary. Long, silky hair that looked cute with a ball cap on backwards, big green eyes, black shirt, tight blue jeans. She even made those hiking boots look sexy! He enjoyed the view for a few seconds before he looked back at her face. God, she was beautiful!

Then it all went wrong for him.

She stopped suddenly, with her left foot ahead slightly, feet shoulder-width apart, knees slightly flexed. Something changed and he saw a glint in her eyes. This wasn't some innocent young girl that was going to take her clothes off in a few minutes, willingly or not. This was danger!

Hairs stood up on the back of his neck. He'd done enough prison time to know the signs and to appreciate when his feral side reacted. There was something wrong, something very bad about this sweet, innocent-seeming young girl. Not bad like prostitution or being a junkie but bad like death. She was a killer.

His whole being was screaming like that robot he had seen on the rec room TV in those old reruns: "Danger! Danger, Will Robinson!"

He saw it in what seemed to be slow motion. Her right hand, which had swung all the way behind her back, returned filled with a pistol. It was swinging up and up to point at him, her left hand coming in to meet her right and to clamp onto the pistol in a secure and practiced grip. He reached for his own weapon but he felt like he was in one of those dreams where a monster was coming after him and he was running in molasses. Too slow, far too slow. Maybe she would just turn the pistol sideways and dump the magazine in his general direction, hoping to get a hit.

That stupid little bitch doesn't know how to shoot, does she?

He felt like he'd been punched in the gut — twice — bam-bam. Pain exploded from that area through his entire body like he'd been doused in gasoline and set on fire, but deeper than that. Fire would just affect the skin and this went down to every single individual cell in his entire body, a blaze searing through him. The hits were low in his belly, right at the beltline. He went back a step to keep his balance and hunched over, the air driven from his lungs. His knees started to buckle and he stopped them from collapsing completely only with a great force of will to remain on his feet. He had learned you never go to the ground in a prison fight. He clutched his arms to the wounds, his pistol forgotten.

He looked up into those big green eyes again. She was watching him. Not shooting, not doing anything, just watching him. She wasn't smiling any more but her mouth was open, maybe like she was breathing through it. And he hadn't even done anything to her! She couldn't do this! He had rights! Things were getting dark around the edges of his vision and he put one hand out to catch himself when he fell.

"I have rights," he croaked.

Her big eyes got even bigger as they widened in surprise and she smiled again.

"Really?" she asked with a broad trill of laughter in her voice.

Laughter! That bitch! He'd beat her to a pulp for laughing at him, right after he raped her.

The pistol had been pointed down at his stomach where she had shot him, so that she could see him without it being in the way. Now she raised it. He started to bring a hand up to hold it in front of him. He didn't move it very far because it seemed so massively heavy, but it didn't matter anyway. It wasn't bulletproof.

She got good sight alignment and squeezed the trigger steadily until it broke. His last view on earth was her emerald green eyes, both open, and then there was an erupting puff of smoke but no noise, and then nothing at all.

The hundred and fifteen grain 9mm hollow point hit him squarely between the eyes and turned the lights out instantly. He dropped like a rock straight down, just slammed down hard on his ass and then fell back, knocking the chair aside. One leg stretched out but the other got trapped beneath his body. Thick, deep red blood poured up out of the bullet hole, coming up about three inches in a little geyser for seven or eight seconds before it tapered off.

Dani saw that Taylor was focused on the dead guy so she scanned three hundred-sixty degrees to make sure the guy didn't have a friend somewhere. She knew Eric was doing the same behind her, and if she turned to the right as she scanned,

50

he would turn to the left. This wasn't their first rodeo. It wasn't their second, either.

Taylor holstered her pistol and approached the body from the driest, non-bloodiest side. She found his pistol and set it aside. She was just dumping his backpack out when a game warden came around the corner.

"State Game Warden! What's going on? Who fired?" he demanded. Then he wished he'd surveyed the scene a little better from cover first. He might have just terminally screwed up.

There was a blonde girl squatting beside a body, a Latina with a rifle at the low ready position pointed not too far off from his direction, and a guy with a big rifle further back, also ready to go. All they had to do was to bring the muzzles up and start firing and he was toast.

The man spoke up immediately: "Justice of the Peace! Do NOT point your weapon at either of those two young ladies!"

The voice lashed out with years of command experience behind it and the Game Warden knew without a doubt that he needed to tread lightly here. If nothing else it was two-to-one odds, even without the blonde joining in, and they had him from two different directions. He would lose if it came to shooting. He might get one of them but the other would turn him into Swiss cheese and he didn't regard that as a fair trade at all.

He kept his hand on the pistol grip of his AR but held up the left in an "empty hand" gesture. He made damned sure to keep the muzzle pointed down, and with only one hand on the weapon he would be unable to bring it up into action with any speed. He looked at the girl with the rifle and she looked back at him coolly, not a hint of doubt or fear on her face.

She had an AR too, a short barreled one with a fat suppressor, and she held it like she knew how to use it. Casually, but ready. She didn't clutch it tightly, like it was a wild beast she was afraid to let go of. Instead, she held it with confidence and expertise. She knew exactly what she was doing with it, where the muzzle was pointed, where the trigger and safety were, and where her fingers were in relation to those controls. That made her very dangerous.

She made the same gesture briefly as he had, left hand up, then allowed her rifle to hang from the sling with a hand on the top of the receiver to keep it from swinging around and banging into her as she moved. She walked a few steps closer to him and looked him straight in the eye, unflinchingly.

"Deputy Ruiz," she stated. A slight nod in the man's direction and "Justice of the Peace Eric Marten. Marten Cattle Company."

"Oh." Of course he had heard of Marten Cattle Company. He had met some of their people several times and had been on the edge of their protectorate. They were almost a sovereign state within Texas. Word had been passed that the Martens were on a first name basis with the governor and they were to receive full cooperation at all times. And then that phrase had been repeated slowly and a little louder by his boss so that there were no misunderstandings: *Full cooperation at all times.*

In addition, Eric Marten was a JP in Rusk and Cherokee Counties and a General in the Texas Army National Guard. Those thoughts flashed through the warden's mind and then he vocalized a much deeper, more thoughtful "Oh!" as he realized exactly who the girl standing in front of him was. Not just any mere MCC employee! If that guy was Marten, then she... "You're —"

"Dani." She nodded as she said her name.

A number of thoughts raced through the Game Warden's mind. For one, it was like meeting someone famous, and not just spotting them in an airport but having them pay attention to you. For another, it was like meeting a high official, someone that you certainly addressed with respect, and not just because you were raised to show respect to everyone. And third, it was like meeting a war hero, with the attendant admiration and, admittedly, disappointment that can bring.

They've done amazing things on the one hand, but they're all too human on the other.

He'd heard Dani was tiny but it didn't really hit home until now that he saw her in person. Despite her small size she had an intensity about her that was like an unstoppable force of nature.

"I... is there anything I can help you with?" he asked.

He was kind of intimidated by that laser-like stare that she had, and those amber eyes. People said those eyes would scan the depths of your soul and could see any secrets, any weaknesses that you had. This was something else that he had heard about but didn't appreciate until he experienced it in person.

There were more than a few people that believed she was either an angel or a demon. Literally one of those creatures, not in an exaggerated sense. People said she had brought fire and brimstone down onto sinners more than once, and had killed men by the hundreds, that she had walked among the dead on battlefields and selected the souls that she would take to serve her in Hell.

Or to select the souls that she would send to Hell, depending on which side she was on. It differed with the teller of the story. There were a number of people in the area that were simply terrified of her.

He knew that she had in fact killed a large number of men but he dismissed those demon and angel stories as tall tales and superstition... but he seemed to lose track of time as those eyes grew to become his entire existence. He seemed to sink down into a world of amber, brown here, yellow there and there, combining to form an unusual...

He shook his head and deliberately looked off to the side to break the spell. He genuinely did not know how much time had passed. It could have been a second. It could have been an hour. He tried to look at the position of the sun to estimate the time that had elapsed. His watch had died with the EMP.

"We're good. We will pay someone to bury the body," she answered his question from so long ago, so far in the past that he had forgotten he had asked it. Or from a second ago.

He knew he needed to focus. The body. The gunshots. The reason he had come here in the first place. He seized on that to bring himself back from the depths.

"What happened here?" he asked.

He saw the girl beside the body look up at Dani, at the back of her head, and she seemed to sense it. She couldn't possibly have seen anything because she had her back to the girl and the girl made no noise. Yet as soon as the girl looked at Dani, she turned to glance at her, then immediately back to him. She made a 'come on' move with her fingers and walked towards the body.

As they walked, she bobbed her chin at the body and answered his question: "He committed suicide."

He opened his mouth to say that three shots to commit suicide was highly unusual when she continued.

"Prison tattoos, especially that teardrop tattoo under the eye, is 'shoot-on-sight'. No questions, no warnings. We do not tolerate that. Him coming here was suicide."

"I heard that that tattoo means they killed someone, but it can also mean other things. Like someone they loved was killed," he countered.

"This one has committed murder. Among a long list of other crimes. Taylor did the right thing shooting him."

"And where did that come from, that 'shoot-on-sight' thing for prison tattoos? Who came up with that?"

They were up to the body now, and Dani stopped and looked him in the eye, a slight smile on her face. "I did." Despite the smile, there was something in her eyes, some cloud that drifted through, some horror from the past that drove her to order men killed.

The blonde stood, breaking the moment. She smiled at Dani and pointed at a pile of scattered items where she had dumped the guy's backpack out and dug through the contents.

"I don't know what this is, but I'd bet meth," she said. She shrugged. "But I've never seen it before, so I may be wrong." There was a plastic bag stuffed with smaller plastic bags with a whitish substance in them.

The Game Warden looked at the substance, surprised at the large quantity, obviously sales weight. Then he couldn't help but look at the body. He'd seen too many dead bodies but they were usually drownings, wrecks, and a few hunting accidents. He'd never seen someone shot between the eyes.

The blood had pooled in his eye sockets, making it look like he had huge red eyes. The blood was thick, too, more like tomato sauce than water. He could barely see the teardrop tattoo that had started this whole thing, though.

"You just... shot him?" he asked the girl.

She looked like the cheerleaders he had known in high school, just very casual. Maybe like she was going to the gym and would shower afterwards, so didn't put any makeup on, just a backwards ball cap to keep the hair under control. But she was a natural beauty, so she didn't need anything artificial.

"Yeah," she replied breathily, drawing it out.

Or maybe that was the dreaminess he felt. She was staring at the body and licking her lips but she was pretty calm for having just gunned a man down. He spotted the pistol by the body so he moved to secure that. He went through the man's possessions, setting aside the suspected meth and also finding some cigarette papers and a small bag of marijuana.

He meant to ask the girl some more questions but it didn't seem too important. He didn't even realize the women and the man were gone until a couple of guys came up. They stopped at a distance and called to him. Once they had his attention, they said they had been paid to bury the body. He took the drugs and pistol and left them to their work.

He sat in his truck for a while after that. He didn't know what had happened. He was fuzzy and unfocussed. He didn't know what that girl had done to him. He wasn't a Star Wars fan but he did know enough about the movies to keep thinking *Jedi mind tricks*.

He went home for the day, fed the animals early, and went to bed before he hurt himself somehow. He was back on his game the next day but he never could explain what happened to him that afternoon. Stress was the best answer he could ever come up with. Just too much built-up stress. It was a good theory. The End of the World has happened, the survivors are more like Mad Max than anything else, people are setting up their own little kingdoms, young women are ordering executions, high school girls are gunning down hardened ex-cons… All of that's entirely reasonable, isn't it? Absolutely normal?

Isn't it?

He needed a vacation.

***

"What do you think about Taylor shooting that guy?" Dani asked Eric, later on that evening.

He shrugged. "We taught her how to shoot. We specifically said that gang tattoos like that are the death penalty. And, as it turned out, the guy was carrying meth in dealer quantities. Now, he wasn't technically on our territory, so maybe that's a gray area, but other than that I really can't say anything bad about that shooting."

"I guess it's just that it's Taylor. I mean, a few months ago she was fourteen. She was a little girl!"

He laughed. "She may only be fifteen now, but she's fifteen going on twenty-five. A lot of people throughout history have done things at an early age. Alexander the Great started leading men into battle at age sixteen and was a general at seventeen. Joan of Arc was seventeen. There were a number of other soldiers who gained distinction at early ages. Taylor is smart — she's scary smart. She's competent and capable.

To tell you the truth, I never thought she would hang with you on the training, but she has."

She looked at him questioningly so he elaborated.

"I knew you were tough. Determined. I knew I could throw all kinds of things at you during training and you'd just knuckle down and carry on. Her, I doubted. I mean, seriously, she's never worked, never had any hardship, never had to get dirty and strain to do anything. I figured she would catch one taste of hard training and she'd throw up her hands and be done with it."

"And yet, she did not. She gutted out everything so far and came back for more."

"Yep. And I'm not going to tell her she did something wrong with that shooting."

Dani thought about it for a moment. "I just hope she's okay with it. I don't want it to affect her. You know, like spiral down into depression."

***

She needn't have worried.

Number four! Taylor wrote in her journal. *It's different to do it without some action going on, like at the bank robbery. This got my adrenaline running but it was a lower dose or something. Less effect. I didn't get the tunnel vision or the hearing loss. It was more like that time Nathan took me for a ride in his father's Corvette and went really fast. I mean, exciting, but not that intense.*

I need to figure out how I can rack up some more kills. I think I'm pretty good at it.

Chapter 7

Dani and Eric were hosting the acting governor of the State of Texas, Trey Marsh, at their ranch. They had given him the grand tour and were back at the house now, sitting on the back deck with a view of the pond. It was mid-November but the weather was a pleasant sixty-seven degrees.

They had toured farms and ranches, the school, workshops, headquarters, clinic, and the ranges. The top rifle shooters, including Taylor, had a small competition on steel gongs at a thousand yards. Everyone could hear the hits when the bullets slammed into the steel.

Then there had been a little demonstration with Taylor putting multiple rounds on targets at various ranges from ten to fifty yards. It took a lot of movement from one target to the next, required a couple of speedy magazine changes in her AR rifle, and then there was a final transition to pistol for the finish.

Eric had planned this one so that she had a ski mask on, with her hair up under it, and wearing loose-fitting camo clothing so there was no obvious indication that the shooter was a female. At the end, he had brought her up to meet the governor. She had swept the ski mask off, shook out her long blonde hair, and dazzled him with a smile.

He laughed later on that the governor would probably have asked for Taylor's hand in marriage if she'd been ten years older. And it also didn't hurt to let him know that this teenaged girl could sit a half-mile off and spread his brains all over the landscape if Eric ever thought that it had to happen.

Now was a little downtime before the big barbecue and battle of the bands, to be judged by the governor. There were two bands and two solo artists on tap.

"When I make a few remarks this evening, I do have one important announcement and I'm going to give y'all the head's up now. You know we have been, of course, trying to make contact with the federal government, as well as reaching out to our neighboring states. We've already established contact with the acting governors of Louisiana and Arkansas and Oklahoma but, just this last week, we got word back from Washington, D.C."

"Really? I don't imagine that's anything other than interesting, is it? Nothing they can do for us, right?" Eric was skeptical.

"I wouldn't bet against you on that. I think the part that perhaps troubles me is that they are asking for inventories on what we have. Now, asking for the status of our oil and gas operations I can understand. This is another story."

"Give them the inventory with the price of things if they want to buy it."

"That may not be a bad idea. Anyway, the point is that there is contact. One of the implications of that is that the federal troops will now come under their control. The soldiers from Fort Cavazos, and I know you have some here assisting with the oil and gas project."

"We need the trucks more than we need the troops. Either way, whether they're under the feds or under the Texas Army National Guard, we're feeding them, so it doesn't matter. Now if we run into another problem like the *Pistoleros*, then it would be good to have the equipment and the troops both."

Eric had crushed the *Pistoleros* in Dallas with artillery and armored vehicles and had sustained no friendly casualties. That little incident had apparently put the fear of God into the Dallas gangs, at least. Governor Marsh had deployed Army units under command of the Texas Army National Guard to other cities to supplement the police forces with great success. When the gang members have a 'shoot on sight' target on their backs, they are less likely to go wild in the streets.

"I'd like for you to think through the implications and see what we need to do. Do we need to try to get some equipment or supplies from the Army now? You know, borrow it permanently? What changes now that we have contact with D.C.?"

"Tell 'em we secede. Texas was a country once. Let's do it again. I think the last figures I saw we would be the tenth largest economy in the world if we were a country. We have one third of the oil in the U.S., we're the leading producer of cattle, cotton, and plenty of other things."

Marsh was silent for a moment. Then he gave a sideways nod and replied "That may be something we have to seriously consider. Texas has always paid more taxes in than benefits it got back. We may have to reconsider that during this present crisis. All of the things you said are correct. We can feed ourselves and more, which, as you know, is the first thing. Nothing follows if you can't do that. Which actually brings me to a suggestion."

Eric gave him a dirty look.

Marsh laughed. "Oh, come on! Whenever I've asked you to do something you've always benefitted. I have no intention of stopping that now."

"Don't pay attention to him, Trey," Dani piped up. "You know we'll do the best we can. What do you have?"

"I want you to expand your operations. The ranching and farming part. Too many people are just doing subsistence agriculture. That really doesn't help anyone but themselves. I don't know if it's the general depression that has struck so many people from Hexen or what. Far too many people have just lost all ambition. They're doing enough to keep the next meal coming but they may not have enough to make it through the winter. They certainly don't produce enough for Texas to start exporting food, which is one thing we need if we were to declare independence." He looked at Eric for this last part.

"If they don't have enough to make it through the winter, there's noth — Well, shit," Eric replied, stopping himself as he realized what Trey was saying. They might have to dip into their own supplies.

"I know." The governor looked contrite. "It would have been nice to start building up an inventory back in April or May, right? On the good side, I will authorize you to take troops from Fort Cavazos and a train to Dallas and fill up a trainload — a *train load* — of whatever you need to take on an additional two hundred people."

"And you already have these two hundred people sitting somewhere? Are you trying to empty out a prison on us?"

"No, no, nothing like that. We do have a group of refugees that we'd like for you to resettle. It's a couple hundred people, a mixed cross-section of society, just like you've integrated here so well. But the best news is that I have a couple of gems for you."

"Gems." Eric didn't phrase it in the form of a question. He sounded distinctly skeptical.

"Yes! One is a veterinarian, specializing in livestock. He was in Somervell County and evacuated from the nuclear power plant meltdown. I mean, not that it exploded like a bomb, but there is an area downwind of the facility that we have to be cautious about. Anyway, this guy has been a travelling vet and would like to settle down more. Your operation would be perfect for him. But —" he held up a finger and beamed a huge smile at Dani — "there is also a priest in the group."

Her eyes lit up and she leaped to her feet. "Really?"

"A genuine Irish priest."

Dani bounced up and down in excitement, a huge smile on her face.

Damn it, Eric thought. *That sold it for her. Now we have to make the best of this. A trainload. Okay, you son of a bitch, that's going to be the biggest goddamn train you ever heard of!*

Trey knew Eric well enough by now that he could tell he was figuring out how to do something. The crossed arms and distant stare didn't mean he was sulking. He was planning. He might not be happy, maybe, but he'd get over it. And this would make it easier to get the next group of refugees in. It would almost be routine next time.

"The land," suddenly popped out of Eric's mouth. "I want the land now. Deeded. All of it. As a matter of fact, double it. Forget all of this crap with our guys out posting properties. Forget all of that waiting a year to apply for ownership. Let's pull out a map and draw some real big lines on it. We have about twenty thousand acres now. Let's go to fifty thousand. That's a nice round number."

Dani stopped doing her little bouncy dance and stared at him, wide-eyed and open mouthed. She had always been the empire-builder. She was always the one pushing to claim more land. It looked like he was going to take that job now.

Eric continued. "If we're going to do this, then let's do it. I'll take three companies of soldiers and a train for a month. No, scratch that. Six weeks. With an option to extend at my discretion."

The governor smiled. This was a deal! He was trying to build Marten Cattle Company up so they could pull him up to the Presidency of the United States. He would need rich, influential people in order to do that and Hexen had killed them all off or the EMP had bankrupted them. The only option now was to create some new ones. And any that he created would be indebted to him.

What Eric was asking for would be no problem whatsoever. The governor would be giving away some materials that he didn't own, providing labor in the form of soldiers that he wasn't paying, running on a train that he wasn't financing, and giving away land that was sitting idle because the owners were all dead. And Eric and Dani would owe him huge favors because of it. What politician would *not* love this deal? Most of them would stab their own mother and step on her bleeding body to make a sweet deal like that.

He had actually been afraid of trying to push too far, too fast, afraid of scaring Eric off. Now he thought just the opposite. Maybe it was exactly the right time to push. Eric was a Marine, and Marines tended to rise to challenges, so he challenged him.

"Do you think you can go full throttle? How about we *really* go full throttle?"

He had Dani and Eric's full attention. He stood and waved at his assistant, sitting in the SUV out of earshot but watching him. The assistant popped out of the vehicle and trotted closer.

"Map. I want that big map," Trey called to him. The assistant waved and swung a U-turn.

Trey sat back down. "This was just a pie in the sky type of thing we were thinking about. You know, for future reference, future expansion. I don't want to give you anything you can't handle, but..." He let that dangle there, sure that Eric would not be able to back down now.

The assistant returned and they spread the map out on the patio table. There were red lines outlining an immense area around their ranch. Governor Marsh started pointing at the boundaries. "Highway 110 on the west, from Troup down to a point between Rusk and Reklaw. Highway 84 at the bottom to Mount Enterprise. Up to Henderson on 259, skirting around the edges of the city limits and then back west to Troup."

"How big is that?" Dani asked.

"It's about 250,000 acres."

"And you want us to..."

"Take it. Manage it. Run it. I want this to be Marten Cattle Company." He tapped the map for emphasis.

"Holy shit." Dani stared at the map, eyes huge.

As usual, Eric was looking at the practical aspects of it. "It would take I don't know how long just to stop at every property in that big an area. There aren't enough people to —". He looked at Trey suspiciously. "What's the intent here? Are you looking to move a bunch of people in here?"

"Some, but not an immense amount. Part of the problem is that the survivors are so spread out now. Look at the Tyler police force as an example. There are probably only three percent of the policemen still on duty. Ninety percent of them were gone with Hexen. Then more went out to a farm or wherever to try to feed themselves. The city couldn't, at first, pay them in money that was worth anything and couldn't provide food to them. So, you have three percent of the police force still patrolling one hundred percent of the territory. Granted, there are only eight or ten percent of the population remaining in that area, but you still have the full size of the area to deal with.

"Or look at electricity. How easy would it be to set up one plant and power up one small city versus powering up ten small cities spread across east Texas when you're dealing with the same population either way? The more people you have in a smaller area, the easier it is to provide electricity and other services to them."

"Where are these people going to come from? What incentive would they have to come here?"

"Snow. It's getting cold. People living up north are realizing that they are going to freeze to death in the dark if they don't head south to a warmer climate. They thought the power would be back on or something and now they're waking up to the fact that they are in real danger. I don't think the majority of people stockpiled food and firewood this summer. Or even if they did, they can't heat their big house all winter long with just a fireplace that was mainly put in for decoration. We are seeing a surge of people coming down."

"And rather than letting them spread out, you think having them in one spot would be better?"

"Sure. Plus, it gives you the ability to use economies of scale. It's too expensive for a small farmer to run a big combine, but it's easy if you have a large property. Or on the bargaining side, if you are the big supplier of beef in East Texas, you can get a better price than the little guys. It's good all around."

"How many people are you thinking about? In total?"

"I don't know. But if we take in refugees like this, it will make Texas stronger and maybe more able to become its own country, like you mentioned earlier. But you will have the full support of the State of Texas. I will have biologists and foresters and agricultural experts and whatever you need out here, whenever you need them."

"Okay, my head hurts. I don't want to talk about this anymore tonight. I need a beer." Eric stood and opened the ice chest nearby. "Baby? Trey? Y'all ready for one?" Dani and the governor both took one.

This was huge. This was life-changing, an immense opportunity and also an immense responsibility.

Chapter 8

Amidst all of the festivities, the governor took the stage.

"Ladies and gentlemen, my fellow Texans, my fellow Americans, I am very happy to be here with you this evening. Even if you weren't born in Texas, you're here now and you're a Texan now. And let me say that I am very impressed with what you have done with the place!

"Seriously, this is the premiere, the best community that I have seen in Texas and I have been travelling a lot! We have all gone through a terrible time, the worst in our history, but we are coming back! And it is you, each and every one of you, who are bringing us back. And for that I thank you. Please keep doing what you are doing because you are doing the right thing.

"I think that when they write history books about us, and they will, they are going to call us 'The Rebuilders'. In the Old West you have the pioneers and the frontiersmen. Now, in this New West, you will have the rebuilders and that is you. Every one of you. Stand and be proud of that fact. Give yourselves a round of applause!

"I also want to let you know that we just did receive a representative from the federal government in Washington, D.C. We had extensive meetings and they are now on their way back to Washington. There is a federal government that is functioning, but I can't honestly say when or if they will be able to assist us. But that's fine. We don't need them. We are Texans and are standing ourselves back up on our feet just fine. Better, in fact, than those around us."

He talked some more and he was pretty good at it, but Eric and Dani both had their heads in the previous conversation.

***

The next day, Eric called a meeting of all of the management staff. They were going to have to move fast.

"Let me say that if I was distracted last night, I have a reason. And if I look like hell this morning, it's the same reason that kept me awake all night. The governor dropped something in our laps that's ultimately going to be a good thing, but it's going to mean a lot of work. We all needed more work to do, didn't we?"

He pulled out the map with the red lines and pushed it to the center of the table. He gave them a few moments to look at it and then turn their attention back towards him.

"The governor wants this to be Marten Cattle Company."

"*All* of it?!" The question tumbled out of Ted's mouth, but Eric could see the blood draining from everyone's face. He took some small satisfaction in that, since he knew the sensation well. Ever since he'd seen the damned map, in fact.

"Well, you know there are some people in that area that have prior claims to property. Curtis has his ranch to the west, and there are the others that have ranches and farms and homesteads, and we don't get those. We're not kicking people off their land. But anything that's unclaimed in that area is MCC property now. Trey will make up the land grant when he gets back to Austin.

"And to populate that land, we're going to be receiving refugees. These are coming down from the north where it's getting cold and they are realizing that they aren't going to survive the winter. Trey has agreed for me to take three companies of soldiers and a train and raid Dallas and Fort Worth. I am going to go through as much of the DFW metro area as I can and I'm going to take anything that's not nailed down that will help us and the refugees survive. I need all of you to make lists of things that you'll need.

"One thing that will be vital is the ability to offload things from the train. I am going to run as many trainloads of stuff in here as possible. How do we unload it? I liked the thing in Dallas where you just drove vehicles on and off of flatcars onto a concrete platform and then down a ramp to the pavement at ground level. Or you could run a forklift into a boxcar and then load the pallets into a truck while remaining on the platform the whole time. We need to build one of those starting tomorrow. We worked with what's-that-guy's-name to get his cement plant and trucks running. Get his ass over here, pouring concrete. He owes us. I want a loading dock. A big one. A huge one. We most likely want to look at Troup. There are four tracks in places, so there's bound to be someplace for us to build a nice loading dock. Also, highway 110 crosses the tracks, so that makes easy access for trucks.

"Next item. I want messengers. A Pony Express. The road between here and Dallas is still jammed but we can do exactly what the *Pistoleros* were doing. They would drive a vehicle down the highway as far as they had cleared it, park it, ride bicycles through the abandoned cars, and then have a vehicle waiting for them where the road cleared out again. We'll have to establish two stations, one on each side of The Jam to protect the vehicles, serve as a place for the messengers to sleep or eat or whatever. We might be able to use motorcycles and pick up a few miles on each end. I want a minimum of five messengers on each side. We need bicycles, tools and supplies for repairs, food, water, whatever they need to maintain the stations and the vehicles. Probably a person or a few people that live in the station permanently and manage it, keep it clean and stocked with supplies and do repairs and stuff.

"Now that I think about it, we need a Pony Express between here and Austin, too. We have the convoys to and from the bank but we may need something more frequent. Set up something every week, a round trip every week. At least we can use trucks on that route since it's cleared. We'll need facilities for the guys to sleep in Austin. I'd like something like a reserved floor of a hotel if we can get it. You get the idea. Do what you need to make it work.

"Forklifts. We need more. We'll have to have some at the ramp where we unload the trains and also for the warehouse here. I don't want to have to shuffle them back and forth. Figure out how many we need and then double it. And then add spares. And repair parts. And propane or whatever they run on.

"Warehouse space. As soon as that guy finishes our train loading dock, get him pouring foundations for more warehouses. Grab some more of those steel buildings from that place in Tyler. If we don't have shelving here then put it on the list for Dallas.

"Medicine and medical. Liz, give me as long a list as you think. If we need to ask the doctor in Tyler, see if there's anything he needs. Let's get a messenger on the way to him right now.

"Manual water pumps. We have a good design, we have a small production line, but we need to start cranking these things out. What do we need for supplies for these things? If we don't have enough stuff to build another two hundred at least, then give me a materials list. Make it five hundred. Hell, make it a thousand. Pipe, iron, welding supplies, O-rings, whatever it takes to make them.

"That goes for anything. If you think we need a hundred, then ask for five hundred or a thousand. I have no idea how many people we're going to end up with."

He sighed, closed his eyes, and pinched the bridge of his nose, trying to tamp down a growing headache. "What else do we need to think about?"

***

They parted while holding back tears. Dani would stay at the ranch. Preparations had to move quickly and they were not going to allow any holdups because someone couldn't make a decision. Not that that had been an issue in the past but they were trying to get out ahead of Mr. Murphy and his rule about things going wrong.

Eric was headed to Austin to the governor's office, then Fort Cavazos, then Dallas. Mark was going back into his previous position as aide de camp for Eric, allowing Taylor to stick with Dani.

Their convoy contained a half-dozen vehicles with trailers for eight motorcycles. Eric had thrown in a couple of extras, plus had the thought that he may need to run messages to multiple recipients at the same time.

They were probably going to have to spend Thanksgiving apart, but Eric promised he would ride the rails back for Christmas. That was another reason for Dani to remain at the ranch, to prepare for the holidays. They were not going to be easy. Everyone had experienced loss and the holidays were the worst time of the year for those memories. Suicides were always up during that time and they fully expected to have some.

There was nothing they could do about it other than to try to ensure a sense of community support. Dani and Eric had convened a brief meeting with the religious leaders of the community, several pastors, ordained and otherwise, to ask for their assistance in keeping everyone safe and sound.

Ultimately, though, if someone was determined to end themselves, there was nothing they could do about it. They couldn't keep guns, knives, sleeping pills, and rope away from everyone, and there were other methods beyond those.

* * *

At the governor's office, Eric received a land grant for the area, a declaration that he had the authority to gather any and all items as he deemed necessary, and an order for Major Batista at Fort Cavazos to supply him with one train and such troops and equipment as General Marten determined, for the duration of time that Marten needed them. In other words, a deed and two blank checks. Eric could work with that!

Chapter 9

"Major Batista, a representative of the federal government did visit Austin and the governor gave them your written status report. They have moved on now. The delegation was apparently making a sweep down through the Midwest and then Texas, Louisiana, and along the Gulf Coast and then East Coast. They had no instructions for the military personnel other than to assist the states just as in a hurricane or other disaster. That means that nothing has changed so far. You're doing the right thing. In addition, I have a request from the governor requesting assistance right here for your records.

"We do have a resettlement program going on. People are coming down from the north to get away from the cold. I guess there were inadequate preparations made and we are going to have to absorb some refugees. There are already two hundred or so coming into my protectorate in East Texas. What we need to do is to get to Dallas and start loading up supplies to handle that resettlement and for an unknown number of additional refugees.

"One top priority is going to be to get your train engineers working to get more trains up and running. We're going to need more than the two we have now. I need to get trains running from Dallas to my place. That is the other top priority: to get a train to Dallas and start loading. I'm thinking we need a security element to establish a base at the loading dock in Dallas and a couple of companies to salvage and load."

***

Two days later they were in Dallas with Humvees, Strykers, and a lot of trucks. Work parties headed out and started loading up with supplies. Solar panels were high on the list. They also needed metal buildings for more warehouse space, tools, ATVs, older trucks and other equipment that they could get running again, building materials, any type of food processing equipment, bicycles, boots and shoes, clothes, blankets, and the list went on.

There were some stores that they simply cleaned out from floor to ceiling, such as drugstores, sporting goods, and auto parts stores. All that remained, that is. Most had already been picked over. If someone was running the store, they moved on. Eric wasn't going to wipe out someone trying to make a living. He was trying to help people, not ruin them.

***

The governor had sent off a messenger the day after the barbecue at the ranch to get the refugees moving in that direction. They were in an area in the north of Dallas and obviously had their own transportation in the way of bicycles and would have to make their own way through The Jam heading east on I-20. Dani had a group ready to meet them and give them a ride as soon as they got out into The Clear on that side.

When there was the panicked evacuation of the cities the roads were flooded with far more traffic than their designed maximums. People even pulled into the inbound lanes to drive outbound. Then the EMP hit and froze all of the cars in place. This was termed The Jam.

As traffic got away from the cities there were side roads and alternate routes for the traffic to take, and at some point, the roads were clear enough for a repaired vehicle to drive on, even if it had to weave around dead cars. This was called The Clear.

Some cities had also made fair progress in moving dead cars out of the way so that there was an open lane. Any area like this was also called a Clear. For the refugees to come from Dallas to Marten Cattle Company, they passed through a Clear in Dallas, a Jam on Interstate 20 and Highway 64 until they reached a Clear. Using back roads and single lanes in Tyler, they had a Clear all of the way to MCC. Obviously other qualifiers could be added, such as "The I-20 Jam east of Dallas".

While Clears had at least room for a car or truck to pass, the Jams could take a bicycle at most. There was frequent debris that required the rider to pick up the bike or push or carry it over, or rerouting around or even over wrecks. A motorcycle was too heavy for this, so they actually had limited advantages. Motorcycles couldn't really go that much further than a pickup truck in many areas, and carried far less. So, bicycles became the preferred mode of transport.

That meant that bicycle scout met bicycle scout when the northern refugees first encountered Marten Cattle Company.

Joseph and T were both seventeen, former high-school classmates who had met again at MCC, coming to it by separate paths. They were friends but couldn't have been more different. Joseph was fairly large and pale-skinned. T was about half his weight but almost as tall, and as dark as Joseph was light. Both were attempting to grow mustaches but Joseph's just looked like he needed to wash his upper lip. Right now, both were standing on top of an SUV in The Jam, looking for the Northerners.

"I don't see anything. I have to pee," announced Joseph, moving a bit to the side of the roof and unzipping his pants.

"Aw, man, go off somewhere. Don't do it off the side here or we'll have to smell it all day," T replied, giving him a dirty look.

Joseph ignored him except to give a loud, breathy sigh of contentment as he started the flow.

"Oh, there's a girl! She's looking at you. Through binoculars!" T announced gleefully, using his own binoculars.

"No, there isn't!"

"Oh, yeah, there is!" he laughed. "HEY! HEY!" He let the binoculars dangle from the strap around his neck and waved broadly with both arms.

***

Shirina's long, dark hair floated off to the side as a gust of wind caught it. She was learning that Texas weather may require bundling up in the mornings against the chill but stripping down to a t-shirt in the much warmer afternoons, especially outside in the sun. The temperature swings could give rise to substantial breezes, too.

Overall, though, she was just so very weary. Her group, the majority of the travelers, was from the Twin Cities, the Minneapolis – St. Paul area, and it felt like they had been on the move forever. She no longer kept track of the days, but it had been months of move, stop for rest and to hunt for supplies, move, stop for this, or that, or something else, and finally move again.

It was frustrating because she had to settle down to get on with her life, but they had to get out of the cold. With no electricity, they had no heat, and winters that were below freezing the entire time in Minnesota. March and November barely got to 40 degrees as a high temperature.

Their group had voted to move south, and she had been accorded a full vote. She was only sixteen but she had taken on the responsibilities of an adult. She had taken charge of two younger survivors from her *gurdwara*, the Sikh temple. She had come to regard them as her young sister and brother: thirteen-year-old Aasha, the girl, and eight-year-old Raftaar, the boy. Aasha and some other girls her age were responsible for the younger children. Shirina spent most of her time as a scout since her small size precluded her from carrying much weight.

She had been outfitted with camouflage clothing and her bike given a mottled green and brown spray paint job that had worn off in many places. A Ruger Mini-14 rifle, also sprayed in camo colors, and also showing signs of wear, was strapped across her back. She had only fired it twice, and only once in the general direction of a person, trying to scare them with the sound rather than seeking to hit them. It had worked, and so she was free of karma.

She hoped she would remain so. She wore a kara, a steel bracelet inscribed with the Aad Guray Nameh for protection. She had been born and raised in America and wasn't sure that the bracelet really had any powers but now was undoubtedly not the time to tempt fate.

She needed protection now because she was deliberately showing herself. She had spotted the silly boys on the roof of the SUV a long way back and sent Robert, another scout, riding back to alert the others. Then she had approached more carefully until now. The boys were armed and there could be others waiting in ambush, although Shirina couldn't spot any. They were also as exposed as they could be, so shouldn't offer a threat.

Exposed, indeed. The one boy who was urinating was apparently unable to stop and had limited room to move off somewhere more discreet on the roof of the vehicle. Shirina had deliberately put her binoculars to her eyes once she had seen that the other had spotted her to try to embarrass him. Why, she couldn't say. Maybe a flashback to the seemingly carefree schoolgirl she had been only a few months ago.

She was too bone-weary now to even smile at her own attempt at humor. She stood fully and pushed her bike around the vehicle she had hidden behind, coming straight at the boys. Her fate would be what it would be, just let this journey end!

Shirina noted that the boys were dressed in Army camouflage and combat boots. She knew they were heading to something called Marten Cattle Company and this was Texas, so she had kind of expected cowboy boots, denim, and Stetson hats. But then, they probably weren't expecting a dark-haired, dark-eyed Sikh girl from Minnesota.

Viking girls, maybe, the big, buxom, corn-fed ones with blue eyes and white-blond hair. They definitely had those in the group, too, just not her. And she certainly didn't look her best. She hadn't bathed in weeks, not any more than she could do with a wet rag and small towel. Her clothes were little better, and ragged. Deodorant was a thing of the past and she hadn't shaved her legs or pits in a really long time. Almost anything that added weight to their burden and wasn't food had long been discarded. Ounces equaled pounds and pounds equaled pain, as the backpackers had said in that long-lost world when people actually used to hike for fun. Now people hiked for survival, but they still started off heavy and threw away things as they decided they didn't need them enough to carry them.

She stopped when she got close enough that they could talk easily. "I am looking for Marten Cattle Company," she stated.

T, now standing on the pavement, spread his arms and smile wide. "And we, my dear, are looking for you." He imagined himself to be a ladies' man.

She didn't know if he was expecting a hug but he wasn't going to get one. "I assume you are scouts? How much further?"

"About two miles. There are trucks that will take you the rest of the way. Welcome to Texas!"

Shirina caught her breath and tears almost came to her eyes. She turned aside to hide it. Could it really be that this horrible journey was finally coming to an end? Would this nightmare that had dominated her every waking moment and haunted her sleeping ones for so long possibly ease up?

She and the boys introduced themselves and made small talk for a few minutes, somewhat shyly. Then Robert came up, having alerted the group and then sped forward back to his position. Then they took their leave of the two boys and headed down the final stretch.

***

The trucks didn't roll in until after dark, in the rain. Ideally, they would have arrived sooner and it wouldn't have rained and they could have had a welcome barbecue. Of course, with no communications they hadn't known when they would arrive other than, 'in a couple of days'. They did get an hour of warning due to the CB radio in one of the gun trucks and they had most of the security detail on duty.

They had opened up twenty-three houses at the east end of their original territory and parceled out ten people per house for the night. They would figure out better accommodations in the morning but right now people were hungry, damp, and tired. Each house had a 'house manager' for tonight and maybe longer, to be determined. This person was to assist as needed, show them around, and make sure they were using the latrine and not the yard. Each house had loaves of bread, beans, sliced ham, and a supply of clean water, in addition to soap, laundry detergent, toothpaste, shampoo, and other toiletries. Beyond that, they would figure it out.

Gunny Fitz had been on hand at the edge of The Clear to greet the Northerner's leaders and bring them with him. There were five altogether, with another three hangers-on of some type, assistants or whatever. Plus the priest. Those he brought straight to Dani at the HQ building. The duty NCO directed them to the conference room, which was equipped with a nice table and plush leather chairs claimed from an office in Tyler. They had even let a carpenter talk them into trimming out the room with nice baseboard and crown molding.

As they entered, Dani rose from her seat and walked to the doorway to greet them and introduce herself. She was amused to see that they were all blinking in the now-unfamiliar overhead lights.

***

"Solar power," she explained. "We're on batteries right now, obviously. Please eat and make use of the facilities out the door and to your left." There were platters of ham and loaves of bread, the same fare that was at the houses.

Dani was dressed in spotless ironed and starched tiger stripe camouflage utilities that had been tailored to fit her. Early on they had found a prepper, dead in his house, who had stocked up on many things, including tiger stripe uniforms in a size that fit Dani. Eric had suggested that she have at least one set tailored for just such an occasion.

She had discussed this whole situation with Brennan, who had retired from the Air Force as a high-ranking NCO. Brennan had been in the Security Forces for her entire career. She regarded this visit from the leaders of the refugees like an inspection. A little spit and polish was applied to people and places, just like had been done for the governor's visit, although less so. She had also suggested Dani show them who was boss without rubbing their noses in it, hence the meeting in the plush conference room with all of the lights ablaze and carafes of hot coffee with fresh cream and sugar. Without anyone saying a word, there was a crystal-clear difference between the clean and well-fed and comfortable versus the have-nots.

Once everyone was reasonably settled, Dani began. "Greetings, ladies and gentlemen. Welcome to Marten Cattle Company. My name is Dani Ruiz. My fiancé is Eric Marten. He is currently in Dallas gathering supplies and equipment for you. This is our operation. What we have been doing is taking the noobs — that's our term for people that have always lived in the city and don't know how to farm or ranch or hunt or do much anything to survive in this new world of ours. Anyway, we take the noobs in and train them. Put them to work. We have people that have been farmers and ranchers all of their lives and they oversee those operations and train people. Then later on, if they wish, people can go off and claim their own farm or ranch and start up their own operation. What we need to do here is to integrate your people into our operation. Our philosophy is you work, you eat."

"We'll work. We have no problem with that. But the growing season is past, as far as I know. What kind of issue is that going to be?" That was Bill Vogel, the leader of the Northerners.

Dani looked him straight in the eye and replied, "It's going to be an issue. I'm not going to sugarcoat it. You're going to cut into our supplies. We may all have to tighten our belts this winter. No one's going to starve to death but we want to do a lot better than that. Eric is working on supplies from Dallas, working with the governor. I am sending out salvage teams to locate herds of cattle that were abandoned and have survived in the wild. We can either bring these cattle in or shoot them as we need meat if they are too wild. But we're going to need your people at work quickly. Like immediately."

"You tell us what we need to do and we'll do it," Bill promised.

"That's great! That's the attitude that we all must have. Now I'd like to introduce a few members of our team. On the end is Lieutenant Colonel Brennan. She is in charge of our Security Force and hunters. If you have any military veterans, police officers, experienced hunters, people like that, she will take them on. Major Ted Fowler is Support Operations. That includes Supply, Housing, Motor Pool, actually a lot of things. Ted may be able to use people from the construction trades, mechanics, welders, um, what else?"

"I wouldn't mind having an experienced project manager. Somebody who knows how to plan and ride herd on a project through to completion."

"Okay. Liz Mitchell is Medical and also Education. If you have any medical personnel or teachers, she needs them. We have a more comprehensive list of the skills we need and we'll get all that sorted out but this should give you an idea. The other big category, the biggest actually, is Ag Ops, Agricultural Operations. I didn't ask that manager to come in here because it's getting late at night and he's up way before the crack of dawn. Plus, his operation is fully staffed. And as you pointed out, the growing season is past.

"I mentioned a couple of military ranks a second ago. We do have a somewhat military structure here. It's tighter in the Security Forces, looser in other areas. Don't worry about saluting or standing at attention or anything like that. We're using the system to assign people to roles, track their training, and reward them. We'll explain all that as needed.

"Anyway, what we need to do starting tomorrow is to get your skilled people pushed out to these guys and then get the unskilled, the noobs, working on improving their living conditions. Right now, we have twenty-three houses that we made habitable as best we could in the limited time we had available. We need to open up more houses, convert wells to manual pumps, dig latrines, build bunk beds, and chop and split firewood. That's going to be a big one. We're going to be burning wood to stay warm this winter. Fortunately, our winters aren't like Minnesota winters." That drew a bit of laughter.

Dani paused for a moment and Liz gently reminded her, "Medical screening."

"Yes, medical screening! Liz and her nurses are going to need to give everyone a quick exam tomorrow. Tell them about that."

"We need to know about any conditions, any injuries, does anyone have head lice, things of that nature," Liz spoke up. "This is just a quick preliminary. We'll do a more thorough screening with both a doctor and a dentist in the near future. Everyone goes through medical and dental once a year at minimum."

Dani followed with "And last but certainly not least, this is Taylor. Taylor is my assistant. If she tells you something or asks you to do something, it comes from me, or treat it as if it comes from me. She knows everything that goes on that I know of."

"If there are no immediate questions, I know it's late and everyone had a long day. Gunny Fitz has a truck available to take you to your housing and we'll get started in the morning."

Bill stood and shook her hand. "Thank you. I know this isn't going to be easy on you, just having a couple of hundred people descend on you like this."

"I won't pretend it's going to be easy. Just help us to help you."

Chapter 10

As soon as they were on the truck and gone, Taylor cut the lights down to a quarter of what they were. No sense in running the batteries down. They had made the impression that they wanted to make with the Northerners.

"What are everyone's thoughts?" Dani asked, looking at Liz.

"They're obviously malnourished. They didn't leave a crumb of food on those plates. Their cheeks are sunken and they probably haven't gotten much in the way of vitamin C. Fortunately, we do have a supply of vitamins and we can treat it. Once they get some food in them, they'll probably be fine."

"Great attitude," Ted volunteered when Dani looked at him. "Which I would expect if they were determined enough to bike and walk all the way here from Minnesota, however far that is. I say we don't baby them. Put them to work immediately."

Dani looked at Brennan.

"I have my guys on the job but I'm gonna be running them hard. We need to get the Northerners integrated quickly before my troops start running out of gas." Brennan always looked out for her people. "What Ted says: put them to work immediately."

***

As soon as the truck dropped them off, Bill asked the Northerners' leaders the same question: "What are everyone's thoughts?"

"Electric lights! When was the last time we saw electric lights? I think we just hit the gold mine here!"

"I guess I didn't expect so many women in positions of command. Not to be sexist or anything. I don't object, just surprised."

"They seem to be very militarized. I wonder what kind of trouble they've had that led to that."

"I think the biggest thing is that they seem to have their operation up and running and they know what they're doing. They're organized, they're efficient, and they're pretty no-nonsense."

***

The Northerner's sleeping arrangements had been hammered out long ago and were just a matter of habit now. The only variable was the new location. With ten people in a three-bedroom house, obviously everyone didn't have their own private room. The other consideration was the fireplace. Sleep on the floor near the fireplace or in a nice soft bed under blankets? The custom that had formed was for the older ones to get the more comfortable accommodations, which was fine with Shirina. There were extra blankets in the house beyond what they had travelled with, so she, Aasha, and Raftaar bundled up on the floor near the fire. Raftaar went out like a light, exhausted. Shirina was almost asleep when something started nagging at the edge of her consciousness. As she drifted back up from the depths, she became aware that Aasha was shaking.

"Aasha," she whispered. "Are you crying?" Aasha went still for a moment, then turned towards Shirina.

She sniffled, wiped her nose, and then whispered back "Are we here now? Are we finished travelling?"

Shirina pulled the younger girl into a hug and held her tightly. "I think so. I pray so." Then her tears began to flow, too, and the girls cried themselves to sleep, trying to be quiet and not make Raftaar start crying, too.

Chapter 11

The no-nonsense came before the crack of dawn. A truck pulled up to the house, blew the horn, and then unloaded breakfast. Right on the heels of that came Medical to give everyone a quick once-over to make sure that there was nothing that needed to be treated immediately. As soon as they left, Personnel arrived for an initial job classification.

At this point they just asked for certain experience, which they had abbreviated as '3M' — military, medic, or mechanic. There were more categories than that, like electrician and plumber, but 3M made a nice, quick reference. The 3Ms were loaded on trucks, barely having eaten their breakfasts, and sent to HQ for processing into their new organizations.

Next came a school bus, one of the classic yellow ones built by the contrarily named Blue Bird Corporation. The driver called for everyone sixteen years old and younger, so Shirina, Aasha, and Raftaar all loaded up. They started to pack their meager belongings but the driver assured them they would come back at the end of the day, so they reluctantly left them.

With the 3Ms and the students gone, that left the noobs. The noobs had no useful skill, or at least one that had not yet been identified or appreciated. Trucks gathered them up and carted them off to locations with saws, axes, shovels, and other tools as required to get things working. They needed more houses for the Northerners, so that meant cleaning and airing out houses that had been closed up for months, washing the sheets, installing manual water pumps, digging latrines and building outhouses, and mowing the grass and cutting back the plant life that had started to take over the abandoned property. Wood had to be cut and split for fires. There was more than enough work to keep the noobs busy.

The 3Ms were evaluated, then sent to section chiefs to be evaluated more closely and either assigned and immediately put to work or sent to the noobs if their skills were lacking.

The students went through their own evaluations. The first order of business was a test that covered different levels of math, English, and reading comprehension. The intent was to find out the highest level at which a student could perform. They would then be able to take the appropriate classes. The younger students were bussed to an off-ranch school nearby that consolidated children from the county and the nearby communities. The older kids, from about twelve on up, stayed on the ranch for school and were usually finished before they were seventeen. That meant that Raftaar would ride the bus.

The classes were more concentrated than a pre-Hexen high school, eliminating some of the softer classes and focusing on subjects that were more immediately useful to life in the here and now. Aasha was nicely advanced for her age and would have to go to two more years of classes, finishing just before she turned sixteen.

Shirina was the one in the gray area. Liz Mitchell spoke to her one-on-one.

"Last year, I'd have said you were definite college material, early admission," she commented. "No question about it. Of course, that was pre-Hexen. Now, I'm afraid I'm unaware of any college that is back in operation. It is probably going to be years before any of them are. What I suggest is that you take a few classes that we offer. Eric is very big on our Constitution and our Government classes. He wants everyone to take those. I'd also like to have you as a teaching assistant. With this influx of people, I think I ought to be able to justify that in my budget. But I guess I'm kind of getting ahead of things. What were your plans before Hexen?"

"College, of course. I was interested in chemistry."

"On the bright side, you are young. Even if it takes the colleges ten years to come back, you'll only be twenty-six. Of course, that sounds like an old lady to you, doesn't it?" Then Liz laughed at Shirina's expression. She was trying to imagine herself that old and at the same time trying to not insult Ms. Mitchell, who was certainly older than that.

"Shirina, let me outline your career choices here. Obviously, they are severely curtailed from the opportunities you would have had before. You're small, so manual labor is out. That leaves things like teacher, nurse, veterinarian, clerk, cook, and some of the construction trades like electrician. Mechanic, maybe. Oh, and Security, but that might not be in your wheelhouse. Those are pretty much the choices regardless if you are a man or a woman.

"Let me mention something else. You're sixteen, turning seventeen in another three months. That puts you in another gray area. You seem very mature so I don't see any issue with regarding you as an adult. Plus, you have Aasha and Raftaar as dopts, so that gives you a household."

"I'm sorry," Shirina interrupted. "What did you say? Aasha and Raftaar are what?"

"Oh, sorry! Dopts. Like 'adoptees'. That's our slang term. One dopt, two dopts. And the term is the same both ways. You are Aasha's dopt, for example. That is, if you want to keep that relationship. Or was that just for the journey?"

"No, we stay together, if we can."

"We're not going to tear you apart. You have two options. One is a house of your own. It will either be a tiny house, really not much more than a single room, or it will be a full-sized house but you'll have to share it with another family. The other option is to become a House Manager and move into the girl's dorm. You and Aasha would live there but Raftaar would be in the boy's dorm. Why don't we gather up Aasha tomorrow or the next day and let you look at all of the options for yourselves?"

Shirina's head swam. She didn't know what the best option was. She wasn't sure she was ready to be an adult. Tonight, she resolved that she and Aasha and Raftaar would pray for guidance.

Chapter 12

The meeting in the conference room that morning had the same cast as the previous night. Dani, Taylor, and everyone on the MCC side was looking sharp in their pressed camouflage. The Northerners, the new MCC people, were looking rather road-weary but were at least showered and newly clothed thanks to the showers and warehouses at HQ.

"This afternoon and evening we want to run everyone through the showers and get them some new clothing. Today we are doing job classification and getting more houses suitable for habitation. I know you're cramped with eight and ten to a house but we are expanding that even as we speak," Dani related.

"Father Doyle, we do have Pastor Michael with us today. I would like for him to show you around today and for you to coordinate schedules to a suitable compromise. We have a single church building at this point, which is also used for community meetings and as a classroom. We may be able to build a separate church in the future but that is not an option right now so we have to share. And Father, I do need to speak with you at length at some point, regarding confession and my wedding."

"Excellent! Congratulations on your upcoming marriage! And I'm sure your confession will be nothing of any consequence." Doyle beamed a toothy smile at her.

There was a sudden dead silence in the room. It was like having hard rock music on full volume and suddenly cutting it off. The silence comes back and almost slaps you in the face. It started to stretch out. Doyle's smile began to slip and a look crept onto his face like he'd committed some blatant faux pas. Brennan cut her eyes at Dani and opened her mouth and drew in a breath to speak.

Pastor Michael beat her to it by suddenly standing and suggesting "Father, perhaps you and I should take that walk now. Let me show you around."

Doyle's smile had disappeared completely now, replaced by apprehension. His mind raced, trying to figure out what he'd said wrong.

Dani held up her hand. "It's okay, Michael. It's something that…" She sighed and waved a hand in an 'it doesn't matter' gesture. "Y'all were going to hear about it sooner or later. You may as well hear it straight from the source and sooner rather than later." She paused for a moment, collecting her thoughts before she continued.

"Eric and I were in Houston when Hexen hit. We had to fight our way up here. I was involved in three gunfights. Then there was a gang that tried to take over the city of Tyler and stole from us and tried to follow us back here to attack us. We took the fight to them instead. We had two big battles with them, one in Tyler and one in Dallas, plus some smaller ambushes.

"After the Dallas battle, we — no, I'm not going to say that. I, not we, I, myself, alone and solely responsible — *I* executed the prisoners. We had full and complete legal authority straight from the governor and I carried the sentence out. Between those executions and battles and the gunfights, I have killed something like a hundred seventy, maybe a hundred and seventy-five men." She leaned back in her chair and looked over the Northerners. Their mouths were all hanging open and she could actually see the blood draining from some of their faces.

She let the silence go on for a few seconds and then continued. "The *Pistoleros*, that's the gang, they thought I was a demon. I actually encouraged that rumor in an attempt to scare them off. On the other hand, there are a number of people, especially in Dallas, who think that I am *Santa Muerte*, who is a saint, Saint Death literally, in Latin American culture. Kind of a female Grim Reaper, with a scythe. And there was an event in which I actually encouraged that rumor also. With several hundred people who got down on their knees and tried to worship me and sacrifice chickens to me and I tried to discourage all that, but there it is."

"But... but..." one of the Northerners stammered, "That sounds like a war. Like killing someone in a war. It's not as if you drove down the street and shot people at random."

"You're right. It was most definitely a war. And there are still bad people out there. We don't run all of this expensive security for the fun of it. But if y'all need to take a break, go to the bathroom, refill your coffee, let's do that now." She stood up and walked out to find something to do for a few minutes. Taylor bounced out of her seat and followed.

Dani walked out to the duty area and asked the duty NCO a couple of questions that were just to have something to say. Taylor sidled over to an unoccupied desk, picked up a clipboard at random, and looked at Dani like she had a question. Dani walked over and they pretended to confer about something while staring at the clipboard.

"Are you okay?" Taylor asked, almost whispering.

"Yeah, I just... I was going to tell them. I just didn't want to be forced into it like that. It was probably a good thing to get that on the table early. I shouldn't be irritated but I am."

"That's one of the perks of being a girl. You can be irritated when you shouldn't be!" Taylor had such a big, bright, beatific smile on her face that Dani had to laugh.

She hugged Taylor, muttered "You crazy bitch," and they killed another ten minutes before they walked back into the conference room.

When the guy got back to his desk from the errand he was running, the duty NCO told him that Dani and Taylor had been looking at one of his clipboards very intently and Dani looked pissed. The clerk spent the next hour rechecking absolutely everything on the clipboard and couldn't find anything until he went back to the warehouse and started counting things himself. He found one miscount and chewed out the guy that had made the mistake and gave him extra duty. He fixed his paperwork but never could figure out how those two had zeroed in on such a small thing like that. Maybe there really was something to that 'angel' thing about Dani. Or maybe the *Santa Muerte* one.

Naw, no way that's true, neither one.

But then how…

Chapter 13

Dani, back in the conference room said, "Okay. My apologies. It has been a very traumatic time for all of us."

"And my sincere apologies for reminding you of it, my child," Father Doyle spoke up. "I certainly didn't intend to bring up anything so dreadful, so..." He shook his head in amazement. "I simply cannot imagine the... I will be glad to hear your confession at any time that is convenient to you, and devote as much time to you as necessary."

"Thank you, Father. That really does mean a great deal to me. Regarding what I told you before the break, does anyone have any questions, comments, concerns?" She scanned the Northerners.

"Is there an ongoing threat?" asked Bill.

"Not from the *Pistoleros* or anyone that I am aware of. We located their headquarters in Dallas and dropped artillery on it. Lots of artillery. Then we shot anything that moved. Then I shot the prisoners. I don't think there are many *Pistoleros* left alive after all that, so no, I don't see them as a threat. Another gang could be. Or there may be Russian tanks coming over the horizon in the next three minutes. I have no way of knowing. We do have ongoing issues with cattle thieves and other opportunistic thieves, potential rapists, criminals like that. Could you address that, please, Brennan?"

"That is an issue. It doesn't happen often but we do have to keep a watch out. We have people on duty around the clock, manning checkpoints on the main roads leading in here, guarding cattle and important locations, plus roving patrols. We have contact with our neighbors and defense agreements, but of course there are gaps where people can sneak through. There have been six incidents where our Security people exchanged gunfire with intruders. We had one man wounded but not seriously and we killed two and captured three altogether."

"What happened to the ones you captured?"

"We hung them. After a fair trial, of course. No one should expect to shoot at our people and get away with a slap on the wrist. That's attempted murder. We don't take that lightly."

There was a short silence, broken when Bill mused "I guess we had safety in numbers when we travelled down here. No one wanted to take on our big group of people. We did have an incident where one of our scouts had to fire warning shots, and Mark here was just reminding me of how one small group that joined ours had trouble. They were attacked and lost two of their members before they drove off the bandits."

"We looked too poor and shabby to rob," one of the other Northerners grumped. "Compared to here, especially. I imagine this place looks like a gold mine. Plenty of people would love to come in here and rob this place."

"And so we run security," Dani agreed. "Moving on to other things, then. I understand that your group is composed of smaller groups and that you are the leaders of those various groups. Or at least of the larger groups"

"Yes, that's correct."

"Okay. You do realize that as we integrate the people into our operation, the need for a separate command structure will be reduced and even eliminated in many cases?" Dani raised her eyebrows.

One of the Northerners spoke up immediately. "Put me out of this job as soon as you can! I never wanted to be the leader but someone had to do it. I want to go back to being an engineer, and I think you said Ted needed a project manager. I've done that. Let's talk!"

"Good deal. As for the others, I'm not saying we're kicking you out of your positions. We need to have a transition period and with increased personnel we'll have an increased need for leaders. But this is an integration. We're not setting you up as a separate community. That would create an 'us versus them' mentality that could get ugly if food starts running low. Or rather, when."

"Of course. I think everyone realizes that, or should realize it," Bill replied. "None of us were politicians. Maybe some middle managers or such but we were all just trying to survive and to help as many others survive as possible."

"That's good. We definitely don't need any internal fighting here. It's going to be tough enough as is. Three days from now is Sunday. If the weather cooperates, we want to do a cookout and have a little down time. The ones that aren't on duty, that is. Someone, many people, are always up and alert and working on something. Not just Security. And then the following week is Thanksgiving. Of course, we will do something for that but it's not going to be an all-you-can-eat feast. We are already starting to ration.

"I want to show you a map of our territory and what our plans are for expansion..."

***

Later that morning they were giving a tour of the ranch to the Northerner command group and then Dani intended to cut them loose after lunch to process them through Personnel and get them to work. She had other things that demanded her attention and she was just easing their transition from leader to worker at this point. Courtesies must be observed, but she thought she had done enough. She was more concerned at this point on how well the work to house the newcomers was going. They had been speaking to Liz at the school and dorms when their driver came trotting up.

"We just got a radio message. A messenger from the governor's office is here. They're bringing him to meet us here."

Dani's blood ran cold. *Oh, please God, please Jesus,* please *don't tell me that anything has happened to Eric!*

Taylor had the same reaction, though less religious. She tried to figure out how to get the Northerners away from Dani but they had just finished the tour of this area and there wasn't really anything else here to show them. It didn't matter. She needed to move them away.

"If y'all will please follow me," she called, waving an arm over her head and then turning and walking. They trooped obediently behind her to the other side of the road and a ways down it. "One of you is an engineer, right? What do you think of an addition to the dorms on this side? Or should we go two-story?" She just started firing off any questions she could think of to keep them occupied but she kept an eye on Dani. She saw the truck wheeling up and a couple of guys get out, one in camo that had to be an MCC guy and one in leathers like a motorcyclist.

That made sense. There was a route open to Austin through a series of back roads. They had done it in trucks a number of times now. At highway speeds it should have been about five hours. In trucks, with rest stops and working slowly around some dead eighteen-wheelers, it could take ten or twelve. On a motorcycle, though, you could get close to that five-hour time if you were familiar with the route and were daring and a little reckless. Taylor turned and interrupted the engineer in mid-sentence.

"I'm sorry. Excuse me for a minute." She turned and started walking quickly towards Dani, who was opening an envelope from the messenger. Then she apparently thought *fuck it* and started to run, her long legs pumping hard. She didn't run like a girl, either, her long, silky blonde hair streaming out behind her.

Dani scanned the document quickly, then again more carefully. She took in a deep breath slowly and exhaled it slowly, eyes closed, and crossed herself. Taylor skidded to a stop in front of her, causing the messenger to step back. Her big green eyes bored into Dani's amber ones.

"Nobody's hurt," she said and the blonde blew out a big, noisy breath.

"Well, that scared the hell out of me," she exclaimed. She noticed that Dani was reading the document again, paying attention to the message that was on it this time, and not just looking for words like *death, hospital, injured*, and things like that. She saw her jaw clench, and when she looked up, she was *pissed*.

Taylor stepped aside because she didn't want to look at her, she wanted to look at the messenger. When she moved and the messenger could see the little Latina's face, he took a step back, bumping into the guy that had driven him here from the HQ building.

"Are you fucking *kidding* me?" she growled through clenched teeth.

The messenger had both hands up in front of his body, palms out. "Ma'am, I'm just a runner. I don't even know what —" He stopped when Dani looked away and put a hand up. She handed the message to her assistant and walked around the truck to burn off some furious energy, a dark expression on her face.

"It's okay. She's not mad at you". It was kind of amusing to see the big messenger — well, beanstalk-thin but very tall — afraid of little Dani. He towered over her by more than a foot. She looked like a toddler compared to him. Then Taylor read the paper and her mouth dropped open. "Are you fucking kidding me? Holy shit!"

Chapter 14

A messenger finally found Eric deep in a warehouse and handed him an envelope. He tore it open, read the contents, and gritted his teeth. "Are you fucking KIDDING me?"

He kicked a nearby metal trash can, caving in the side and sending it flying across the room. It almost beaned a soldier, who ducked and then looked at Eric wide-eyed.

"Shit! Sorry, man!" Eric apologized and waved at him. He looked down at the paper again and said slowly, "Son of a bitch." He took a couple of deep breaths to calm himself. He didn't need to yell at people who hadn't done anything wrong. He handed the message to Mark, his assistant, to read.

He turned to the messenger. "Tell the governor I received the f-f-f — the message."

Next, he pointed at the sergeant who was in charge of his escort. He travelled with three Humvees loaded with soldiers and weapons. This was potentially dangerous territory and no one travelled alone or unarmed.

"I need to be face to face with Major Batista ASAP. Find out where he's at and get us there soonest." He turned towards another sergeant, further off. "Keep this running. Just use your best judgement. If in doubt, take it all. More is better."

He started walking towards the Humvees and his little entourage followed.

"Mark, when we get stopped, compose a message. It goes to Cavazos. I need the engineers, the train engineers, to get me four, repeat four more train engines, locomotives, whatever the fuck they call them, four more up and running *now*, and I need them here *now*. I'll get the major to send it under his signature."

He looked at Mark.

"Here's a command secret and a negotiating secret: if you want two, demand four. If they get me two then I'll be happy but I sure as hell won't tell them that. Instead, I'll bitch at them that they only gave me half what I wanted." He was silent for three or four steps.

"Well, fuck me. I just realized that's what the governor did to me with those refugees. Son of a bitch."

***

Meanwhile, back at the ranch, the Northerners, Dani, and Taylor were all gathered by the SUVs in the driveway of the school.

"This is a message from the governor," Dani waved the paper. "I'll let you read it, but what it says is that there are another *six hundred* refugees headed this way. And when Trey Marsh says six hundred, I have found out it's going to be closer to seven hundred fifty. The one redeeming thing he says is that he is giving us supplies from a FEMA warehouse. I don't know if that's enough food to get us through the winter or what, but it's in Fort Worth and Eric is in Dallas with a train so at least we have transportation."

"Oh, my God! How is that going to work? If two hundred people were going to strain your supplies, and then you add another seven hundred and fifty on top of that…"

"FEMA is federal. How is a state governor controlling that?" someone else asked.

Dani looked at that guy like he was an idiot.

"Where have you been the last eight months? They used to say that possession was nine-tenths of the law. Now it's a hundred percent. You reach out and you take it, that's how. You go out there and you stand on the thing with a rifle in your hand and you make it yours. Now load up. Everybody in the trucks. We're going back to the HQ and there is a huge amount of work to do."

Once they were back at the office, Dani turned to the refugee leaders.

"My apologies to everyone but we have a crisis on our hands. I have to ask you to go through Personnel and have them place you where you can start doing the most good as soon as possible. I still want you as leaders of your groups but I need to deal with one person and not each of your groups separately. I am going to keep Bill here since you elected him as your overall leader.

"Bill, you are going to be the Refugee Integration Coordinator. I just created that position. We need to find someone to work with you, someone experienced in how we do things here. I want you in all the meetings."

"Thank you for having the confidence in me," he said.

"I don't know if you'll be thanking me in a few weeks," she commented dryly. "Or even in a few days."

She turned to the duty NCO.

"Since you just heard me say 'crisis', here it is. We're getting six hundred more refugees. I don't want any wild rumors starting. Get on the radio and bring in the management group. Send runners if you can't contact someone. I need them here now, like right now."

Ted was standing in the doorway of his office, attracted by the noise and trying to see what was going on. Dani wordlessly handed him the message.

He read it and said "They have got to be —" He finished the rest of it under his breath. Everyone else had said it. "Okay, so that's my afternoon migraine starting up early." He closed his eyes and pinched the bridge of his nose.

Dani nodded. "Yep. Let's head to the conference room. Come on, Mr. Refugee Coordinator."

***

The FEMA warehouses were huge, two of them, actually. The governor's signature on the document accompanying the message had gotten Eric inside through the State Police guards. He looked down a row of shelving that was stacked to the ceiling with cardboard boxes secured with shrink-wrap, then at the staff sergeant that had accompanied him.

"We're authorized a quarter-million MREs and fifty-thousand liters of water. What's your plan for loading it by tomorrow morning, staff sergeant?"

The sergeant shook his head.

"Not a problem, General, if you can throw enough men and equipment at it. And it would help if I could choose at least some of the men. But if I can get all that, I'll get your train loaded, Sir."

"Let's go back and pick your crew, then. You have a gold card. Whatever you need, you get." He looked at the guard. "We'll be back in an hour or two. Then we'll be here all night."

Chapter 15

There was an uneasy quiet in the conference room. People were simmering in their own thoughts without a lot of small talk. This wasn't a problem where the company might lose money, or suffer some bad publicity, or maybe was in danger of being bought out by a competitor. No, this was an issue where people may go hungry. People may die over the winter. This was serious.

Dani and Taylor came in and took their seats. "Okay," Dani said, and sighed. "So, six hundred more people coming in, which is probably a low estimate. I'm going to guess more like seven hundred and fifty, so I am going to start calling this group The 750. I don't know when they're arriving, but they are on the way.

"One advantage we have is that we just got things opened up for The 200 group that just arrived. We can use that experience to help us do it better and more efficiently this time. With that in mind, Bill, here, is our new Refugee Integration Coordinator. I haven't fully worked out the details of what that position means, but my intent is that it will be more on the personnel side of things. We can do the math and figure out how many beds we need, how much food, how many outhouses. It's not that.

"Bill will be more on getting the kids sorted out to the proper dormitories and the proper schools, getting everyone through medical, getting them to personnel to integrate into jobs, and so on. Something like, this group goes to medical today, that group tomorrow, and get a manageable flow going rather than everyone descend on medical all at the same time. Bill will talk to all of you and make schedules. And he'll need an assistant, someone with experience here at the ranch, who knows their way around and how we do things. Suggestions are welcome.

"Housing, food, water, and sanitation are going to be the big four. There's enough housing if we go out far enough, but then how do we transport people? I think we're going to have to go with the plan that we considered with the 200, which is to use the school as a dormitory as much as possible. It'll be easier to take the students somewhere else for classes if we have to.

"Sanitation goes right along with housing. Sure, I know guys can just whip it out and go anywhere in the woods, but you can't do that with large numbers of people over any length of time. You'll contaminate the water supply and spread disease. So, we have to have outhouses. I guess I need to get Ted to address that issue."

"Of course," he said. "Last time, with The 200, we tried to round up those fiberglass portable toilets from construction sites but that turned out to be a waste of time. We found out that there would be maybe three or four at any one site, if that. So, we tried to find a place that rented them. I mean, somebody owns them, right? But apparently business was good and most of them were out... at various construction sites scattered all over three counties. That put us back to square one.

"We have a well-drilling machine that can dig a hole for an outhouse pretty quickly, but we need a lot of them. If you figure we can put bunk beds in houses and put ten people per house, on average, that's seventy-five outhouses. Now, that's a simple wooden structure, just a box like a deer blind, but you have to cut and nail it up, roof it, and paint it to keep it waterproof and have it not warp and rot.

"The short-term alternative is that you can use a regular toilet if you fill up the tank with water. But that takes a lot of water."

"Yeah, we don't want to do that," agreed Dani. "Get the guy who had project management experience, I forget his name, get him to take a chunk of your work, Ted. Give him this as a project or something."

"Another thing on the housing," Brennan broke in, "is that the further out you go, the thinner you're going to stretch Security. You're talking seventy-five additional houses now.

The houses around here aren't that close together. That's a lot of territory."

"Good point." Dani crossed her arms and leaned back, gazing at the ceiling for a moment. "Let's do this — we'll start with the school. Turn that into a dorm for now, and that gives us some breathing space to open more houses. And the houses that we open up, seventy-five or whatever, are going to be the only ones we open for ninety days at minimum. That gives people a limited time to be crammed in all together. After ninety days we will reevaluate and see what we can do. No promises other than we'll take a look and make plans."

She turned to Bill. "Our method is that we divide people into three categories: families, singles, and nodopts. The nodopts go into dorms —"

"Wait. What did you call them?" he interrupted.

"Sorry. That's local slang. Not adopted. Taylor's a minor and we adopted her, so she's our dopt and we're her dopts. It runs both ways. A nodopt is a minor that has not been adopted. They live in dorms with a house manager, or it could be a couple. You're going to have to call for volunteers or something to get people for those positions. Of course, you don't know how many house managers you'll need until the entire 750 group gets here." She gave him a big, bright smile.

"I guess I have not yet appreciated all you did to accommodate us," he said slowly.

"The part that scares me is the food, more than the housing. We don't want to wipe out whole herds of cattle for food over the winter because that will impact everything going forward. We could eat like kings this winter and then starve because we have no cattle left for the next year. The good thing is that the governor is releasing FEMA food supplies to us."

"Are there lakes around here? For fishing?" Bill spoke up.

"We have some ponds that are stocked, and there are nearby lakes, but we haven't really made a big effort in that direction. It always seemed to be a lot of time and effort for not much return to me."

"We could try trotlines," he replied. "They aren't legal in all jurisdictions, but I guess that may be kind of out the window at this point. It's a line stretched across a large section of water with multiple hooks hanging down from it. It's like a trap. You just set it, or set multiple ones, and come back later on to check it. We were able to feed a lot of people that way on the trip down here."

"You get a lot of fish?"

"Yeah, that's why they're illegal in some jurisdictions. That is, if you have the right bait and everything."

"I guess none of us are fishermen except you, so I want you to follow up on that. As a matter of fact, your real duties won't fully begin until the 750 start to arrive, so tomorrow would be a great time for you to do a proof of concept. Ted can get you set up with a vehicle and equipment and let you get on the road first thing. Do you need a boat?"

"Yeah, nothing big. Just a little Jon boat."

She turned to Ted. "Do we have boats?"

"Oh, yeah," he answered. "There were lots of people that owned them. We have plenty of boats. But we haven't worked to try to get any of the motors running."

"We can row it tomorrow," Bill volunteered, "but if this works out, we'll need to have some working motors. Just a couple."

Dani sighed and looked at Taylor as she flipped to a page on her pad titled 'Motor Pool' and made a note. She didn't have to tell her to take notes; she was looking at how many items were already on the list.

She was scared. She'd been scared fighting her way up from Houston but after that, things had settled down, become comfortable, even. Then the ranching operations had given them enough of a surplus to be able to sell beef, and they got the banks started up, and there was the land grant, and she'd started to feel rich. That's when the world jumps on you with both feet. Like almost a thousand refugees coming in with absolutely nothing, just hungry mouths to feed.

For just a second, she wished she was in her first semester of college, where she would have been if civilization hadn't ended, stressed about something as minor as a term paper instead of keeping people alive. And keeping things like food riots from becoming a reality. But that was gone immediately, and she got a surge through her body, determination that she was not going to be defeated.

She was going to attack the problem head on. She stood abruptly.

"You know, I think we all had the same reaction when we read the message from the governor. We all said 'you've got to be freakin' kidding me'. Only I don't think we said 'freakin'. I know I didn't. But we can do this. We *will* do this. It's going to mean cramped quarters and I imagine we'll all shed a few pounds over the winter.

"But this is going to be a good thing. We have a quarter million acres here now. We are going to get out there and bring all of those ranches and farms and oil wells and whatever we find out there, we are going to get it all up and running and producing and we are going to rebuild this world.

"I came in here this morning with a glum face because I was thinking about how much work this was going to be. And it will be a lot of work. But I'm looking forward to getting that 750 in here because those people represent opportunity. There will be rough patches, but this will be a good thing. A great thing."

She smacked her hands together, a single clap, loud in the silent room. A smile creased her face and her eyes danced.

"Let's do this!"

***

I'm fucking exhausted, Taylor wrote, a couple of days later. *The only reason I'm writing this is I'm so tired I can't sleep. I don't know if that makes sense or not. I'm too tired.*

Dani managed to spare a little bit of time, about an hour, to talk to Father Doyle. I guess that was a confession. I don't know. I'm not Catholic. I'm not the right person to ask.

When she came back, I could tell she'd been crying. And I heard in passing that the good Father spent a long time in his room. A really long time. I guess he was praying for guidance or something. Or maybe performing an exorcism in absentia. I hope I'm not being disrespectful with that little joke. Not meaning to be if so. I'm just saying that I think he was pretty shaken up. Dani looked better, though, and that was the important part. Let someone else take on some of her burden.

We were going to do something for Thanksgiving but that pretty much went out the window with a battalion of refugees coming here. Eric had started gathering some data points he wanted to talk about in a speech, some good numbers about how well we were doing. Dani and I and some of the others had a whole plan going for decorations and activities and bands and all that. The cooks had a big menu planned.

Scratch all that.

Well, not completely. The menu got cut down to a regular meal for everyone, not a big all-you-can-eat food orgy. We've already started rationing now. For the rest of it, we gathered up a committee of high school girls and dropped the planning for the activities on them. Dropped it completely, like, "here was our basic idea, run with it and don't talk to us about anything, just make you own decisions and do it."

That's good, actually. It gives them a little real-world experience and responsibility and if things don't turn out great, then oh well. No big impact. Eric and Dani both like to challenge people, push their abilities. If you can do ten of something now, they want you to do twelve. You get to twelve, they want fifteen. Like me with shooting, for example. I'd never even held a gun before I got here. Now I can hit targets at the full length of our twelve-hundred yard rifle range. All because Eric pushed me to do it.

He's actually here at the ranch now, which was unexpected. He just popped off of the train that came rolling in with the FEMA MREs.

That was pretty cute. Eric just came riding up in his SUV, which looks like the other two, so you couldn't tell it was him until he got out. Dani saw him and ran into his arms at high speed. Crash! Probably left bruises on both of them. I bailed out of the house and slept at HQ for a couple of days. There are some bunks there for the runners and the next guard shift. We call it the Doghouse, like a guy pisses off his wife or girlfriend and has to go spend the night in the doghouse. I just claimed one of the bunks to give those two lovebirds some alone time.

But whatever they were doing in the privacy of their own bedroom at night, they were up before the crack of dawn and running hard and fast. That group of 750 is going to hit us like an eighteen-wheeler at high speed. We're still working to get the 200 squared away.

And I got my first taste of MREs. Eric said we'd better introduce them into our diet now, otherwise we'll get to the point where they are all we have and no one wants to eat them for breakfast, lunch, and dinner.

Oh. My. God. Meals, Ready to Eat? No, no, and no. The only word that's not a lie in that name is 'to'. I've never been a real big fan of heavy spice and barbecue sauce and steak sauce and Tabasco, but when it comes to an MRE I am. I'll almost pour used motor oil on it to cover up the taste. Fortunately, we can mix them in with some good meat and onions and bell peppers and beans and stuff and they are more edible. Not actually edible, just more edible. Less inedible. But I understand MREs are twelve-hundred calories per pack, so one MRE with some supplemental real food per day will keep people alive through the winter.

That's a good thing, but I never imagined I'd have to think in those terms. Never thought I'd have to plan in terms of how many calories to keep someone alive.

And while we're desperately running to keep the incoming mob fed and watered and housed, we can't forget our existing operations, like the banks and the oil & gas support, both of which require constant movement of supplies back and forth. Which reminds me of something I need to remind Dani about tomorrow. I have to write myself a note on that so I'll end here.

OMG so f'ing tired.

Chapter 16

"Tell me about your experience today," Dani prompted, late one afternoon.

"As you know, I went out with a crew that was opening houses up for the 750," Bill began. "You could barely tell a house was back there, with the first one. It's been less than a year, but the foliage has grown up so much that it almost covered up the driveway. They ran a bushhog down it and around the yard. Then they had some other string trimmer on wheels thing to cut a path up to the door."

"The soil around here is great for agriculture, I understand," Dani agreed. "Tyler, the biggest city near the ranch, is known as the Rose Capital of the U.S., and it used to produce over half of the rose bushes sold commercially in the country."

"That doesn't surprise me. Stuff grows very well here. Anyway, they had kicked the door previously. Actually, not kicked it in, but broke out a single pane of glass on the window in the door and opened the lock that way. And they had nailed plywood up over the window afterwards.

"There were no dead bodies, thank God. The house was musty, of course, and we opened windows to air it out. Other than that, it was mainly a survey to figure out how many bedrooms there were, and how many bunk beds could fit in each one."

"Yeah, that was part of the learning process." She looked disappointed. "If you kick a door, you have to be damned sure you can get it locked down when you leave. Otherwise, any door or window that is broken or ajar will let in bugs, rain, and small furry animals that are not cute at all when they are nesting in a house. All that can trash it in no time. We've had to simply burn a few houses that were just too far gone."

"Burn them?"

"Yep. You can't have a house full of rats and black mold close to inhabited dwellings. You have to torch it. It's sad. It's heartbreaking, actually, but we've had to do it.

"Here was a place that was someone's home, more than likely multiple people. Maybe multiple generations of the same family. It's still filled with their possessions. Photographs of ancestors on the walls. Kid's toys. A comfortable recliner.

"We watched them do it once, me and Taylor. The owners were probably dead and gone. I don't know. We didn't see them die. But we saw their memories and dreams burn down to ash. We both cried. Once was one time too many."

"I'm sorry. I didn't mean to bring you down or anything."

"No, it wasn't you." She drew in a deep breath and let it out slowly. "You have to do a lot of hard things in this world. Or maybe that's just being an adult, only with different things."

They talked some more, but Bill left the Headquarters building thinking that the tough young Latina who had killed so many men had a soft side, too.

***

With all of the work going on to integrate The 200 and make ready for The 750, Thanksgiving was a non-event. In retrospect, that was probably a good thing. The holidays always show a spike in suicides when people sit around and contemplate those who are no longer there, and that number was considerable after Hexen. MCC did have three suicides, which was actually less than expected. It had been discussed in one of the countless meetings. But the celebration was very low-key. The weather was rainy, the meal was adequate but no feast, and many people preferred to just rest.

The first parts of The 750 started arriving the next day, a young group of about forty. They weren't scouts or an advance guard. The group had no such organization and was really just a mass of people in singles, couples, and groups, all heading for MCC. All with nothing. All hungry.

Dani wasn't going to waste time welcoming every little group. There were far too many other things she needed to do. There had been more promotions and they had some good staff sergeants and lieutenants now that could handle the small groups.

Eric was back in Dallas and he was tearing through that city and Fort Worth and grabbing everything he could think of that would assist them. They went through smaller locations like quick oil-change or auto parts stores in minutes, leaving nothing but empty shelves. It was like a swarm of locusts. It was a waste of time to pick and choose items to keep or leave. Just take everything.

At larger locations like retail stores and warehouses, it made sense to be more selective, but not a lot. Footwear, for example. Anything that resembled a work boot or hiking shoe, rubber boot, or athletic shoe, in any size, male or female, was scooped up.

Houses near the MCC loading dock, miles from the ranch, had been taken over and people lived there, just to be ready whenever a train came in. And come in they did. The men from Fort Cavazos that had repaired the other trains were brought up to Dallas and got a couple more running, plus some smaller switchers that are needed to move cars around a yard or side track.

Other houses were turned into temporary warehouses, with all of the furniture stacked in one room and the others filled with boxes. The influx of the 200 and 750 groups were turned to building if they didn't have anything more pressing. MCC needed more warehouse space of its own, temporarily at least, until items like shoes could be given out to the needy. They needed more dorm and school space for the kids on a longer-term basis. They needed more kitchen space, more shower space, more… more… more…

Shirina's decision on housing was made for her with the news of The 750 refugees coming in. She didn't mind having her options taken away. She was happy to help. These people were giving her food and clothes and a nice place to live. Who was she to complain?

She found herself assigned as house manager for a mini-dorm. It was all girls, so Aasha was there and she saw Raftaar every day after school. He slept in the boy's dorm right next door to the school, although he rode the bus to the county school.

Things were a lot better for them now, better than they had been since Hexen. Except for the one young man who kept coming around. She wasn't interested in him but he wouldn't take 'no' for an answer. Until the time that he grabbed her and she used the little knife she had carried for months. Modern society had made carrying a knife in a city fairly unacceptable until Hexen and their journey south made it indispensable. The knife symbolizes a Sikh's duty to come to the aid of those in danger, and she didn't use it maliciously, just a jab into his arm to get his attention.

***

The good thing about The 200 (actually two hundred thirty-two) coming in was that it was a dress rehearsal for The 750 (actually seven hundred twenty-eight). They were called The 200 and The 750 groups because they didn't know the final numbers at the start and had to call them something. All of the departments, Personnel, Housing, etc., were on their game when the 750 showed up. Fortunately, they didn't all show up in one group. In several big groups, but also a lot of smaller ones. And there was no rest and relaxation at the end of a long trip. They were fed, put to bed, processed and medically prodded and questioned the next day, and at work later on that morning in many cases.

If nothing else they were hands. Unload this lumber from that truck and put it over there so we can build more dorms to house the kids you brought with you. You know how to drive a nail without bending it? Okay, start driving them into that outhouse over there.

They didn't have to dream up any make-work. There was too much actual work that needed to be done. Overwhelmingly, the refugees bent to it and performed the task. They realized that they were in a fight for their own health and safety and well-being. There were some that were rubbed the wrong way, though. Conflicts were inevitable, but generally fairly low-key. Some, not so much.

That's why Brennan brought one to Dani's attention. Brennan ran a minor court every Wednesday night and Dani fully endorsed her judgements, but this one had the potential to blow up more than just a fistfight between a couple of hotheads. It involved an alleged attempted rape and a potential assault with a deadly weapon. Worse, it involved an MCC male and a 200 Group female. The outcome could seriously affect relations between those two groups and interfere with, basically, everything.

That being the case, Dani invited a number of people important to both communities. As much as she wanted them to all be one happy family, she realized that there were groups within groups and therefore influential people in those groups. In addition, she made sure everyone knew the court was open to the public on a space available basis.

What was not disputed was that a girl named Shirina, sixteen, had cut the arm of a boy named David, eighteen. It was not serious enough to make him miss work but would leave a scar, and having people cut one another up was not conducive to a polite society.

Shirina claimed she thought he was going to rape her, that he had put his hands on her without permission and that she had told him to stop to no avail. David claimed he had not done such a thing.

Dani looked the both of them over with her arms crossed. "On the one hand, we don't want people cutting other people up for no reason. That should only be done as a very serious matter to protect yourself. On the other hand, rape is a very, very serious matter. Deadly force, killing an attacker, is justified to protect oneself against rape. The bottom line here is that this is a 'he said — she said' situation. You two were the only witnesses and each has a different story, so it is impossible for me or anyone else to determine who is telling the more accurate story. Therefore, I am not saying anyone is guilty but I do have some assignments."

"David, do you go to church?"

"No, ma'am, not really."

"What religion are you?"

"Southern Baptist, ma'am"

"Well, you go to church now. You will attend Pastor Michael's services every Sunday for the next twelve weeks at minimum. And if the Pastor has any additional work he needs done, any cleaning or setup, then I'll bet you will be delighted to volunteer to do it." She glanced at Pastor Michael, sitting front and center. He smiled and gave her a thumbs up.

She looked at Shirina. "Shirina, you are a Sikh?"

"Yes, ma'am."

"I must confess I don't know anything about that. Are you the oldest Sikh here?"

"Yes, ma'am."

"We need to talk sometime. I should learn more about Sikhism. About this matter, I want you on twelve weeks of KP duty at the chow hall every Sunday morning."

"Ma'am? I don't know what that is."

"Kitchen Police. That means you wash dishes, take out the trash, whatever the cooks tell you to do."

Taylor waved at Dani to get her attention, then stepped closer and whispered something to her.

"Oh! Yes, that's brilliant. Shirina, we are also enrolling you in a self-defense class. You were going to take it anyway at some point but you're going to the top of the list for the next one that starts."

Chapter 17

MCC was very concerned with firearms safety. There were a lot of firearms around at all times and it was vitally important that everyone go through a safety class at minimum. Beyond that they could train them to do anything, with classes roughly categorized as pistol, rifle, and long-range rifle depending on which range was needed. Optimally, the majority of people would be proficient enough with pistol and rifle to defend themselves.

There was a group on the rifle range, having completed the safety class, when Taylor saw a gross violation right in front of her. She was pulling coach duty on the range because she was actually one of the most highly trained shooters they had, thanks to the work Eric had put into her and Dani's training early on.

What she saw was one of the newest refugees, Greg, turn and start to sweep the barrel of his rifle across the people on the firing line to the right. The rifle should have been empty at that point but she didn't know that it was and it didn't matter anyway. One of the four basic rules of firearms safety is that you do not point the weapon at anything you do not want to destroy.

She stepped up and shoved the rifle hard back into a position where it was pointing safely downrange. She figured if it hit the guy in the face that would make a lasting impression on him about safety. It did. It hit him in the bridge of the nose and the Picatinny rail on the top of the rifle raked a flap of skin loose. He shoved the rifle back at Taylor. It slammed into her hands and jammed one finger painfully.

Bad mistake.

That just pissed her off, and she was also one of the hand-to-hand combat instructors. She stepped back and then forward to put the weight of her body into a below-the-belt punch. Guys are usually pretty good about protecting their groins from kicks. It's fairly quick and easy to turn and take the kick on the thigh instead. Not so with a punch to the groin. It's more difficult to turn enough to get out of the way and a punch doesn't actually have to hit the jewels to be effective. A good shot south of the navel is almost as good as one to the balls.

It drove the wind out of him and he bent partway over. Taylor ripped the rifle out of his hands completely and then drove it forward as hard as she could, right into his face. She also twisted at the hips so that the rail hit his face and slid along it, ripping a substantial amount of skin off of his forehead. He fell back on his ass when the rifle slammed into his face, blood flowing from both wounds.

Strong arms suddenly encircled Taylor from behind, clamping her arms to her sides. No problem. In fact, this was one of the defenses they taught. She dropped the rifle to free her hands and snapped one of her knees up as far as it would go. Then she drove her boot heel down as hard as she could onto the top of her attacker's foot.

There are twenty-six bones in each foot, plenty of small, delicate bones that don't hold up well to being stamped on. The guy grunted in pain and surprise and his grip loosened. She thrust her body away from him and twisted to one side, opening his grip up even more. Now she could get an arm out and do some damage.

When she twisted back, her elbow was up, and she could estimate about where his face was located. An accurate estimate, as it turned out, because she caught him right in the nose. She immediately performed the maneuver twice more, twisting away and then slamming her elbow back into his nose. The last time was a glancing blow because he was backing off and putting his hands up to block, but she still got a piece of him.

And she wasn't finished.

Completely free now, she quickly moved around in a circle to come up slightly behind and to the side of her attacker. She clamped one hand on his wrist and the other on the back of his arm just above the elbow, on the triceps. Then she pushed them, hard, in different directions.

The elbow doesn't bend that way. His only choice was to lean forward, and she kept the pressure on until he went to his knees.

"Don't break it! Don't break it! Please!" He started coughing from the dirt he was breathing in since his face was pushed into the ground.

"Shut up. Now listen to me very carefully," Taylor spoke slowly through gritted teeth. "If you ever lay hands on me again, I will break both of your arms and then I will *hurt* you, very badly. Do you understand me?"

"Yes, ma'am! Yes, ma'am!" *Cough! Cough!*

She let go of his arm and stepped back. She surveyed the firing line.

"Everybody put your rifle down. Just down. Do not touch it, do not unload it, do not fuck with it, just put it down and step back. Now!" There was a rush to comply, many people holding up both hands to prove they were empty.

"Take a break. Fifteen minutes." She pointed to the break area, away from the firing line, and the group moved quickly off towards it.

She looked at the two guys still on the ground, both sitting now and both trying to staunch the blood from their wounds. The one she had raked with the rail had a mask of blood flowing down his face and dripping off of his chin since facial wounds bleed profusely. The other had a nosebleed and a filthy face since it had been down in the dirt.

"Get off of my firing line. Go see Medical." Nosebleed reached for the rifle on the ground and Taylor exploded. "DON'T TOUCH THE FUCKING RIFLE, DICKHEAD! DIDN'T YOU JUST FUCKING HEAR ME TELL EVERYONE TO STEP BACK AND NOT TOUCH THEIR FUCKING RIFLE?!"

He snatched his hands back from it like it was on fire. "I'm sorry! I'm sorry."

She stood there, hands on hips, as they slunk off down the road to seek medical attention. They were going to have to walk, since she wasn't giving them a ride. She picked up the rifle, cleared it and locked the bolt open, and placed it on the table. She noticed bits of skin stuck in the rail and wondered if it was going to leave a scar. Or scars, rather.

She walked over to the break area, which was in the shade of some trees, with benches, fresh water, and a couple of outhouses. She was thinking about what she was going to say when the class got back to the firing line. Obviously, she was going to make this into a lesson about safety.

She noticed three girls huddled together, one in front and two kind of hiding behind her. They were all staring at her.

"You three look like you're up to something," she commented, trying to use a friendly tone and a smile while she was still hyped up from the little tussle.

"Can you teach us how to do that?" the front girl asked. The other two, one peering over each shoulder, nodded vigorously.

"Yeah, I'm going to. When are you scheduled to start the hand-to-hand class?"

"Ummm."

"Go to Personnel. Check the schedule. And don't be late!" She smiled at the girls and they chatted some more. Taylor had a little fan club now, apparently.

***

That night, some of The 750 were gathered in a house with Jim, one of the group leaders.

"So, you're telling me that the hot little blonde girl that runs around with Dani, that skinny little girl, she's a hundred and freakin' nothing pounds, she kicked both your asses? And you had her grabbed from behind?"

Greg and Dennis just hung their heads.

"Jesus H. Christ. Now that's a great way to make an impression on the Texans. Let's take two of our studs, not one but two, mind you, and let them jump one of their little teenaged girls and the next thing you know they're on the ground, bleeding into the dirt and begging the little girl to not hurt them any more. What a fine example of manhood you two are!"

"Okay, Jim, I think they know they lost that fight. What are we going to do about it?"

"Do about it? What do you want to do? Take revenge? I think that's a real God damned good way to get your ass planted six feet under. Do you have any idea at all how many people these Texans have shot? And hung?"

"No, no, I'm not saying revenge. I've heard the stories, too."

"What, then? You want me to go complain? Oh, Dani, boo hoo hoo. I've got two big studs here, close to four hundred freakin' pounds between the both of them, and one of your little girls that weights a quarter of that was sooooo mean to them! So very mean. Please make her stop."

"All right, all right. I guess I'm… just embarrassed or something. I don't know."

"Okay, then I'll tell you what we are going to do. You two are going to make friends. You are going to go apologize to what's her name, Taylor? Apologize and beg for her forgiveness. And be sincere about it. Then you are going to learn everything you can from her because obviously she knows more than you do.

"If she asks you to do something then your answer is 'yes, ma'am'. I don't give a damn what she asks, you do it. Look, you have an opportunity here. She may teach you something that will save your life someday. Think about that. Or think about this: what if she had been some guy that wanted to tie you up and keep you as his sex slave for the rest of your life? What could you have done about it? Nothing, obviously. So, any time that girl tells you something, you just think that maybe she can save your ass — literally, *your ass* — from being some pervert's sex toy.

"Oh, and that makes me think of something else. Don't try getting in her pants. Please don't be that freakin' stupid. I have a feeling she would hurt you pretty bad just for asking. Or she might mention it to Eric and, well, you're going to be on your own, there, bud. I'm not getting in front of that man.

"And that goes for everybody. We're the beggars here, much as I hate to say it. They are sharing their food with us, keeping us safe, teaching us how to feed ourselves. If you don't like them, then spend six months or a year here or whatever, learn the skills you need, and then go find your own farm. Until then, keep your God damned mouth shut and keep the attitude to yourself. Do what they say and learn everything you can from them. You'd be a fool not to.

"And you two — come talk to me tomorrow after you apologize to Taylor. I want to know how that goes."

"We have to work tomorrow. We'll have to find her after work."

"Okay, so find her after work. Talk to me after you talk to her."

Chapter 18

Taylor was at HQ, just finishing up something and thinking that she might make it to bed at a decent hour for once, when she heard the duty NCO at the door. Dani was feeling a bit under the weather but still worked until Taylor had almost physically pushed her in the door to the house and put her to bed. That was a couple of hours ago, after Dani had put in only an eleven-hour day. Taylor was headed out as soon as she did this one last thing and didn't really want any delays. But duty called.

She looked up and the NCO said, "Visitors for you."

She sighed, stood up, and said "Bring them in." Her eyebrows went up when she saw who it was. She almost crossed her arms but stopped herself. "Good evening. What can I do for you?"

Dennis had a black eye and he was the one that looked good. Greg looked like the Lone Ranger in reverse. Instead of a black mask over his eyes he had white bandages above and below his eyes, across his forehead and the bridge of his nose. He cleared his throat.

"Ma'am, we want to apologize to you. We did wrong. Both of us." He looked at his friend.

"Yeah, I'm sorry. Believe me, I'll never grab you again!" He gave a short laugh. "I learned that lesson."

"Okay, apologies accepted." She came out from behind her desk and shook their hands. "But I need to see y'all again in my Firearms Safety class. Especially you." She gave Greg a no-nonsense look.

He nodded. "Yes, ma'am. I understand that."

"Can we get our guns back?" Dennis asked.

"*You* can." She looked at Greg. "I'll have yours in the class."

"Yes, ma'am. I understand."

She looked at the two for a moment, then said "Look, let's bring it down a notch or two, okay? My name's Taylor. You don't have to call me ma'am or Miss Taylor or anything like that. I don't mean to come off like a hardass, but we just took in almost a thousand extra people who came here with no supplies and virtually nothing except hungry mouths to feed. We've been scrambling desperately to try to get all y'all fed and clothed and housed.

"I'm only putting in a thirteen-hour day today. That means I'm getting off early. I'm fucking exhausted. I'm really a nice person most of the time. This month is not one of those times. Next month probably isn't, either. But things will get better."

The two young men both looked surprised. "I guess we were kind of taking it for granted. You know, just kind of figuring you had this huge operation here and... I don't know."

She looked him in the eye and firmly shook her head. "No. There could be one little thing go wrong and we're all out in the cold and starving to death. All of us."

"Is there anything we can do to help?"

"Probably the thing that would help the most is to get people to work with us and not against us. We know what needs to be done to survive here. So, realize that we know what we're doing and go along with it, at least until the winter is over. Once we get through the winter, things will be a hundred percent better. A thousand. Believe me." Taylor smiled tightly.

"Okay, we can do that."

"There are also notices on the bulletin boards asking for volunteer help for some things. Maybe y'all could sign up for some of those. Maybe take on some training. The better you are, the more skills you have, the more valuable you are here. The more you can do, the more you help yourself and the whole community.

"You can build something here, in this world. I think there are more opportunities for advancement now than there were before Hexen. Maybe not as many different career fields to go into, at this point, but that will come."

The boys looked at each other. "I guess I never thought about things that way," Greg said slowly, mulling the idea over.

***

"Okay, sounds like you did good, smoothing things out with Taylor," Jim said, a little later that night. "I asked around a little bit about her. You boys got off easy. Real easy. Especially you, for grabbing her. You're lucky you're still above ground." He had everyone's attention. The half-dozen men and the two boys in the room were all looking at him. "She's a killer. Three men and a woman. So far."

"That little girl?" exclaimed one of the men. "She seems..." He stopped himself.

"Yeah, that's what other people thought, too. She seems so sweet and innocent, doesn't she? Until she starts kicking people's asses or shooting them in the head. That's what she does. She busted up a bank robbery. Shot a man and a woman in the head. Shot the woman *four times* in the head."

"Jesus!"

"But the worst part is she shot one of the bank robbers with a double-barrel shotgun. Blew him pretty much in half, right at the waist. Then she crouched down by him while he was trying to hold his guts in and stared at him until he bled to death. Looked him in the eye and just watched him bleed out. That sounds to me like she enjoys it.

"And then another time, she saw a guy with tattoos she didn't like. Prison tattoos. She just pulled her gun and popped him in the head. Bam!" He thrust an index finger to his temple for emphasis.

"Holy shit."

"That's cold. That watching the man die. That's savage."

"You got that right. I'm going to say this one more time. These people are willing to be our friends. Be friends with them. Don't piss them off. If you don't like something they're doing, do yourself a big favor and shut the hell up.

"Like Taylor was telling these two, get in there and take advantage of the opportunities they're offering us. What do you think things would be like in some ragged-ass little refugee camp? Or some smaller operation? This place is like the Hilton. Sure, we may be crammed in, all on top of one another right now, but that's because so many of us just dropped on these people all at once. When we get things straightened out, and that's going to take a few months, but we'll be in good shape. Really good shape."

Chapter 19

Christmas came rushing up and it was a little more organized than Thanksgiving had been, but not a whole lot more. There were still groups coming in, sometimes only three or four and sometimes forty or fifty. But by this time, the organization was running like a well-oiled machine, getting them assigned to housing, classifying people and assigning them to jobs, unloading the trains, and making things happen.

The people from the 200 and the earlier 750 Groups had adequate training and knowledge now that they could take over some of the tasks that the original MCC people had been working double shifts to accomplish. The joke among them was that all they wanted for Christmas was a day off, and now they were able to take one.

Another thing that allowed people some rest was that Eric shut down the Dallas operations until after the holidays. He kept the soldiers with him, bringing them to MCC "to treat them to a Christmas". He figured that a holiday at the ranch would be better than one at Fort Cavazos. Plus, he didn't want to send them back to Fort Cavazos and then have to ask to get them back. It was easier to just keep them. Besides, they didn't have anything to go back to at Cavazos.

Dani was exasperated when she got his message. "Oh, seriously? Eric is going to bring his soldiers here for Christmas? That means we need yet *more* houses opened up, water wells, latrines, food… Aaaaah! I'm going to kill him!"

Then she started thinking about how much she missed him and tears came to her eyes.

***

Eric came roaring in like a conquering hero, with a troop of soldiers and a trainload of alcoholic beverages. They had found a warehouse for a liquor distributor that was relatively intact. Surely some survivors knew about it but they may not have had the means to transport away more than they could carry in their arms or in a shopping cart. Eric and his crew did.

When they rolled up in a neighborhood, in force and with all weapons manned, the locals that remained either fled or approached. Those that fled apparently had guilty consciences and thought that the government was after them. Those that approached generally wanted something, usually food, protection, medical assistance, or just information. In this case, a couple of teens had gladly accepted some MREs and pointed out the liquor warehouse.

"It's nothing but trouble. There have been probably eight or ten people killed there, fighting to control that alcohol."

The soldiers looked at one another, the sergeant in charge of the scouting party pointed, and the drivers accelerated. The front of the building was a decently designed office with the warehouse behind it. On the sergeant's instructions, the gunner of one of the Humvees gave anyone inside the building a wake-up call. He was firing the .50 caliber Browning M2 machine gun, and he traced a line across the bricks at the top of the office part.

The intent was not to hit anyone, but to announce that the big dogs had arrived. The M2 shoots a massive six hundred and sixty grain bullet, about eleven times the size of the bullet fired by the AR and M16 series of rifles. The huge projectiles blew bricks to red powder where they hit and threw partial and whole bricks in all directions from the shock waves.

Following that little display of firepower, the troops drove slowly around to the side of the building where the loading dock was located, and did it again. The brick tapered off as one got further from the office, to a plain concrete here, but the result was much the same when the gunner fired again. The concrete was more cohesive than the brick but still fractured and chipped off from the impact of the bullets.

The sergeant radioed the find in and Eric jumped on it, sending a whole crew there with trucks and forklifts to load up.

***

Actually, it wasn't a whole trainload of alcoholic beverages. Eric played Santa Claus, too.

He had specifically targeted some toy stores and the train contained a couple of boxcars packed with toys, plus equipment for soccer, football, and baseball. He had been proud when he showed off the liquor. That was something he knew about. Then he turned sheepish when he started talking about the toys.

"Um, I hope I did okay with the toys. Other than the footballs and stuff, I didn't know what to get." He looked at Dani.

"I don't know exactly what... um." Her voice trailed off and she looked at Taylor.

Her eyes went wide and she held up an empty hand. "Wrong person to ask," she protested. "Talk to the house mothers."

"That makes sense," Eric mused. "They deal with the kids every day. They'll know best. And I'd rather the gifts came from them rather than me swooping in here like a helicopter parent and giving them out. I feel guilty that I haven't been here more."

"You're in Dallas because you're trying to keep us fed and supplied. That's a good thing," Dani murmured, nuzzling his neck. "But the sooner you can come back to stay, the better. Much as I hate to bring up business now, we really need to have some meetings."

***

One of the meetings was with the refugee leaders, the 200 and the 750 groups. They had all come down from the north and Eric wanted to see what opportunities may be there. They gathered in the community center the next day.

"Greetings," Eric scanned the group from the podium. "Wow, I feel so out of touch. I've barely even met half of you, I think. I've been in Dallas trying to gather up as much stuff as possible to send here. My name is Eric Marten. I belong to Dani."

That got a big laugh. Dani's mouth dropped open in surprise and then she burst into laughter, too. Eric was usually pretty serious in meetings. That went doubly true if he was going to play the bad guy to her good guy. At those times, he looked like he was just barely keeping himself restrained from climbing across the table and beating someone unconscious.

"Really what I wanted to ask you all today is to think about a few items. One is what things did you see on the trip down here that we may be able to use? Is there anything that would be worth the effort to go get? One example would be solar panels. I always want more of them. As you know, we only have power for a few buildings. So, give that some thought.

"The next thing is trade opportunities. When I think of Nebraska and Kansas and the Midwest, I think of wheat and corn. Is there an opportunity for us to trade with farmers there? Obviously, we would have to have some open routes to be able to transport the wheat or whatever.

"Let me talk about refugees for a moment to get us all on the same page. There are going to be several waves of people fleeing. Some have already occurred. The first wave was the people leaving the cities to get away from Hexen. Fear drove them. I'm including people like me and Dani who waited a few days and then took off. That wave was confined within a short timeframe; a matter of days, maybe a week.

"The next wave happened when the cities ran out of food. This one was spread out over weeks or a month or even two, depending on when people ran out of food. When there was no more food available to them in the city, they went out to the country looking for it.

"The next one is an even longer timeframe. This one is where people living up north realize that they are going to freeze to death if they don't head south to a warmer climate. That was y'all.

"First off, I realize that people have been surviving in cold climates forever. However, they knew how to do it. They built their houses to be warm, and they stockpiled firewood and food to tide them over through the winter. I don't think the majority of people can do that or did do that this past summer. So, we saw a surge of people coming down as soon as it started to get cold and they realized they were unprepared. Then we're going to see another surge next spring when the people that did survive the winter decide that they are not going to go through that again.

"What this may mean for us, I have no idea. If you look at a map of the U.S. and Canada there is a lot of territory north of us. It may turn out to be a nomadic thing, where people farm the Midwest during the growing season and then retreat south during the worst of the winter.

"If I was going to do that, I'd try to form a cooperative where some people stayed south and kept a safehold while others farmed up north. Then the farmers could come south for the winter and meet up with the community down there. I don't know if we need to do something like that or what. I'd like for y'all to think about it, discuss it, come up with arguments for and against, and let's see if it would be a good idea.

"Maybe we end up with some part-time farmers that are snowbirds and head south for the winter. Maybe we just trade with farmers that stay up north all winter. I don't know what would be best but let's come up with some ideas.

"The other thing is that we need to change the way we are doing things here. Not overnight. This change may take a year or two or even more.

"What we are doing now is providing everything to everyone. Food, clothing, housing, education, medical. What I want to do is to go back to a more capitalist model. That means a transition from working and getting all of these things to working and getting paid and buying what you want. That is going to be a big transition and I am going to rely on you to provide the majority of the work in doing it. I don't have all of the answers. I have some ideas, and some things I want to do and some that I don't.

"Here's an example of what I am thinking. We start paying people, let's say $100 a month. Then we sell a meal ticket for $75 a month. Now you have food for a month and $25 spending money. Or you don't buy a meal ticket and you have $100 to feed yourself and spend any way you want. We'll phase pay in and phase services out or charge for them. We'll continue to cover medical and dental but we'll start charging for some services. If someone comes up and wants us to farm out something to them, then we will definitely look at that. Maybe someone wants to open a laundry service or a snack bar or, I don't know, food truck.

"Also, as far as paying someone goes, there will be at minimum a six-month period with either no pay or very reduced pay. If we bring someone in and feed and house and clothe them, then that six months is the payback. But I can see us making a judgment call on a case-by-case basis. If someone comes in with a running truck and a load of supplies, then they are in a different position that someone coming in with nothing more than the clothes on their backs. That's not a slam at any of you that came in in that condition. I specifically want your input on these ideas that I'm throwing out.

"Anyway, I want you to talk amongst yourselves and come up with a group of people with business experience that can work this problem out. I want people that can come up with good solutions and implement them. Emphasis on the 'implement'. We are not going to talk about this endlessly and never get anything done. I get more than enough of that at the state capitol."

Chapter 20

One thing that was high on Eric's list of things to do was to make some time for the kids. Dani had spent a few days as a prisoner of the *Pistoleros* before one of them got sloppy and gave her the opportunity to grab his pistol. The rest of the day didn't go too well for him and his friends, and on the walk back, Dani had gotten food and shelter at a Catholic church in Athens, Texas.

They had later returned and taken a busload of orphaned girls back to the ranch. Eric had wanted a bunch of big, strong boys that could do a lot of farm- and ranch-hand work. The problem was that everyone wanted those kids, so the church didn't have any. What they did have was girls, and Dani wasn't about to turn down a bunch of girls. She could be cold-blooded as the devil himself when it came to dealing with criminals, but she was a softie at heart.

Eric had cussed a little at that, got in trouble with Dani for cursing on church grounds, and they had taken the girls. Plus, the Wild Girls.

The Wild Girls were a different breed than the orphaned girls. The orphans were too young to fend for themselves or were old enough and just didn't know how. The Wild Girls were tough. There were six of them, two twelve- or fourteen-year olds, one about sixteen, and three in the eighteen to twenty range. Two were black, one of the older and one of the younger, and one of the older was Asian. They kept quiet about where they came from but had been with a 'community' and had decided to leave. They had rifles and other weapons and the Asian girl was wounded slightly, so Eric assumed they had had to fight their way out of that other place.

That being the likely situation, they had placed the Wild Girls in a house that was out on the edges of their territory and assigned them to Security. That gave them some time to themselves, to become secure at the ranch while still connected to it, and allowed them to integrate as they felt comfortable to do so. The exception was the younger girls, who went to school. That was a non-negotiable point with Eric and Dani. No one was going to grow up uneducated under them.

The Wild Girls had integrated completely, though. They were all in school or working and were fully a part of the community. One had even become a member of Dani's personal security detail. That was Diff. Her real name was Meredith, which her little sister couldn't pronounce. The closest she could come was 'Diff', and the whole family picked up on it as a nickname. And the name suited her because she was different. She went heavily towards the Goth look when she could, everything black, but toned it down to not stand out when she was on-duty with Dani.

That had been one of Eric's demands after Dani was kidnapped, that she travel with substantial security whenever she was off the ranch, or even out at the edges. Her minimum was three vehicles. Her own had her and Taylor with their rifles and pistols, plus a driver and co-driver, both fully armed. The lead and trail vehicles held another eight people, all heavily armed. That wasn't cheap but it was more than worth it to Eric. Dani was the most precious thing in the world to him, and he wanted her safe.

They had done what they could to insert armor plate into the doors and the side windows were heavily tinted to prevent targeting. Until they came across an actual armored limousine that they could get running again, or pirate parts from, that was the best they could do. Dani drew the line at riding in an armored Humvee unless she was knowingly going into a firefight. Those things had never been built for comfort or anything approaching it.

The rest of the orphaned girls were not tough like the Wild Girls. They were either too young to fend for themselves, or couldn't do it. They had fled to the church for sanctuary. That was fine. Not everyone is a warrior or a hunter. Throughout all of human history, not everyone has been. MCC was very militarized but was not a military organization per se. The intent was not to fight wars. Even if it was the intent, there are still plenty of people in the military who are not fighters. This is termed the 'tooth to tail' ratio and expresses how many fighters there are, the tooth, versus the tail, those that support the fighters, such as medical, cooks, clerks, mechanics, and so on. Usually this is something on the order of fifteen to twenty-five percent actual fighters, so most are actually support.

MCC needed many people to do many tasks so the girls found a home. Mainly they went to school and then had after-school duties. They were not yet so rich and secure that they could allow a lot of time for play, for athletics, for band practice. It was work, in the kitchens, the laundry, or other chores.

And the girls attracted men.

MCC wasn't running a brothel, so the underage girls were closely supervised. The older ones were freer to do as they chose. Not completely free. They could have boyfriends but not a line of clients. Due to the dormitory-style living, there weren't that many opportunities for much privacy anyway.

Word got around, both that the ranch was a safe haven for girls and women, and that it was a great place to meet females. Eric laughed that it was like the idea of bars and nightclubs having ladies' nights, where the drinks were free for the girls. Once the girls were there, the men would invariably follow.

That made for a back-and-forth, where girls would come in seeking shelter while others were getting married. Lots of the newlyweds left the ranch to go to their new husband's property, but that went the other way, too. Plenty of men joined the ranch. So eventually the workforce that Eric wanted was being built up.

And the pregnancies that inevitably happened came out okay. The entire community was holding a collective breath about that, wondering if the babies would die from Hexen. They did not. They survived, but that didn't necessarily mean that they were immune to Hexen as their parents were. There was probably no way for them to become infected with Hexen at this point, so there was still a weight on everyone's shoulders. But now the easy travel from Asia was gone, so that was probably a better barrier than anything.

Overall, the survivors were young. Hexen had hit the younger and the elderly especially hard, something fairly typical with a pandemic. The young and the old tend to have weaker immune systems and stamina, so they take on a disproportionate number of casualties. The overall survival rate was about ten percent, but teenagers survived at about seventeen percent. Younger than that, it dropped off sharply. Older, it gradually declined until a sharp drop came in at age sixty or so.

A disaster like Hexen brings out the best in some people and the worst in others. It's kind of the same thing as winning the lottery. It doesn't really change people; it just allows them the freedom to do what they wanted to do all along. If a guy wins a million dollars and blows it all on cocaine and hookers, it only shows that he's always wanted the drugs and the whores.

During Hurricane Harvey, when the Houston area and southeast Texas received up to five feet of rain in a four-day period, the 'Cajun Navy' came in and rescued five thousand people from flooded areas. These were just guys that owned bass boats and airboats and drove over, at their own expense, to rescue people. They wanted to help people and they happened to own the equipment needed at the time.

That's exactly what Eric and Dani were doing, rescuing people. Not everyone in the world was willing to do that.

Chapter 21

There was a scare with some bikers. Three of them cruised down the county road into MCC territory. There were perimeter guards on this road, two of them since it was daylight. There would be three during darkness. They had the truck parked per regulations, which is at an angle across both lanes, but the trucks aren't long enough to completely block both lanes. It is more of a warning, a big signboard that tells people to either go away or to stop and talk to the guards first.

The bikers didn't do either. There was enough room to get by the truck so they motored on by at twenty or thirty MPH. The guards yelled at them to stop and got the finger for their efforts. They couldn't shoot in such a situation, but they did have a radio to call in.

Dani and Taylor were both in the office, just back from lunch and not started on anything yet, when the call came in.

"HQ, East Two, we have three bikers, motorcycles, coming in from the east. They didn't stop, just blew by us," came over the radio.

"Everybody grab a rifle!" Dani yelled, running back to her office and jumping into her chest rig with its row of magazine pouches. Taylor duplicated her move, then they ran out to the truck in front. Three clerks had snatched up their rifles from the racks and gotten the truck started by the time they got there.

"Go! Go! Just drive up to the gate and stop!" Dani ordered. The gate fronted on the road that the bikers were coming down. She didn't know what they were up to but she wasn't going to let them in.

They saw them within seconds, still cruising at about thirty or thirty-five, checking out the area. That's what Dani didn't like. The area had changed drastically in the months since she had first seen it. It was no longer exclusively a region of trees and farms and ranches. They had a village of sorts at the headquarters, with more buildings going up even now. Eric was plundering the Dallas-Fort Worth area of anything he could think of that would help them, and the riches were there for anyone to see: warehouses, tankers full of gasoline and diesel, tractors and farm machinery, construction equipment, fields full of steel cargo containers, shops that refurbished vehicles and produced things like manual water pumps, food processing operations that smoked meat and canned vegetables.

God, I'll bet we look like the richest, juiciest target in the world! Dani thought. *In fact, we might actually* be *the richest, juiciest target in the world right now.* She seriously thought about just gunning down all three of the bikers, but figured that would just mean that more would come looking for them. And they'd be pissed off when they came. And then she mentally kicked herself. *No, no, don't think like that. We're trying to reestablish safety and law and everything. We can't just shoot people like that. That is not a valid option!*

"Don't shoot unless they make a move," she called out to the clerks. "Weapons ready to go but don't actually point directly at them." She hoped that was the right decision.

The bikes came by, big Harleys with straight pipes, no mufflers. They slowed a bit and the lead biker reached up and raised his sunglasses so that he could take a better look at the girls. He gave Dani a tight smile and looked her up and down as he passed.

Taylor stepped half in front of Dani protectively, flipped him off, and shouted, "FUCK YOU!" as loud as she could. He didn't react. Maybe was far enough past that he didn't even see or hear her over the loud exhaust, and they kept on going.

Dani turned to one of the clerks. "Run back to the HQ and get on the radio to the guards down that road. Tell them to get out of the way and let those bikers out. Everyone else in the truck. We're going to follow them out."

She hopped in the back and Taylor followed her as always. They stood in the bed and hung onto the rollbar as the truck accelerated after the bikes, then matched their speed about a hundred yards back. A few minutes later they could sight the other guard truck, off to the side of the road with a clear lane outbound. The bikers rolled on through, giving the guards the finger and accelerating off.

***

The driver stopped alongside the guard truck. Taylor looked at Dani.

"What do you think?"

"I wish I knew. If it's only those three then I'm not worried. But I have no idea if it's three or three hundred." She stared down the road but the bikers were out of sight. "This is something Eric would know what to do about."

They located Brennan and discussed the situation with her. She didn't look happy.

"Damn, we were just now getting to the point where I could cut my guys some slack. I wanted to give them some decent time off. But I think we need to add guards now. Let's run four at night and three during the day, with two trucks instead of one. We probably need some extra guys on call. We could have a fire team bunk at HQ. What would you think about machine guns?"

"Let's have a couple, or more, ready in the office. Eric didn't want to put machine guns out with the guards because someone might take them out and then they'd have a machine gun. I'm not going to go against him on that. I'd rather have some in the headquarters available to that fire team you were talking about. And we need to put the word out so that everyone is on the lookout for more bikers."

"I'll break out some SAWs and start running people through a familiarization course if they haven't already done it."

Brennan used the old name, Squad Automatic Weapon, for the M249 light machine gun. This weapon fired the same 5.56mm round as the M16/AR-type rifles, but in a linked belt. Each cartridge case had a metal spring device clipped to it that connected to the next cartridge in what could be a never-ending belt. The M249 mechanism dragged the belt into the weapon so that the round of ammunition could be stripped from the belt and fired, and then the belt link and empty brass casing were both ejected. A one hundred or two hundred-round belt could be carried in a canvas pouch or hard plastic box that attached to the weapon so that the belt was not hanging down, catching on underbrush and dragging in the mud and dirt.

The weapon was termed 'light' because it fired the 5.56mm instead of the 7.62mm round more common to machine guns. Despite that terminology, it weighed seventeen pounds empty and about twenty-two pounds loaded, close to three times the weight of an M16/AR rifle. That was lighter than the M240, for example, which weighed in at about twenty-six pounds empty and used ammunition that weighed about twice as much.

"I want to be in on that," Taylor spoke up, unnecessarily raising her hand as if in class.

Dani smiled as she looked at the young blond.

Anything with weapons, that girl wants in on it, went through her mind. Then she had to laugh at herself as she raised her hand, too.

But weeks went by with no trouble, so they stepped the alert down again.

Chapter 22

In a rare moment of quiet at the office, Taylor wrote in her journal. She told the guys to go on to lunch, that she would watch the radios and hold down the fort. She actually wanted a little time to herself. With ninety percent of the world dead, you'd think there would be more private time, and yet there was not.

It's cold in the HQ since we have no central heat or air, she wrote. *For the summer there are wide porches that let us open the windows even when it's raining, to get some air flow through. We don't have enough power from the solar panels to run anything but the lights and the radios, though, not even a fan.*

The winters are not that bad in East Texas but it does get down to freezing some, with occasional light snow. The building is insulated and has double-paned windows but there is no heat, not even a fireplace. Eric is worried about burning the building down, so we just dress warmly. It's leggings and wool socks and layers of warm clothing.

I think I've grown up ten years in the past ten months, maybe more. Certainly, I have more experience in many things than I might have ever gotten, some good, some bad. I'm a better person, one who contributes to society, helps the community. Had Hexen and the EMP not hit I would have existed in a shell, insulated from many things. Certain other people, for one thing. My parents didn't like blacks and Latinos and gays and probably a long list of others. But they would never mention that, never say it in so many words.

They paid lip service to being tolerant of everyone and then kept us isolated from them, except for those they employed to mow the lawn and service the pool and clean the house. We lived in a gated community, they went to a country club that probably had only a few token members of any other race, and sent me to an exclusive school.

Obviously, we don't do that here. Eric says it's like the Marine Corps, pretty damned color-blind. You might have to go into combat with that guy right beside you, rely on him to keep you covered, give you first aid, save your life. His color, his religion, his beliefs, his family's financial status, none of that mattered. What mattered was his character.

"You work, you eat" was the philosophy he started with and we all follow. Some of the other communities that have formed are rather less tolerant, shall we say. There are enclaves that you don't go into if you are the 'wrong' color.

Chapter 23

Shirina and Raftaar came into the office then, as Taylor was writing, sitting at one of the front desks instead of her usual one in a shared office with Dani. Taylor had taught Shirina in a couple of self-defense classes. She taught most of the classes for the girls, not that she pulled any punches for them. Someone else had taught her firearms safety, but Taylor knew her by name.

They chatted briefly, and then Shirina showed Taylor how tight Raftaar's sweater was.

"God, I'm surprised he can breathe," Taylor exclaimed. "He is growing, isn't he? Let's swap him out for a bigger one." She stood up, then hesitated as she eyed the radio.

There was supposed to be someone on radio watch at all times, 24x7, and she would have to walk pretty far back into the warehouses to get to the clothing.

Maybe I can go partway and then point Shirina in the right direction, she thought. *The radio is quiet today and they're not due for a check-in for forty minutes.*

She started to walk, with Shirina and Raftaar following, and got a dozen steps before the radio came to screaming life.

"HEADQUARTERS, HEADQUARTERS, THIS IS EAST TWO! WE HAVE A TON OF MOTORCYCLES COMING AT US!"

Taylor spun around and headed for the radio as soon as it started making noise.

"SHIT!" she spit out when she heard the screaming and launched into a full run, zigging around Raftaar, ricocheting off a wall, and skidding to a stop at the radio desk. She tried to reply but the guy at East Two was transmitting continuously without a pause.

"THEY'RE SHOOTING! THEY'RE SHOOTING! HOSTILE!"

"Fuck! Fuck! FUCK!" she screamed in frustration and almost threw the microphone. Instead, she stopped herself with an effort of will and set it down carefully. She spun around and speared Raftaar with a look that made him move to hide behind Shirina.

Taylor forced herself to smile while her mind was racing, counting down how long it would be until the bikers reached the office. Not long. She took a step forward and knelt down to be less intimidating.

"Raftaar, I need you to do something very important for me. I need you to run to the chow hall as fast as you can and start screaming that we are being invaded by bikers. Scream loud. Tell them I sent you. Okay? Run fast. Go, go!" She swept her arm in an arc towards the door.

He hesitated, eyes wide, then bolted out the door.

Shirina was also looking at her wide-eyed but Taylor had used up all of her ration of nicey-nice for the day.

"Grab a fucking rifle and one of those belts with magazines!" Taylor ordered, pointing at the rack of AR rifles.

There were web belts with pouches filled with loaded magazines at the base of the rack. A rifle isn't much good without them. While Shirina moved to do that, Taylor ran back to her office and pulled something bigger out of the closet, an M249 machine gun. After slinging the strap across her shoulders, she picked up its corresponding bag of magazines and headed out the door with her heavy burden.

There were trucks right out front but it would be more trouble to start one up than to just run to the front gate. Halfway down the driveway, Taylor had the thought that they could have pulled a truck across the road and blocked the motorcycles. But then she heard gunfire and stopped second-guessing herself and kept running towards the road.

Apparently, the bikers were just shooting at anything they saw, houses, cows, people, whatever they saw. Maybe they were shooting to scare people, like a band of cowboys charging an enemy in those old Western movies.

They must be stoned to the gills on something Taylor thought. At least the gunfire would alert people to grab their rifles and come help if they were ignoring Raftaar. She had a bad feeling that someone would yell at the boy and tell him to be quiet, and he'd be so intimidated that he'd obey. That would mean no one was coming to help. That would mean that she'd probably die here, today.

If there was even time for reinforcements to get there. It didn't look like there was going to be.

There was a drainage ditch down the side of the road, not much of one, less than a foot deep, but enough to provide some cover. Taylor pointed at it, on the side of the driveway opposite the bikers.

"You get in the ditch. Shoot at the bikers when they come up." The roar of the unmuffled exhaust was already a dull roar.

Shirina looked at her wide-eyed but followed her instructions, loading a magazine into the rifle and chambering a round halfway competently. Then she stared at the side of the receiver to make sure it was off safe.

Taylor looked at the options for her position. The other side of the road had even less of a ditch, and there was nothing to set the bipod on over there. That was going to be more important than her having cover.

Screw it, she thought, and knelt down right in the middle of the road. *Either I'm going to stop them or it doesn't matter. I just can't let them get by me in the first place.*

And then she concentrated on loading the SAW. She first snapped the bipod legs out to hold the weapon upright. Next, she locked the bolt back and ran the handle forward, opened the cover, slid the two hundred-round plastic box underneath, pulled the ammo belt out and into the feed tray, and slapped the cover down. She settled down into a prone position behind the gun and stuck it into her shoulder for a test fit, looking down the sights.

That was it. The engine noise had been ramping up and up.

She was as ready as she was going to be. She took a quick glance over at Shirina to see if she was in position. Whether she'd shoot was another question, but the SAW was going to be the queen of this battle, right now, anyway. There was no time for any gallant words or anything.

The bikers were coming fast, riding three abreast, and shooting. Bullets cracked over their heads like whiplashes. Taylor breathed in, let half out, sighted in, and firmly mashed the trigger.

Her first shots tore into the guy in the middle, then she moved her body back and forth to slew the barrel so that the rounds went into the guys to his left and right. One of the bikers tumbled off the back of his Harley and it kept on going without him, veering off and crashing through a fence and into a field. The other two bikes went over in the road, sliding and spinning, sparking and shedding parts, causing all of the other bikers to jam on their brakes and end up in a disorganized mess.

Some small detached part of Taylor's mind thought *So that's what Eric means when he calls something a clusterfuck.*

But she stayed on the trigger, ripping out long twelve- and fourteen-round bursts, sweeping the crowd of bikers back and forth. She could see men and machines going down like dominoes, see her tracers going in and things flying off from the bullet strikes, pieces of humans or machines, she couldn't tell. She ripped bursts of bullets out at anything that moved and anything that looked human. All too quickly her weapon ran dry and she bent to the task of reloading.

The incoming fire had dropped to almost nothing when all of the bikers were busy trying to avoid wrecking. Now it came back with a vengeance as the bikers had dismounted and were prone, using the bikes for cover. Rounds cracked overhead and one hit the pavement near her face, sending a spray of dirt or something to slap her face. She took a second to wipe a finger at the corner of her eye to clear some debris out before finishing the reloading drill.

As she pounded the cover down on a fresh belt of ammo, she scanned the situation. A fire had flared up in the mass of bikers. The bullets had punctured several gas tanks and either hot exhaust or the SAW tracer rounds had lit it off. Men who had hit the ground and taken cover behind laid-down Harleys now had to jump up to get away from the fire.

That meant she had fresh targets.

She chased the runners with her bullets, torquing her body side to side to swing the barrel onto the men. Some new ones that jumped up stood straight up into the path of her fire and went right back down — this time to stay.

One moron, shirtless despite the brisk weather, charged them.

He leaped over the crashed bikes, right in the middle of the action, and ran at her. He apparently imagined himself to be Rambo, nine feet tall and bulletproof. He had a bandanna around his head, filthy jeans, and boots. That was all. He was built; you had to give him that. He obviously spent a lot of time in the gym. All of his muscles stood out in sharp definition. He fired a shotgun as he came. He'd trigger a round, turn the shotgun up to point at the sky while he pumped the action to chamber another shell, and then drop the barrel back down to fire from the hip.

It was totally useless, from a tactical point of view, unaimed shots with a lot of wasted motion thrown in for good measure. Taylor stopped shooting for a moment, surprised by the idiot's actions. She even raised her head up to get a better look at him, but just for a second. Then she got back on the sights, got the Rambo wannabe targeted, and fired him up with a good, solid burst of 5.56mm to those well-developed abs and up into his chest. He went down immediately, dropping the shotgun, momentum carrying him forward a couple of steps before he flopped down onto the pavement and skidded a bit face-first.

Then those in the back were turning to run. Maybe seeing their hero go down so easily broke them, or maybe they were already running and Taylor just now had the opportunity to pay attention to them. Some had managed to get their bikes turned around if they had stopped quickly enough. Others were on foot, their bikes shot up or inextricably tangled in the cluster. Taylor shot them as they tried to flee, letting loose an eight- or ten-round burst at one and then swinging over to the next to give him a dose.

That was her training from Eric. If someone proved they were willing to attack you once, then they would be willing to attack you again. You would therefore be foolish to retaliate, but allow them to survive. That just gave them the breathing room to build their forces up, maybe to something bigger than your own, and then make a sneak attack against you when you were vulnerable.

No, if someone attacked you, then the answer was to wipe them out entirely. People who attacked you and then ran away were simply moving targets and should be shot quickly and efficiently.

She did.

She mowed down the bikers trying to flee until her weapon was empty, and that was all of the ammo she had with her. She turned and looked at Shirina. They locked eyes momentarily and then Shirina wordlessly stretched her arm out, giving her the rifle. She also pushed the pouches of magazines towards her.

Taylor raised up a bit since there was no longer any incoming fire and scanned for targets. She could barely see a couple of bikes in the distance and racing away, really too fast and too far to hit, when movement to the side caught her eye. There were two men running away from the fire and the clusterfuck, one helping the other towards the woods. They had figured out that the road was a killing zone and were trying to get away from it. She swung the rifle towards them.

Shirina, behind her, saw what she was doing and pleaded, "No," but her throat was dry as the Mojave Desert and almost no sound came out.

Taylor lined up on the man that was helping the other. Always take out the most dangerous target first, and that was the guy that wasn't wounded. She squeezed the trigger and the shot was true, right into the center of mass. He became a rag doll and went down immediately, legs and arms flopping loose.

The wounded man went down too, with his support gone, but tried to get back up immediately. He grabbed a small sapling, just a big weed really, and tried to haul himself up with arm strength until he could get a leg under him. He kept the other, bloody one straight. Taylor shot him and he stopped trying to stand but stayed clutched up to the sapling. She fired again and it was like she had electrocuted him. His whole body convulsed and his arms flew back and he fell.

Then there weren't any more targets that she could see. The fire was quickly burning out since motorcycles don't hold much gas. All she could see were bodies.

There seemed to be a long moment where no one moved, while a little smoke blew away in a chilly breeze. Then Shirina stood up and walked away from the scene, head down, with one hand over her mouth and one across her waist like she was going to throw up.

Taylor grabbed a full magazine from the pouch and did the swap while she looked around, evaluating the situation, scanning for targets. The only noise came from behind her, so she glanced that way. What looked like a wave was coming down the road. There was a truck in the lead with more behind it, and a swarm of people on foot, running towards the sound of the guns, with their own rifles in hand.

Tears suddenly came to her eyes and her throat clutched up.

What the hell? she thought. *That's never happened before.*

Then she realized it wasn't the adrenaline or the gunfight or the excitement. It was the fact that all of these people were running to save the community. To save each other. To save *her.* All colors, all religions, male and female, young and old and whatever other divisions and descriptions one cared to name. Tears streamed down her face as her heart swelled with love for these people.

She'd never felt that before. Sure, she'd loved certain people. She loved Dani and Eric. But she'd never loved a group like this. It was something she'd never felt before. She couldn't even adequately put it into words.

Oh, God, I can't let them see me like this! She suddenly thought, and started wiping the tears from her eyes and taking deep breaths to settle down.

Then the first trucks were there and people were jumping down, covering the area with their guns, asking if she was okay, and she was telling them that some of the bikers had escaped and answering questions.

She just kind of stepped back and let someone else take charge at that point. It was almost like she'd had too much to drink. Things were dreamy. Fuzzy. Voices seemed to echo and be far away even when the speaker was right there. She got someone to carry the rifle and magazines back to the office while she toted the SAW. She had radio watch. She had to get back to it.

And reload the SAW.

Chapter 24

Brennan got onsite quickly and took charge of things. Dani was onsite, too, but Brennan grabbed some of her security people and hustled her off.

"No! I want to stay here!" Dani protested. "It's my responsibility."

"It's my responsibility to keep you safe." Brennan countered. "Eric will shoot me if I let anything happen to you. Won't he?"

"Well. Not really shoot you."

"Bullshit. With all due respect. Now please go with these nice young men and women and allow me to do the rest of my job, which I need to start doing right now." She emphasized the last phrase rather sternly.

The two strong personalities locked eyes for a few seconds, until Dani sighed loudly.

"I'll be at Headquarters," she declared, and turned to walk up the driveway to the building. Brennan looked at the security people and made a 'go!' gesture with both hands, telling them to follow the pissed-off little Latina.

***

She found Taylor in the front office, sitting at the duty NCO's desk, with a thousand-yard stare and a reloaded SAW in her lap. Her fingers were drumming on the weapon, not a tune, just something random.

"*Chica*, are you okay? Taylor?" she questioned.

She looked up, but not at Dani. There was some gunfire going on back at the road, scattered shots here and there.

"Do I need to go back out there?" She looped the strap of the SAW over her shoulder and stood.

"No, no, it's good. That's just Brennan doing some cleanup. You did everything else. Don't worry about it."

The radio came to life and she turned towards it, but one of the security people that had come in with Dani was closer and grabbed it first and replied to the caller.

"Come on," Dani said softly, putting her arm around the shellshocked blonde and turning her back towards the offices. "Everything's under control. Brennan is on the job. Let's get out of their way. Right now, I need you to tell me everything that happened."

"Did I tell you that I looked up Brennan's personnel record the other day? Her first name is Vanessa. That's not embarrassing or anything, but she always wants us to just call her by her last name."

"Really? I didn't know that. How about we go back to the conference room and talk? The chairs in there are nice and comfy. I'll make us some tea."

***

Brennan formed up a base of men and women ready to bring fire down on any bikers who still wanted to fight and had an assault team move slowly and carefully in from the side. At the end they found nineteen bikers, eight of them wounded but still alive. Two of those made aggressive moves and were shot on the spot. One of the others went into convulsions and died fairly quickly.

The next one had a fatal case of smart mouth. Brennan asked him what they thought they were doing with this little stunt. He said, "Fuck you," so she shot him. That motivated the others to talk, right there in the road, with Brennan squatting beside them in blood puddles. The main question she wanted answered was the location of the biker's place. When she was finished, she delegated some guards.

"Tie their arms and ankles. Duct tape their mouths," she directed. "Drag them over there by the side of the road and stay with them until I get back."

"What about first aid or something?"

150

"No medical treatment. None. Understand?"

"Yes, Ma'am."

***

A crowd of people cleared a path, pushing bikes out of the way and carrying bodies to the side of the road. They had the vehicles up and loaded quickly. They were all kept in a state of readiness so any delay was for the people to go home, get their gear on, make a bathroom stop, and load up.

Brennan was taking the team. They got medical and some security out to East Two to replace the one dead and one wounded guard they found there.

Then they went to go wipe out some bikers.

***

Apparently, there had been a three-day nonstop party with alcohol, weed, and some homemade pharmaceuticals, over and above the usual nonstop party the bikers had, and some criminal mastermind had hatched a plan to take over the ranch. The plan was based on the one ride that the three bikers had taken through the area a while back. No one with any sense would have considered that a suitable recon mission, but this crowd did.

Based on what they had seen, there were only a few guys and some girls there with guns. There were some people here and there in the fields, but man, did they have some cool stuff! Tanker trucks full of fuel and steak on the hoof and pallets of stuff just laying out in the sun! Just go roaring in there with guns blazing and scare the crap out of them and take it all!

It never entered their drug- and alcohol-addled minds that a little fifteen-year-old girl would have a machine gun and four hundred rounds of ammunition and know how to use it to put hits on target quickly and accurately. Not until they were the targets, and by then it was far too late. They had jumped into a brawl that was considerably beyond their capabilities, and they had no way to get out of it.

Brennan's combat team rolled up on the dump that the bikers called a home. It was a few acres with a rundown house and two rundown mobile homes, plus a barn and a selection of rusting cars, motorcycle parts, and washing machines in the yard. Those seemed to be the permanent fixtures. The moveable ones were a pickup truck and six Harleys that looked like they ran.

She had twelve armored Humvees, half with .50 caliber heavy machine guns and half with Mark 19 grenade launchers. Half the vehicles crashed a gate across the county road from the bikers and positioned themselves in a field so that they could bring fire on the compound from the side. It wasn't as neat a maneuver as she would have liked but they could practice it more. It would work for today.

She called for her gunner to put two bursts of .50 into the ground to wake everyone up. The M2 heavy machine gun fires four hundred fifty rounds per minute which sounds fast but is actually slow enough that one can count the rounds. Typical bursts are three rounds and it hits *hard*. For comparison, a 5.56mm fired from an AR or a SAW will hit with about twelve or thirteen hundred foot-pounds of energy. A .50 BMG hits with about thirteen thousand, five hundred. The bursts definitely guaranteed that everybody in the neighborhood was wide awake.

Brennan didn't have a loudspeaker but she bailed out of the vehicle and yelled in the direction of the house, figuring that was the structure most likely to be occupied.

"Come out now with your hands up! We're going to burn this place down in about ten seconds."

She was close enough to hear some yelling inside. The door opened and a girl appeared momentarily, holding up a hand in a 'wait a moment' gesture. Another girl pushed past her and ran for the Humvees. The first girl looked at her, thought about it for two seconds, and followed her. A man appeared at the door next, with a double-barreled shotgun that he started to point at the girls, then thought better of it and stepped back to close the door.

As if .50 caliber BMG rounds would bounce off of a cheap wooden door.

They sailed right through it, leaving half-inch holes. The door was simply not substantial enough for the bullets to impart any more damage. If it had been sturdier, it would have actually suffered more damage. The man behind it offered a little more resistance but the bullets, three of them, still passed through his body almost like it wasn't there. The half-inch entry wounds became even larger exit wounds and hydrostatic compression basically crushed his internal organs into mush. Before his dead body hit the floor the 40mm grenades were already coming in and .50 caliber bullets were cutting all the way through the house from multiple directions.

The first girl ran between Humvees, crossed the road, jumped the fence, and kept going. They never did see her again. The other one took part of the same route but turned and crouched down behind a Humvee. Brennan could have almost reached out and touched her but the guns were making so much noise they couldn't have talked.

Another man came out of one of the trailers and ran as fast as he could in the other direction. He didn't make it. A moving target attracts a lot of attention and a Mk 19 gunner and at least two, maybe three .50 gunners swung on him and fired. They all seemed to catch him in a crossfire at the same time, and the results were pretty horrific. Fortunately, two things shielded the gunners from the nightmarish sight. One was the dust and dirt kicked up by the grenades. The other was that the trailer blew up.

Brennan figured that the trailer had been their meth lab and a tracer round had set it off. They didn't bother with any forensics on it, so that was the explanation that stuck. The whole interior burst into flame, blowing out the windows and peeling the trailer like a huge banana. The sides flapped and waved and then drooped in the heat from the billowing flames.

Everything paused for a moment when the trailer went up, and then there was kind of a 'Hell, yeah!' moment and all of the gunners went back at it with renewed enthusiasm. Brennan figured that Eric may bitch about the ammunition expenditure later on, but he also said that ammunition was cheap, life was expensive. They blew the shit out of everything in the compound except the truck and the motorcycles. They would keep those.

As things were winding down, a cat ran out of the barn and made a break for it. One of the .50 gunners fired at it and hit the ground just under it. The angle was just right, going up some slightly sloping ground, that one round picked up a clump of dirt and weeds with the cat on top of it, and sent the whole thing flying straight up into the air. When it came back down, the cat hit the ground running and got away, seemingly unharmed.

As the firing died down, Brennan started yelling "Cease fire!" then, "Reload but hold your fire!"

Both trailers now looked like peeled bananas and the house was mainly collapsed. One corner was still somewhat upright but the others were gone and the roof had fallen in. Nothing was left alive in any of those buildings.

Brennan hauled the girl to her feet, told her to assume the position against the vehicle, and frisked her. Finding nothing, she pointed to the nearest Security guy. "Cuff her. Keep her safe, but if she tries anything, don't hesitate to blow her head off."

The girl's head snapped back like she'd been slapped, her eyes and mouth wide open.

The Security guy apparently liked what he saw because he smiled widely at the girl and said, "I'll take care of you," as he reached for his cuffs. Maybe Brennan was being a bit rough but the girl did just come from the enemy camp.

Half of the troops and trucks remained to see if any survivors crawled out of the wreckage. They also didn't want someone to come waltzing up from somewhere else, jump on a Harley, and ride off into the sunset, free and clear. Brennan briefed the staff sergeant in charge of this element.

"This is a combat zone right now. If any bikers come down this road, detain them. If they try to run, shoot them. Detain means in handcuffs. If anybody else comes down this road, stop them, check them out and detain if you think it is necessary. Anyone that looks like trouble gets cuffed and I'll be back to make a call on them."

She took the other half of the unit back to MCC to get some trucks and trailers to load the motorcycles up. They also got some rope and tossed the dead and wounded bikers into one of the trailers like bags of dirt.

Once back at the biker's place, they dumped the bodies in the yard, found an appropriate tree, and hung the prisoners.

There was no ceremony to it. They just tied ropes around the men's necks, threw the ropes over some tree limbs, hauled them up, and tied the ropes off. The long drop method of hanging, in which a trap door falls open beneath the prisoner, breaks the neck if done correctly. This was the suspension method, which causes death by strangulation. The condemned prisoner loses consciousness within about fifteen seconds but may take twenty minutes to die. They will almost certainly kick and convulse even after unconsciousness as muscles spasm, hence the phrase 'dancing at the end of a rope'.

The girl that had run from the biker's house asked to walk up to the hanged men. She spat on them one by one, then started crying.

***

There was a funeral that evening for the dead man from East Two, and there would probably be another one soon for the wounded one. He didn't look good at all.

Brennan talked to Taylor and Shirina, one at a time, to get their take on what had happened. Afterwards, Taylor asked how she'd done.

"How did you do? You saved all of our asses. You were the hero of that gunfight. Shirina was firing single shots, maybe fifteen, and she doesn't claim that she killed anyone. Now maybe part of that is being a Sikh with the karmic debt thing. But she probably didn't hit anything.

"You, now. You were in the prone position with a weapon steadied on a bipod, and you fired four hundred rounds. Clearly, you were the one that took down the bikers. You dominated that fight. There were twelve dead at the scene and I am ninety-nine percent sure that one of the ones we hung was dead already from his wounds. You did a great job."

Brennan leaned back in her chair and looked thoughtful. "I don't even want to imagine what would have happened if nineteen men with guns had descended on us like that and no one had stopped them. Based on that, I have to rethink my security. I'm thinking about a series of gates across the road. As long as people keep them closed, that would slow down any attacking force. And if we expand our territory, we just move the gates. They wouldn't be permanent and it wouldn't be a constant drain on manpower to keep someone on each one of them."

Chapter 25

There was what Eric called the E Club and the name had stuck. E meant Enlisted. On military bases, there are various clubs established. At the top, the Officers Club is like a nice restaurant with a bar: waiters, linen, steaks and lobster. At the bottom is the Enlisted Club, which resembles a neighborhood sports bar, with beer only, burgers and fries, pool tables, a jukebox, and maybe a DJ or even a live band on the weekends. In between is the NCO club for corporals and sergeants, and even a Staff NCO Club on the larger bases for the higher-ranking enlisted.

Realizing that people like to drink, and not wanting to have a black market spring up that sold booze and, even worse, made moonshine that might blind people, they established an E Club. For now, there was no officers club and all ranks were welcome, so the name was kind of a misnomer but it stuck.

They had also equipped some guys that had homebrewed beer in that other life. Once they proved they could turn out an acceptable brew, and once the pre-Hexen beer was gone, they would be in business full-time.

The good thing about running the E Club was that they could impose some limits like closing time and drink rationing. Of course, that led to people trading and selling drink coupons, but they weren't going to stamp out every workaround in the system and weren't going to try.

Jim and some of the other 750 group people were having a beer in the E Club.

"There has been a lot of bitching going on about the training that the Texans require," he began. "A lot of people think that they have too many guns around. They don't want to learn gun safety. They don't want to learn anything that's related to the military in any way. They don't want to stand guard duty. On and on and on.

"I think today proved that the Texans are doing the right thing." He surveyed the men around the table. Some nodded.

No one seemed to object. "Who stopped that motorcycle gang? Two teenaged girls who had quick access to firearms, right? Taylor and Shir — Shar — whatever her name is. Both of them are fifteen, sixteen-year-old girls. And one motorcycle gang is dead tonight, solely because of them and their guns and their training."

He looked at Greg and Dennis, who had had the run-in with Taylor at the rifle range.

"When you talked to Taylor, she said you could help by getting people to go along with them and not resist. Well, that's what we need to do. I'm not talking about beating people up but I'm sure we can bring some pressure to bear on the slackers. We need to make sure all of our people are on board. I know they're saying we're all one big family but the truth is that we are the newcomers." He thumped his knuckles down on the table. "I want everyone on board with the Texans. I don't care if they want to bitch but they are going to do it. Everyone. Quickly." He scanned the faces, making eye contact with each person at the table. "Put the word out."

There were nods all around. They had relied on this man for survival for months now, put their very lives in his hands, and they were still alive, so he must be doing something right. He was fully and completely behind the Texans, so they were, too. And everyone was going to be. They would see to it. There were ways other than beating someone up. Peer pressure. Quiet words with heavy meaning whispered in ears. Accidents, if it came to that.

These men weren't gangsters. Just a few months ago, in that other world, they'd been truck drivers and plumbers and small business owners, accountants and salesmen and middle managers. Now they were just men trying to survive in a dangerous world. It's amazing how perspective changes attitude and one's willingness to commit certain acts. What was completely out of the question then was something they would do without a single, solitary word of objection now.

"Taylor with a damned machine gun." exclaimed one of the others. "She looks like a beautiful little cheerleader but then... it's scary."

"She's not just shooting people at random. She and her machine gun saved your ass earlier today. Mine, too. All of you. What if those bikers had pulled up to the chow hall and just started shooting everyone? Did you have a gun on you?"

"No, that's not — I didn't mean it that way. It was nothing against her. My daughter —" His throat clutched up on him and he struggled to get the next words out. "She would have been —" Tears started streaming down his face and he dropped his head but he didn't wipe them away. "She would have been thirteen next month. Taylor reminds me so much of her. And to think that she's killed all of those people. That's got to be traumatic. I can't imagine my little girl —"

He started sobbing then, and the men on each side of him tried to help him out with a squeeze on the bicep or some slaps on the back. Most of the men at the table blinked back tears of their own.

"I think she's okay," Jim said in a smaller, quieter voice than he normally used.

He remembered hearing the story about Taylor watching the man die, the one she had hit with the shotgun blast in the bank. He had just figured she was a psycho and left it at that. Maybe the truth was deeper. Maybe she was going to have some huge psychological issues at some point, if not already. He felt like a shit for not even considering what she was going through. No little girl like her deserved that kind of burden. His throat clutched up, too. He tried to wipe a tear away without anyone noticing what he was doing.

Three people at the next table stood up to go and one leaned in towards their group.

"I couldn't help hearing you mention something about Taylor and her machine gun. Well," he swept a hand to indicate the whole bar. "I think everyone's talking about it. I prayed earlier. I thanked Jesus for Taylor and Dani and all of them. These have to be the End Times, and they are angels sent to protect us. Those two girls, certainly, and maybe some of the others. That's what I think, anyway. You gentlemen have a blessed night." He nodded and turned and walked away.

Chapter 26

Today was the thing with the bikers, Taylor wrote. *Brennan thinks I got twelve of them so that would bump me up to sixteen kills. Double digits!*

I'm still processing some of what happened. The community thing. I want to talk to Eric and ask him about that Marine Corps camaraderie. I asked Brennan about it but I suspect that things are different between the Air Force and the Corps. What she had to say didn't really satisfy me.

The event itself was kind of like the bank robbery but different. Longer. When the guy started screaming on the radio it was like a jolt of electricity went through my body and I had to pee. I knew I didn't have time, so I just had to hold it. I was scared, too. I wasn't scared at the bank robbery. Realistically, I was never in any danger at the bank. The first guy never knew what hit him. The second had his back to me and his attention elsewhere. The woman never got her pistol more than kind-of pointed in my general direction. Same with the guy with the teardrop tattoo. He was reaching for his gun but it wasn't in his hand.

Today was completely different.

I was scared today because there was a shitload of guys coming at me and shooting. Shooting AT ME. I doubt they could have aimed accurately while riding a Harley, but lucky shots can kill you, too. And once they weren't riding, then they could shoot better.

I'll write up the details later on but it's late and I want to get some other things down on paper right now.

One is the fame or whatever. There were all kinds of people at the scene of the gunfight as soon as it was over. Well, duh, of course there were. They were coming to help defend the community! What I meant was sightseers. There was a big crowd there looking at the area just like they had to slow down and look at traffic accident scenes pre-Hexen.

I didn't see all of that up close since the HQ is set back from the road about a hundred yards or so, but people told me about it. We had our own self-appointed CSI guys out there, pointing out where people had fired from, laying down in the road and sweeping an air machine gun across the target area to see what it was like. They were even collecting the empty brass and links and putting them together to make bracelets.

A lot of them wanted to come up to the HQ building but Brennan had locked it down before she left, thank God! She posted guards who weren't letting anyone in except people that worked there so I got some peace and quiet. We were still in the middle of an ongoing fight so we didn't need any distractions.

It helped a lot when Dani got back and we could talk some, and yes, there were a few tears shed. Not many. Just a little sniffle or two. I don't like to be scared and having a big fucking bunch of bikers roaring straight at you and shooting at you is very intensely fucking intimidating. Maybe that's why I shot them up so badly.

Brennan mentioned that I shot those bastards to hell. They had six or eight bullet holes instead of one. Damned right! I wanted those bastards dead, right now. If I saw anything that looked remotely human, I put bullets into it. Anything that moved, I put bullets into it. You want to run away now? Well, guess what? Fuck you, you son of a bitch. Say hello to my little friend Mr. SAW. Let's see how eight or ten rounds of 5.56 feels in your ass.

Anyway, I was wired and kind of messed up and I didn't need to deal with anyone that wanted to chit chat. I stayed at HQ because I needed to, what with us firing up the biker compound and then meeting afterwards. Then I caught a ride to Shirina's place, which is the next thing I wanted to mention.

Shirina was pretty upset, but you have to give her a huge amount of respect for grabbing a rifle and plopping down in that ditch right beside me. And shooting. Maybe she didn't actually hit anything, but maybe she did, or maybe she kept someone's head down and kept them from shooting me.

Aasha was able to go to the chow hall and get us some food and we ate at her place in some privacy. I say her place. She's a house manager for a mini-dorm, a house turned into a girl's dorm, so it wasn't private but we got to talk some. I told her than Brennan thought she didn't kill anyone but I don't know if it did any good. She did mention something in Sikhism that related to protecting the weak and I agreed with that. That is what she was doing.

I think she'll be okay. I'll try to come up with something that will help her. I think the kids will help, too. The way we assign house managers is that the older women who have had kids get the younger ones since they know about childhood illnesses and things like that.

The younger house managers get the older kids. Since Shirina is sixteen, her kids are all about thirteen and fourteen. They thought Shirina was rock-star cool for shooting at the bikers. Of course she put it off of herself and onto me, telling them about me shooting the machine gun. They were impressed by that.

And then I was shocked when I realized that I was less than a year older than some of the girls. I was within a few months of one of the girls. That close in age, yet there was such a huge gulf between us.

Thinking about it now, I want to laugh, but at the time I wanted to say "but they're kids and I'm an adult!" They are just little girls! I guess that's the difference between innocence and whatever I am.

I don't know what I am. I'm not innocent. I'm still a virgin but I've killed sixteen people. I have blood on my hands. Justifiable, but still. I'm not a kid. I act like an adult all day every day, but I may not actually be one. I realize that I never was as nice as Shirina, and I doubt I ever will be as nice as her.

At one point today, just for a fraction of a second, I wished I were back in pre-Hexen times, safe and secure and protected and rich. I wished my biggest decision was what color BMW I wanted for my sixteenth birthday. And then I realized how useless and cold and empty that existence was, and how warm this one is, and I didn't want that old life any more. It almost literally left a bad taste in my mouth.

I was scared today, and I didn't like that. I was also proud today, of having defended my community. Brennan and Dani were proud of me. The little girls and some other people thought I was cool. Shirina was kind of shocked and horrified that I had killed men.

I'm not sure what to feel now.

Do normal, non-psycho people keep a count of the number of men and women they've killed? They'll always be a part of me. How can I not know the number?

I might have to cry a little bit now and then I'm going to try to sleep.

Chapter 27

At first, he thought they were witches.

The first witch appeared behind John out of nowhere. He was splitting firewood at the edge of the treeline, both for shade from the sun and for concealment in the shadows. For the same reason, security, this wood-splitting stump was located a quarter mile or so from their house. If anyone or anything zeroed in on the sound of chopping and splitting wood, they wouldn't walk right into camp without any warning. And there were a half-dozen wood splitting stumps, used in rotation, scattered around the camp in different directions.

John sunk the axe into the stump and bent to pick up the split chunks to stack them when a chip of wood hit his arm. That happened, chips flying up and landing on his hat or in his hair, to fall out later. Not now, with his head shaved clean last week because of the lice infestation, but when his hair was longer. He ignored it.

The second chip hit him in the back, harder, obviously not falling off of his ball cap. He glanced briefly up at the nearest tree, thinking that a squirrel had dropped something on him, but then turned to look behind him.

At the figure that had silently appeared there.

"A witch!" he gasped, eyes going wide as he spun to fully face her and stepped back.

He ran into his woodpile and stopped. No exit there. He looked to the side for a way to run, then back the other way and down at the axe. His hand moved towards it until she spoke.

"No."

Just the single word, in a normal tone of voice, but a voice of authority. It wasn't shouted in fear of what he might do to her, or said timidly as the opening offer of a negotiation. It was a command, and the end of the discussion.

He snatched his hand back away from it, looked at the other way out, and then stood awkwardly, not knowing what to do with his hands. He ended up crossing his arms.

"I'm not going to hurt you," the witch said. "But I do have friends back there in the woods, watching you, and they are very protective of me."

She smiled at him and he realized that she was very pretty. Hispanic, probably, with dark hair, but the eyes were the mesmerizing part. She had eyes so light brown that they were golden. He could stare into those eyes and lose —

No, no, she's a witch, his mind screamed. He started to panic, breathing hard.

"Why don't we sit and talk?" she asked, taking a couple of steps closer and then squatting. That wasn't the most ladylike position but it kept everything out of the dirt except the soles of her boots, and had the added advantage of being the quickest position from which she could react, to stand or to dive out of danger's path.

John followed her lead, unsure of pretty much everything. He was supposed to do what adults said, but she wasn't exactly an adult, maybe only a few years older than him. And yet he felt she was undoubtedly in control here.

Movement caught his eye and he saw another witch coming out of the woods. She was in camouflage, as was the first one, but heavily armed, with an equipment vest full of loaded magazines and a wicked-looking rifle in her arms. She carried it with the casual familiarity of long acquaintance, gripping it adequately but not tightly. She always knew where the barrel was, maneuvering it around a tree and some bushes without having to look to see if it would clear the obstacle without crashing into it.

He also noticed that she was scanning. First there would be a glance downward to plot out her footing, to make sure she didn't slip or trip, then her head came up and to the left, then pivoted to the right, in an endless loop. Her vision was focused out at some distance, looking for any threats.

Very protective, the first witch had said. It had been a warning.

The second witch glanced over at him, their eyes meeting briefly, then hers moved up and down him and his immediate area, and then back out to her scanning. Apparently, she had taken a second and a half to evaluate his threat potential, dismissed him, and turned her attention to more important things. He probably should have felt insulted that she thought so little of him as a danger, except that he was fascinated by her looks.

The first witch was very pretty, but the second one was beautiful. She had big green eyes and long blonde hair and John could imagine her as a character in a graphic novel or video game. She would be the Viking or barbarian princess or something, wielding a huge sword while clad in a skimpy steel and leather bikini. With knee-high boots. And —

"She's not hard to look at, is she?" the first witch asked, smiling mischievously.

There was a flash of embarrassment that snapped him back to reality. He hadn't seen anyone other than his group of survivors in six months, maybe longer, maybe shorter. He wasn't really keeping track of time. A long time, anyway, and he was fascinated to see anyone, much less these beauties.

"Her name is Taylor," the first witch continued. Taylor interrupted her slow scanning to glance at him briefly, with a tiny smile, and twiddled the fingers of her left hand. Her right stayed on her rifle, near the trigger.

"My name is Dani. What's yours?" The first witch, *Dani*, drew his attention back in with her question and those golden eyes.

"John."

"I assume you live around here. Are you doing okay? You're eating?"

"Pretty regular. Hogs for meat, mainly."

She laughed a little and he was proud of having said something that she liked.

"Feral hogs are saving the lives of quite a few people. We eat a lot of bacon and pork chops and ham sandwiches."

"Sandwiches? You have bread?"

"Of course," she replied, starting to say it fast and then slowing as she realized that John's group did not have bread. "Is your group not trading with anyone?"

"Mr. Mason said that everyone else was dead and gone, that only cannibals and witches and zombies remained."

Which, if he thought about it, meant that he was going to die soon, if these girls really were witches or cannibals or zombies. He wasn't sure if that was a bad thing. His first eleven years of life had been okay at best. The last few months had sucked. Overall, his life was a thumbs down.

"As near as we can determine, it was about ninety percent. That means most people died, but not all. There are still plenty of people around, but no witches and things. We have a big ranch a few miles from here, with a lot of people. Nothing like Dallas was or anything like that, but we've been taking in refugees. We have schools and churches set up. We have a little electricity, from solar panels. When was the last time you saw a doctor or dentist?"

He shrugged. "I don't know. Before."

"I notice you keep scratching your leg. Is that a bandage?"

He stopped scratching, as if caught out doing something embarrassing. "I cut myself. It's not healing."

"Show me."

He changed position to sit on the ground so he could better pull up his ragged pants leg and untie the scrap of t-shirt that covered the wound. It wasn't a bad cut, maybe a couple of inches long, but it had been poorly treated. Dani pulled her head back when she saw it and her face showed immediate concern. She turned towards Taylor and a glance passed between them but no words. Taylor started to swivel back towards the woods from which they had come and stopped, a puzzled look on her face. She looked back at Dani with a little smile.

"I can't think of a hand and arm signal for medic. Is there one?"

Dani smiled back. "I can't think of one, either. I was hoping you knew."

Taylor laughed and her eyes danced, showing a little hint of the teenaged girl she really was, and not the heavily armed warrior. But just a hint.

She walked back to the treeline as far as she had to go to make their needs known. John noted that she moved quietly, almost as if she were walking on air, except she left boot prints. Then she was coming back, still scanning, and another witch appeared out of the woods behind her. The third witch was an Asian; a petite little thing even smaller than Dani, who only cleared the five-foot mark by a couple of inches.

"This is Susan," Dani confided. "She's a medic. My husband is a Marine and we call most things by Marine Corps names, except for a couple. 'Medic' is one. Marines use Navy doctors and medical personnel and they would call Susan a 'corpsman'. But we thought 'medic' was more immediately recognizable."

Susan scrubbed his leg with a strong soap and water from her bottle and it hurt. John was trying to be brave and not cry in front of the witches.

The girls, he corrected himself. *They're just girls. Not witches. That was a lie.*

Dani was talking, trying to distract his attention from the pain.

"Another word is 'secure'. All of the military services use that word differently. If they were told to secure a building, the Navy would turn off the lights and lock the doors. The army would put bunkers and barbed wire around it and guard it. The Marines would kill everything inside, outside, or anywhere near the building. And the Air Force would sign a three-year lease with an option to buy!" She laughed at her own joke and John smiled back at her through his pain.

Susan examined the wound, turned to Dani, and mouthed, "hospital."

Dani forced herself to look at it again. It looked better than it had without the crusted blood and dirt and God knew what embedded in it, but it was still nasty.

"It's infected, isn't it?" she questioned.

"Oh, yes. No doubt about it."

"John, we're going to take you to see the doctor. Otherwise, you could lose your leg or even die from infection." Dani stood and looked at him expectantly.

He put his hand on the stump with his embedded axe to help himself to his feet. He never saw Taylor's head snap over towards him as soon as his hand came near the axe. If he had touched the tool, then she would have flipped the safety off and swung her rifle onto him. If he had pulled it from the stump and looked like he was going to go after Dani or Susan with it, he would have been dead before his body hit the ground.

But he ignored the axe entirely and lived.

***

They picked up two more girls from the treeline and met up with four more at the trucks, all of them in camouflage and well-armed. Their trucks were old but actually ran, and didn't just sit, rusting, locked into massive traffic jams with engines that would never start again.

Seeing all of the females, John thought of witches again. *Maybe they are going to boil and eat me,* he thought. Aloud he asked the question: "Why are you all girls?"

That drew laughter and he was embarrassed again.

"We needed security and food, and we're smart enough to make the right choice," Dani replied. "We'd rather carry rifles than work in the fields, farming and raising cattle. The men can do that. Besides, we're better shots than the guys." That caused more laughter, but it wasn't a joke. The girls proved it on a regular basis.

"The truth is that there's a mix of male and female in all of the professions, but sometimes I like to go out with my girls. And we're trolling through all of the churches in the nearby towns and gathering up the orphans. Most of them were female because the boys were highly prized as laborers and had already been taken."

They passed armed guards at the ranch gates and drove for a while longer until they dropped John, Dani, and Susan at the hospital. Over the next couple of hours, he was sent to the showers, examined by the doctor, treated, and assigned to a bed.

Taylor was in and out a couple of times, talking to Dani about what was going on 'back at the office' and then bringing food.

"*Nosotros tenemos tacos*," she said. *We have tacos.* "All the ingredients are separate so John can leave off the onions and jalapeños if those will be too spicy for him."

"*Excelente.*"

At first, he had thought they were witches, but now he thought they were angels. The fact that they had tacos made that an easy evaluation.

***

"John has assured me that there isn't any abuse going on," Dani told Taylor. "This Mr. Mason is apparently just very afraid of the outside world. Understandably so." She widened her eyes with that last statement.

"He does have a rifle, a lever-action 30-30, which apparently is just about out of ammunition. The question is, how do we convince him that we're the good guys? The ranch is expanding and sooner or later we're going to have a conflict. Someone is going to be hunting deer and run into them, or they're going to try to steal one of our cows at night and get shot."

"Is he religious?" Taylor questioned.

"As a matter of fact, yes. John says the Bible is almost the only book they have."

"See if Pastor Michael can talk to him."

She considered the suggestion. Asking Pastor Michael to walk up to an armed man wasn't something she took lightly. She didn't want to ask anyone to do that.

"I hate to even put him on the spot by asking him. I'd rather do it myself."

"Oh, no, no, no, *chica*. Eric is coming back home tomorrow and I am not going to tell him you got shot doing stuff that's not your job. That's why you have promoted people, so that they can take that responsibility and do something so you don't have to."

Dani hated that argument. It was not the first time she had been boxed in by it, and she champed at the bit, wanting to be in the middle of any action. That was why she had gone out with Security earlier, to get a little taste of adventure again. She crossed her arms and gave Taylor a sour look.

"We'll go first thing in the morning. We'll have time. Eric won't be back from meeting with the governor until the afternoon. And we'll stay back near that woodpile and let others go up to make contact. Satisfied?"

Taylor smiled. "I'll hold you to that. We have to talk to Pastor Mike tonight, then. And cookies. We'll bake cookies. The smell will bring the boys running."

***

The advance team went in quietly, just after dawn. The woods were very thick, which actually reduced the grown of underbrush. That and the thick mat of pine needles that smothered most sprouts. Once they had secured the area around the woodpile, the others came up. They included Dani,

Taylor, a medical team, John, and Pastor Michael. The last two moved up from there, towards the camp. The advance team followed.

The camp was an abandoned house, badly overgrown and left that way on purpose.

Pastor Michael sighed. "I can understand the reasoning behind hunkering down, but it really doesn't help anyone, themselves or anyone else."

Just then, someone called out "John! Hey, it's John!" and there was a little flurry of activity.

Pastor Michael glanced at John and murmured "Game on." He said a quick prayer that he wouldn't be shot today.

Back at the woodpile, Dani was frustrated. They were too far back to hear or see anything.

"We need to move up. We're not doing any good here." Taylor gave her a sour look, sighed, and then they slipped through the woods in stealth mode. They didn't want anyone to think there was a stampede coming in.

They got close enough to hear, but not see, the loud conversation. Loud, because the Pastor and Mr. Mason were standing at some distance from each other. Mr. Mason was armed, as expected, but he was keeping the rifle pointed down. That was good for him, because the advance team included those accurate female shooters that Dani had mentioned to John the previous day.

"If you feel that Mr. Mason is about to shoot someone, then shoot him," she had instructed them earlier. "It's his choice. Take him out to protect our people. It's all we can do. It's what we have to do."

"Sir, we believe in the Word of God," Michael was saying. "We are rebuilding civilization just a few miles from here, with schools and a church and hospital. We are bringing people in out of the cities, and people from up north who are going to freeze to death because they have no heat up there. We are growing crops and livestock and feeding them. We are working with the governor and with oil and gas experts to get

173

that industry back up and running, and get trucks running again, so we can transport food."

He remembered the basket he carried, and laughed to himself. "And we have cookies," he announced, raising the basket and turning his head to the side to include the boys, some he could see and some he could only hear in the woods.

"Poison!" yelled Mason. "These are the End Times and we will not be swayed by your gifts and false promises. Go away and leave us alone!"

But his attention, everyone's attention, was attracted by one of the boys, probably only fifteen or sixteen years old, who started to walk towards Michael and John.

"Jacob, stop," Mason ordered.

The boy slowed, his back stiffening as if expecting a blow, but he did not stop.

"They don't look like monsters to me," he said. Two or three of the others boys tentatively moved forward.

"Jacob, stop!"

"And if they are monsters, then I would rather they kill me than live another day like an animal." Jacob was within a step of John and Michael now, finally halting and appraising them.

"Look at them. Look at John. Yesterday he was as dirty as the rest of us, and wearing filthy clothes. Today he's clean and has new jeans, new shirt, new shoes." His voice almost broke when he mentioned shoes. He glanced back over his shoulder at Mason, then turned to look at the basket of cookies.

"Jacob!"

He reached for a cookie, the pastor holding the basket out to him.

Mason moved quickly, his rifle coming up and firing from the hip. That caught everyone off guard, even those watching for it. They all expected a longer setup, with the rifle coming up to his shoulder, then a second taken to aim, giving them plenty of time to shoot before he could fire.

No one was able to prevent Mason's shot, but they delivered the consequences immediately.

Five shots came from three different sources, three slamming into his torso, and two more bullets sailed over his shoulder as he instantly dropped out of the line of fire.

"Damn it!" Dani cursed as she took off running towards the camp, Taylor right behind her, rifle at the ready. The medics were only steps behind them.

They arrived to a scene of confusion, people screaming, shouting orders, and running around. Dani took one look and focused her attention on Pastor Michael and John, both kneeling by the fallen Jacob. His eyes were closed, face contorted in agony, his heels slowly digging into the dirt and pushing, one after the other, as if he were climbing a ladder.

The medics came in, moving them all aside to get to him. Someone went running to bring in a four-wheel drive truck as close as possible to serve as an ambulance.

Dani marched over to Mason and kicked him in the short ribs as hard as she could. He was thoroughly dead so it didn't affect him, but it would have driven the air from his body had he still been among the living. She almost kicked him again, but stopped herself.

Instead, she stepped back and surveyed the scene. Things were being sorted out. She didn't need to do anything and might even hinder progress if she started issuing orders. Taylor was right, of course. Find good people, promote them, and then get out of their damn way and let them do their job. Of course, that meant she didn't have anything to do to take her mind off of the situation, and that allowed her to sink into a foul mood.

The truck with Jacob and the medics took off as soon as possible, then most of them drove off together in a second wave. The last group, including Dani and Taylor, waited until the boys were gone to carry Mason's body out to the remaining two trucks. He would receive a proper burial.

***

Dani and Taylor received the bad news in the front room of the hospital and came through the doors of the emergency room at a fast walk. Dani's eyes already had tears in them. She wore her passions on her sleeve. Taylor, more reserved, was dry-eyed. She scanned the roomful of boys when she walked in, assessing who was there and probably devising how to kill them all if necessary.

Be polite, be professional, but have a plan to kill everyone you meet.

Dani wordlessly looked at Jacob's sheet-covered body and placed her hand on the shoulder for a moment. She shook her head in frustration.

After all of the death, why do we have to continue to kill each other? She turned and hugged Taylor, who whispered in her ear and patted her on the back, which only seemed to make her cry more. They slowly turned and moved towards the door. There was nothing more they could do here.

At the door, Taylor paused just long enough to sweep her gaze across the boys and say "I'll be back later to get you guys squared away." John could see she had tears in her eyes.

The youngest boy, just ten years old, turned to one of the others and asked "Why are they crying? They didn't even know him."

John knew the answer but he didn't think he could reply without choking up. At first, he thought they were witches. Then he thought they were angels. Now he knew that they were only human.

Chapter 28

As if there wasn't enough else to do, they had to maintain two banks. One was in Austin, and if that one broke even they would be satisfied. It wasn't really there to make a profit at this point. It was more for symbolism, to have something in the capital city and as an icon for the governor to point to, to show the progress that Texas was making in rebuilding. Later on, it would be profitable, when there was an actual flow of deposits and loans. Right now, it almost served as a pawn shop. MCC always had a long list of items it needed and the bank was willing to buy them with gold and silver coin.

The good thing was that expenses were fairly low. They didn't have to run extensive security measures since it was close to the state government offices and benefitted from their security presence. It was also close to the Austin Mint, so getting the coins from there to the bank offered less opportunity for robbery, and therefore required fewer guards. They had taken over an existing bank building, so the place cost nothing and there was no remodeling needed. Other than a lightly-guarded shipment of goods which the bank had purchased going to the ranch every week or two, it was pretty self-sustaining.

Not so the bank in Marshall. They had beefed up security after the robbery attempt that Taylor and the lone guard had shut down and didn't have another incident. But they did have to run convoys from the mint to the ranch, and then to Marshall, to supply it with gold and to take the Louisiana paper money back. That wasn't cheap.

Although once word about the bank and the Texas gold got around, it was wildly popular. The overwhelming majority of customers were from Louisiana, as intended. It was less than twenty miles to the Louisiana line and less than forty miles to Shreveport, the state's third largest city.

Louisiana was issuing paper money, not backed by anything other than the trust the people had for their politicians, something that was understandably low in the state. Texas was stamping out actual gold and silver coins. If you asked any individual which they would prefer, only a complete fool or a liar would choose the paper. People flocked to Marshall to trade their Louisiana dollars for Texas metal, glad to lose a substantial percentage of the supposed face value to get the security of actual gold.

The bank bought paper at two-thirds of face value, $67 in gold coin for $100 in paper. Marten Financial Services then transported this paper to Austin, where the Texas government was happy to buy it at a discounted rate, paying out $87 in gold for $100 in paper. That made for a $20 profit for every $100 exchanged, minus the costs of the bank, the security, the transportation, and all of the personnel. There was also a partner in the banking operation, a group of the governor's associates, who took thirty percent in return for their expertise and connections.

Even with the expenses, it was fantastically profitable. Dani had seen the possibilities of making money on the exchange rate but was floored when she saw what it actually totaled. If they took a bundle of paper money that they bought for a million dollars to Austin, they got $1,200,000 in gold back. And people jammed the bank, trying to get rid of the Louisiana paper. They could bring in that $200,000 every week, and sometimes ran out of gold between convoys. They had to lay on more trucks and security and more trips to handle the demand.

The Texas government took that discounted money and primarily bought Louisiana state-owned equipment and oil and gas mineral rights. The Louisiana government couldn't refuse to accept the money that it had issued. That would destroy any faith the public had in Louisiana paper. The value of the money would plunge.

Louisiana just had to smile and act like their money was as good as gold… and lose on every transaction. They lost when they bought Texas products, too, because Texas could legitimately insist on being paid with Texas gold. And basic economics meant that Louisiana couldn't simply print more money because that would drive the value of all of their money down.

Louisiana realized that Texas was going to own the state if this kept up. Buying up the oil and gas leases was probably the worst part, because they were ninety-nine year leases. Texas was buying Louisiana's future at a discount. And acting governor Marsh had said that exact thing to Eric on more than one occasion. He didn't want Louisiana as a part of Texas, he just wanted to own all of the important things in the state. And in all of the surrounding states.

So how would the Louisiana government get Texas gold at a more favorable exchange rate? A Louisiana trade representative put that question to one of the governor's aides over a small, private dinner one night. That started the ball rolling.

Marsh tossed it to Eric, on the theory that it was right up his alley anyway.

Mr. Lee accompanied Eric to the Marten Ranch to meet with Dani. He was a longtime associate of the governor and partner with them in their banking operations, actually incorporated as Marten Financial Services, Inc.

"Let me get this straight," Dani asked. "The state of Louisiana will come to us to do the same exchange that the citizens of Louisiana are doing now at the Marshall bank, but they want a better discount. So please check these figures and make sure that I'm not doing something wrong.

"If they want, for example, $20,000,000 in Texas gold at a twenty percent discount rate, that means they have to put up $25,000,000 in Louisiana paper. Then we take that paper to the state of Texas and they give us a thirteen percent discount rate, so they pay us eighty-seven percent of face value, which is $21,750,000. The bottom line of that is we make $1.75 million to move the paper around."

"Yes, and to keep the deal quiet," Mr. Lee confirmed. "That is very important. Most important. That is why they do not simply go straight to the state of Texas and ask to exchange at the thirteen percent rate themselves. Plus, the fact that Texas doesn't offer that rate to them. I believe that is an exclusive arrangement with Texas banks. But Louisiana would be admitting that their paper is worth less than full face value. If they did that, then the value of their money would crash and the consequences of that would be considerably worse than simply paying you a premium.

"And there would be leaks. No deal like this could go through the state government without the details coming out, so they want to go through a small private enterprise that can keep a secret. You, in this case."

"Of course we want to do this!" Dani had exclaimed. "And I have an idea. Tell me if this is crazy. Let's come up with a list of equipment that Louisiana can give to us in order to get a discount."

"Equipment?"

"Books for our schools. Medical supplies, trains, trucks, oilfield stuff. Whatever we could use or sell. I know Eric would like some military machinery of his own to play with. Let's just ask for the moon and the stars and see what they'll settle on."

Mr. Lee chuckled. He was not prone to emotional displays, so that small sound was like an enthusiastic belly laugh from someone else. But his eyes were dancing.

"You are setting a mousetrap," he commented, looking delighted. "The mouse sees this very attractive cheese, this very attractive discount rate, and rushes forward. He grabs the cheese and the trap snaps down on him, this laundry list you have. But you snap the trap down so softly that the mouse never even realizes there was a trap."

He looked thoughtful for a moment.

"As for the equipment you seek, the politicians did not pay for it, so they will be glad to give it to you. The trains, the oil and gas equipment, the trucks, all of it is owned by private companies. The original owners are probably deceased, and if not, their headquarters may be off in another state or even another country. The equipment could be considered abandoned and the state will simply claim ownership of it. The military hardware, from their National Guard units, was given to them by the federal government. They paid nothing for it. You should demand that they give you every single item that you ask for. They may make noises but they have no real interest in keeping it, and a great deal of interest in giving it to you so that they get the discount."

Mr. Lee wouldn't profit directly from the equipment, since he was a partner only in banking, but some of the equipment, like armored Humvees, would be used in banking operations. Other pieces would put the Martens on a better footing overall, which would allow them to grow the banking — which he *would* benefit from.

They arranged for messages to be passed by couriers and a date set.

Chapter 29

And so, a delegation from Louisiana found itself in a conference room in an anonymous office building in Carthage, Texas, seated across from Dani, Taylor, and Mr. Lee. Eric was in Dallas, gathering supplies and working for the governor. That was what he hated, being pressed into service like that, but it was the price to pay for getting deals like this thrown their way.

Besides, he had every confidence in Dani as a negotiator, born to the task and then trained at her mother's side.

The city of Carthage had been chosen as a discreet site, about twenty-five miles south of Marshall and fifty southwest of Shreveport. Pre-Hexen, the population was about sixty-six hundred and the city had been known for agricultural, timber, and oil and gas production. It also boasted the Texas Country Music Hall of Fame. But it had no connection to the Martens, which was its biggest virtue.

Dani had sent a small team to scout out a suitable location the previous week. They had made the police station their first stop. Small town cops may have been reduced in number, but they were extra vigilant now, it seemed, and very suspicious of any strangers coming into their territory. They could have tried to sneak in, but that might have blown up in their faces.

No, the better approach was to simply waltz in, ask where they could rent a conference room, and pay someone. The trick was to act as if it was to be a secret meeting, but throw the authorities off the scent with a false trail. Since Carthage had an oil and gas connection, the cover story was that people were looking into restarting petroleum production in the area. It was an impossible story to check out, without phones and computers and the Internet.

That got them the use of the Carthage Civic Center. The mayor was disappointed that they were going to bring their own wait staff and security, rather than hire locally, but brightened when they offered to pay a substantial fee for cleaning and 'outer perimeter security'.

***

Dani, Taylor, Mark, and Mr. Lee rolled up the morning of the meeting in a convoy that was toned down from their usual 'military invasion of a small country' theme. They used their stealth vehicles, no markings, and people in civilian clothes. Civilian clothes with concealed weapons, for the most visible people, but others inside the building in full battle gear: vests full of magazines, rifles, pistols, and with M240 machine guns close at hand if something heavier was needed.

The Louisiana delegation came in with a loose convoy of SUVs to be more discreet. First was a scout vehicle, which pulled into the parking lot and was stopped by the guards. Once everyone was satisfied that they were who they said they were, the scout radioed in and the rest of the vehicles rolled up. They were smart enough that all of their vehicles displayed Florida tags.

At the front door they were met by a tall black woman in her early twenties or maybe even late teens. She was nicely dressed in a blouse and slacks, but in running shoes and with a holstered pistol, knife, and extra magazines on her belt. Tameka was a sergeant and in charge of this security detail. Brennan had recognized her responsibility early on and promoted her directly to lance corporal when MCC instituted ranks. In the short time since, she had gone to corporal and now sergeant.

She invited them in and directed their inside security team to remain in the lobby. Courteously, of course, but firmly. There was comfortable seating and fresh pastries and coffee.

Then she led them to the conference room where Dani, Taylor, Mark, and Mr. Lee awaited. Mr. Aucoin, heading up the Louisiana delegation, was Creole. Creole and Cajun cultures both inhabit southern Louisiana and are frequently confused. But then, they frequently overlap and merge. Both started out French. The Cajuns settled in Acadia, which is now the Canadian maritime provinces. During the French and Indian War, over two hundred fifty years ago, they were kicked off of their land by the British and settled in southwestern Louisiana. Cajun culture is more associated with country and small-town versus big city.

Creole was originally a term used to indicate someone born in America, usually in or around New Orleans, rather than a European that emigrated to America. However, as time went on, the term came to mean a person of mixed race. The races could be any combination of white, black, and American Indian, and also Latin leftovers from when Spain owned Louisiana. The famed ironwork railings in the French Quarter of New Orleans are actually Spanish architecture.

Aucoin smiled, looking at the tasteful and expensive business attire all the Texans wore, and decided to make a little joke.

"When I learned that the parent company of the bank was named Marten Cattle Company, I thought I'd be dealing with people wearing boots and cowboy hats." He smiled.

Dani smiled back. "Oh, we do have boots and cowboy hats. We also have camouflage and machine guns."

She cut her eyes over to the side and Aucoin followed her look. Leaning up in the corner were two wicked looking black rifles with suppressors and long magazines sticking out. He took a second to think of how these ladies had carried those weapons into the building and had a mental picture of them just casually slinging them over their shoulders and strolling in, high heels and expensive clothes and machine guns, just like it was nothing.

That was actually exactly what they had done. There was considerable security inside and outside of the building, but these young ladies liked to bring their own.

He didn't quite know what to say to that so he moved on.

"As I'm sure you're aware, we need to have Texas gold coins in order to make purchases from Texas. We are here to establish what we hope would be a more favorable exchange rate. We would like to sign agreements to buy gold at a set rate that would be good for both parties. We're looking for a win-win."

They all agreed that there would be a variable discount rate. That was obvious. The next thing was to determine how that rate would fluctuate. Once they determined that index, the question was the amount of discount.

He made his first faux pas by speaking mainly to Mr. Lee, figuring that he was the oldest person and therefore likely the one at the top. He had taken the lead in the discussion of the index. Mr. Lee helped him out by subtly pointing at Dani. He took the hint.

He proposed a ten percent discount rate and there was no reply. Nothing. The silence stretched out until he kind of laughed and said "Okay, so that didn't go over too well. I'm surprised you didn't jump on that offer."

"We're currently at thirty-three percent," Dani replied. "Ten percent is an immense difference. Did you have an initial lump sum amount that you needed?"

"We can start with ten million. At a ten percent discount that would —"

"I can do math," Dani stated flatly. "If you want ten million in Texas gold at a ten percent discount, you have to put up Louisiana paper in the amount of eleven million, one hundred eleven thousand, one hundred eleven, and eleven cents."

Her eyebrows were raised, and just like raised hair on the back of a cat, it meant to beware.

"I do apologize. I did not mean to imply that you couldn't do the math."

Dani ignored the apology. That was a trick that she used, to make the other party think that they had insulted her, and put them in a less aggressive mood.

"Do you have any idea of the volume you will need over the next year?" she asked.

"Not really. We are, of course, in completely uncharted territory. I can certainly envision a hundred million but there is no way I could guarantee that."

"We can do a discount of twenty-eight, but I don't know if we can do any better than that."

There was about an hour of talk after that, with Dani slowly dropping to twenty-five but staying there. Throughout the whole time the Louisiana team had been conferring amongst themselves in French, and Taylor and Dani had been conferring in Spanish.

It never occurred to Aucoin that Taylor spoke French and was then feeding their conversation to Dani in Spanish.

Taylor's mother had thought that being fluent in French was the height of sophistication, so she hired a French au pair and put her to work teaching a young Taylor the language. Living in Texas, it probably would have been more useful to learn Spanish, but her mother thought that was the language of the maid, the pool boy, and the gardener, certainly no one that she wanted her daughter to marry or even associate with.

But her mother probably would have approved, maybe grudgingly, of Dani. Dani was the daughter of a doctor and was of pure descent from Spain, not a mestizo, which would have been important to Taylor's mother. Of course, it was a moot point. Without Hexen, she would have never met Dani.

Taylor had no problem understanding their slightly-odd French, especially since one of their number was not so fluent and they had to use simple terms and less slang in their speech. Then she converted their comments to Spanish, learned from Dani, and let her know exactly what their position was going to be. To make it less obvious, they often looked at a sheet covered with numbers and simply chatted randomly. But one of the others on the Louisiana team must have decided to test her by speaking directly to her in French.

Taylor looked at him blankly and replied with a slightly exaggerated Texas drawl. "Oh, I'm sorry. Could you say that in English?" She never claimed she didn't speak French.

"My apologies. Would you like a refill on your coffee?"

"Yes, please."

The same tactic, bringing in a Spanish speaker, would never work in reverse because Dani knew what her position was going to be and did not need to discuss it with anyone. She and Mr. Lee were already on the same page.

After a while, Dani spoke a bit of Spanish and Taylor produced a folder from her briefcase. Dani slid it across the table but kept her hand on it.

"These are some items that we want. They're just lying around your state somewhere, not doing anyone any good. All you have to do is to send someone out to load it on a train and send it to us. If we get these items, I'll make you a hero." She focused that intense amber-eyed stare of hers on Aucoin.

"For your first ten million, twenty-three percent. When I get these items, you get the next ten million at fifteen percent."

Aucoin's eyes widened in amazement. He never expected to get anywhere close to fifteen percent.

"After that initial twenty million, there is a sliding scale," Dani continued. "From this point on, you must buy in twenty million dollar blocks. This one will be at twenty-two percent. The next twenty million will be at twenty-one percent, then twenty, nineteen, and eighteen. Maximum discount rate is eighteen percent. Mark will draw up a chart so everyone can see the numbers in black and white.

"The converse is a situation where we don't get that equipment. In that situation, the discount is a flat twenty-eight percent unless you have shown a very strong good faith effort to send the items to us. Why don't we take a half-hour break at this point? We'll have that chart ready and then discuss." She took her hand off of the folder and sat back.

Aucoin pointed at the folder.

"Unless you're asking for the state capitol building and all of the oil and gas in the state, I think we have a deal. And I'm sure we could throw in the capitol building if you really want it."

Taylor was already up and moving, bringing in the three mid-teen girls that they had brought along for the occasion. They were dressed in crisp white shirts and black pants, and would show people to the rest rooms, provide tea, coffee, and snack service, and keep the room clean.

And one of them, the one that would stick closest to the Louisiana delegation, was the best French speaker that they could find on the ranch. She wasn't completely fluent, even with Taylor tutoring her intensely over the past week, but she was the best they had, and she knew to keep it secret. If she was able to pass any tidbits of overheard conversation to Taylor after the break, it was worth the effort.

Chapter 30

Mr. Lee looked at Dani with only a small smile but his eyes were dancing. They were going to make almost $1.3 million on the first transaction. When they got the equipment, that fifteen percent would bring in only $235,000, but that wasn't the real prize there. The real prize over and above that was the items that were "lying around the state".

That list started with six running train locomotives. If Eric couldn't get them, then she would. It went on for six pages through oilfield equipment and supplies, medical equipment and supplies, entire libraries of books, solar panels, military trucks, running eighteen-wheelers, Bradley Fighting Vehicles with spare parts and tons of ammunition, armored Humvees, artillery pieces with tons of ammunition, and so on.

Dani had no idea what all of it would cost but she wouldn't have been surprised if someone had told her it was seventy-five or a hundred million dollars. Unlikely, but she didn't know. The military equipment was probably outrageously expensive. She also didn't think they would get every single thing on the list, but that was why they had doubled or even tripled the numbers and the items that they had requested.

Even if they got absolutely no equipment, the rates Dani had set out would mean a little over nine million dollars profit for a hundred million, once they sold the Louisiana money to Texas. Mr. Lee and the group he represented, which Dani was sure included the governor, was a thirty percent partner, so that meant close to six and a half million for MCC. This was completely on top of the $200,000 per week they were averaging through the Marshall bank. That added up to another seven million for MCC for the coming year.

Thirteen five, Dani thought, then started as she realized what she was thinking. *That's well over a million dollars a month coming in.* She was awed by the number for a moment, and then in the next moment asked herself *What can we do to double that?* Followed by *Please, Jesus, I am not being greedy. I am helping people. If I have more I can help more.*

She resolved to make another run by the churches in Tyler and surrounding towns and bring in more orphans, or at least provide some more assistance for them.

***

During the break, Mr. Lee brought up some news with her.

"On another subject, the governor wants to have a ring of banks around the borders of Texas. The city of Orange is an obvious choice since it is on Interstate 10, Wichita Falls on I-44, Amarillo or another town in the Panhandle, and then El Paso and either Brownsville or Laredo."

Dani's eye grew wide.

"I'm assuming that he is getting some other people to start banks? Because there's no way we can expand to El Paso or the other cities on the border anytime soon."

El Paso was over seven hundred fifty miles from the ranch, the same as the distance from Paris to Vienna. Brownsville was 'only' about five hundred fifty. She was not enthusiastic about running those.

"The governor does want some other players on the board with banks, so the border cities would be more appropriate for someone else. But Wichita Falls and Orange may be possibilities for us."

"What about hurricanes? Eric doesn't want to be on the coast, especially now that we would have no warning until one was right on top of us."

"True," Mr. Lee agreed. "Even with all of the modern marvels of weather satellites and Doppler radar and computer models, it was no more than a somewhat-scientific guess where hurricanes would go. We did get warning that one was out there well in advance, just not where it would go. But all of that is gone now, so it would definitely be a risk to factor into the equation."

"What would be your evaluation of the situation?"

Mr. Lee pulled a map of the U.S. from his briefcase and spread it out on the table.

"Orange could potentially be very lucrative since it is on I-10 with access to Houston, Lake Charles, Lafayette, Baton Rouge, and New Orleans. However, I feel sure that there are extensive traffic jams this entire distance. These cities are all only about an hour apart and access is severely limited by numerous bridges. The Atchafalaya Bridge here is eighteen miles long and only four lanes. A single wreck could completely stop traffic in one direction. I would suggest we ask our guests how they got here. That might prove insightful. But I think that Orange will not be very accessible for some time yet, and therefore not profitable yet. And hurricanes will certainly hit the coast at some point and may render all of these cities uninhabitable. Bridges may fall or be blocked and there would be no easy way around the swamps.

"The Marshall location here takes in Shreveport and the northern half or more of Louisiana and the southwestern half of Arkansas. Wichita Falls is on I-44 out of Oklahoma City, with Tulsa and maybe Wichita, Kansas feeding into it, but virtually all of Oklahoma. I think if I were in Oklahoma City I would go to Wichita Falls rather than Amarillo. It's closer and you can combine it with a loop into Dallas. Amarillo only has Albuquerque and it looks like it would be closer to go to El Paso, anyway. I think Amarillo is a loser. I would say we set up a bank in Wichita Falls. But I am only a minor partner in this." A minor partner he may have been as far as percentage of ownership, but he was an experienced banker and closely connected with the state government. He could get things done for them.

"Oh, don't sell yourself short. We need your expertise." Dani sat in thought for a moment. "And Oklahoma money is paper, not backed by gold? Because they don't have a gold depository?"

"New York has private and federal gold depositories but they are far away and I can only imagine how absolutely terrible the Jam is in the northeastern states. All of the states are on paper money except us. Oklahoma is trying to back theirs with oil, but that does not look very favorable so far. Any attempt to back paper money with the promise of something valuable will fall short of actually holding something valuable in your hand." He gave a small smile. Small but predatory.

"What is the exchange rate with Oklahoma?"

"From our viewpoint, not as favorable as Louisiana. We could discount it to perhaps seventy-five percent. They produce more than three times the oil that Louisiana does and have a larger population, so they are on a better footing."

"Really? I thought Louisiana was at the top of oil-producing states."

"It's in the top ten and there are large reserves in the Gulf and many of those operations are supported out of Louisiana. But both Oklahoma and Colorado produce triple what they do."

"What rate will Texas give to buy Oklahoma money?"

"Ninety percent, but they may have a slightly lower rate for blocks of ten million and up."

"Still a fifteen-point spread, but with a higher population. That could be a stream bigger than Louisiana every week. That's definitely worth going after. Okay, I want to confirm with Eric but I think we need to go for Wichita Falls. Let me ask about Orange but I think he is going to be leery. I guess we need to see about running some more gold and jewelry to the mint for coins. We'll have to establish not only a bank but a secure location in Wichita Falls. People, trucks, convoy routes. Oh, my God. Like I needed more to do."

She turned towards Taylor and smiled expectantly.

"No. I'm busy that week," she deadpanned.

They both laughed. Neither of them needed more work. But they also had to strike while the iron was hot. And to make a list of equipment that Oklahoma had 'just lying around the state'.

***

Once the meeting started back up, Mr. Aucoin had a comment.

"We do have a potential concern with some of the items on your list. Some of these are military equipment. Artillery guns and ammunition, for example."

"We believe strongly in the Second Amendment." Dani smiled. "And you have to realize that we may be on track to get that equipment from somewhere else. If we do receive it from them and not you, then that would reduce our interest in giving you a discount. The quicker we get that equipment, the quicker you'll get deeper discounts."

"You're negotiating with other states, then? And you gave them the same list of equipment that you want?" Aucoin was now looking very concerned.

"Of course, you understand that any such meetings are confidential, just as this one is confidential. Why don't you just deliver the equipment to us first and there won't be any question?"

Taylor almost had to bite her tongue to keep a straight face. Aucoin had gone from thinking he was going to be a hero to sweating. Sweating hard. She imagined him as a cartoon character, maybe an Indiana Jones wanna-be, reaching up for a prized artifact and hearing the boards beneath his feet creaking and cracking. The footing he thought was firm was crumbling. That was a good thing. That showed him that he did not have a lock on that hero's cape yet and that he had better make some things happen quickly to get them their equipment.

***

The rest of the meeting was fairly quick. Dani's baseline of twenty-three percent was a lot better than thirty-three percent and it just got better from there. Once the equipment was delivered, that is. The Louisiana delegation agreed to take an initial ten million at that rate and there followed about an hour of signing paperwork in multiple copies and then wrapping up. Rather than actually receiving ten million in gold coins, Louisiana accepted a promissory note in that amount. Dani accepted a promissory note for $12,987,013 in Louisiana currency. The Texas State Treasury would pay them $11,298,701 in gold for it. Subtracting the ten million that they gave Louisiana, the Martens stood to make a profit of just under $1.3 million, less the thirty percent to their banking partners.

The next step would be for Aucoin to take the list of equipment back to his bosses and get trains rolling towards the ranch. The next money they exchanged would be at twenty-eight percent if they didn't ship the equipment. They set another meeting for two weeks in the future at a location in Nacogdoches which they had already scouted out. Taylor made a note to send a team out to find another couple of locations in different towns. Maybe they were being paranoid, but they weren't going to keep a regular schedule or use the same locations or route every time.

***

Once in the back of the SUV and driving away, Dani was quiet. Taylor looked at her worriedly. It was just them and the driver and co-driver. Mr. Lee has his own vehicle and they had giggled as they pushed Mark into riding with the sixteen-year-old girls that they had brought for hostesses. Maybe a girlfriend would be good for him. But now Taylor was concerned about Dani.

"Is something wrong? Didn't everything go just like you wanted? You're holding a check for thirteen million dollars. One point three million profit."

Dani put her hands over her eyes for a minute and replied "Oh my God, I feel like such an imposter sometimes! I mean, look at me! I'm only eighteen years old and I'm negotiating deals for tens of millions of dollars with the state government of Louisiana and I have authority from the state of Texas to do this and do that and I sit as a judge in legal cases at home and who am I to be doing all that? Seriously, I should be in my second semester of junior college! I should have graduated high school less than a year ago. I can't even buy alcohol under Texas law!"

She ran down for a moment and stared at Taylor before she started up again.

"*You* should be in high school. A sophomore. We're teenagers! We should be giggling about boys and dates and stressing over homework and tests and, and — " She waved a hand.

"It is kind of weird, isn't it?" Taylor replied with a half-smile, opening a water bottle and handing it to Dani. "I always wanted to be older, always wanted to be doing what the older kids or the grownups were doing. And now that I'm doing that, sometimes I want to go back. Just be a little girl and not have the weight of the responsibilities crushing down. But when I feel like that it passes quickly. I'd say I'm good ninety-nine percent of the time. Which, if I took that to the Texas Treasurer's office, they'd give me a thirteen percent discount rate, which means an eighty-seven percent —"

"Nooo! No! No more percentages and discount rates today!" Dani cried.

Taylor dissolved in laughter and Dani had to join her, but not until she had given her a dirty look.

Chapter 31

Eric had been using soldiers from Fort Cavazos to raid Dallas of anything he could find that would assist Marten Cattle Company, especially since the governor kept sending groups of refugees their way. Now, after almost three months, he thought he would give it a rest. He wanted to get back to Dani. He detoured to Austin on the way back to pay a courtesy call at the governor's office. Marsh was glad to see him and ushered him to a seat.

"Let's talk about oil for a minute," he started. "Texas is obviously a big player in that arena. As in, the major player. Forty-one percent of the crude oil in the U.S. comes from Texas. No one else even comes close. The Federal offshore production, that's the big oil rigs way out in the Gulf, generate a little over sixteen percent. That's the closest competition. That gives us a big stick.

"Now, let's look at things as they currently exist. Offshore is dead right now. We have no helicopters and no work boats running to service those rigs, so they are out of the equation. I think Alaska, which generates about four percent, is also out of the equation. It was hard enough to work the oilfields when you had electricity and running machinery and all of that. How are they going to do it now? Plus, they are seventeen hundred miles from Seattle, to say nothing of the rest of the country.

"The snow and ice is also going to be a problem with North Dakota and Wyoming, which together add up to another seventeen percent. But let's leave them in the game. If you just take offshore and Alaska out, then Texas' percentage jumps up to fifty-one percent. Now suppose we made an alliance with the states surrounding us, Louisiana, Oklahoma, and New Mexico. That coalition would control two thirds of the entire oil reserves of the United States.

"You could even expand that out a little. Colorado would add another five percent. Kansas or Mississippi would be another one percent each. Now we're getting real close to controlling three-fourths of the oil.

"Let's talk beef. Texas is at the top, again, with over thirteen percent of beef production in the U.S. If you add up the surrounding states that I've mentioned, we get to about one-third of all of the cattle in the country.

"There are some other things, like the port of Houston being vital to Gulf traffic, and if we're talking Louisiana, that gives us New Orleans and Baton Rouge. That locks up the Mississippi River. Any traffic on the river from other states going to the Gulf can be taxed."

Marsh picked up a sheet of paper and read from it.

"Listen to this. 'Minnesota alone ships eight million tons of corn, soybeans, and wheat annually by barge to New Orleans'. All of these states that produce farm products for export go through New Orleans. Now admittedly, we're not going to be exporting grain for a while, and not in these quantities, but you see how vital these ports are."

He picked up another sheet.

"If you look at the top fifty ports in the U.S., they account for ninety-five percent of the total shipping. Actually, this includes Puerto Rico, Alaska, and Hawaii, none of which are going to be players for the foreseeable future. Anyway, the Texas and the Louisiana ports each make up about twenty-three percent of the total U.S. tonnage, so that's forty-six percent combined. Half of the tonnage of goods coming into or going out of the country goes through our ports."

Eric noted that he was already referring to the Louisiana facilities as 'our ports'.

'We're in an immensely strong bargaining position, and I think it's time we started calling the shots for a change. Not Washington, D.C." He sat back in his chair and gazed at Eric.

Thoughts were racing through his mind, one after another.

"Are you talking independence? For Texas and this coalition of surrounding states? Or remaining part of the U.S. and throwing our weight around?"

"Some of the things I have in mind would make that a difference without a distinction. For example, ignoring the federal laws that we don't like, and not paying federal taxes. Texas has always paid in more taxes than benefits that it has gotten back. So, let's just stop paying taxes. We'll provide our own services and we'll come out ahead. And who knows? That may be an intermediate step on our way to complete independence."

"It would have to be a peaceful deal," Eric replied, his thoughts still swirling. "I can't be a part of any armed conflict with other Americans like that. I mean, I don't want Texas jerked around by any stupid regulations from the left coasts, but no war. Not even an armed standoff. If you have two groups facing off with weapons, sure as hell some idiot is going to fire off a round and then everyone starts shooting."

"No, no, I certainly don't want a shooting war either, but I don't see how we would have one. We have a totally unique situation here. The federal government is incredibly weak. It has nothing. Our population is back to what it was in 1860 but we are in worse shape in many cases. Back then, we had working telegraphs and trains that connected the populated sections of the country. Now we are all in isolated pockets. We're probably doing worse in feeding ourselves than we were back then. No, no battles are going to be fought over this.

"If you look at the Civil War, we don't have any divisive issue like slavery here. There is no easy rallying cry like that that Washington can put out. The states right now are kind of like the survivors of a ship that has sunk. Each of us has to cling to whatever debris that we can reach that will keep us afloat. There is no us versus them mentality now — no divisive, polarizing issues."

He sat quietly for a few moments and Eric felt no need to break the silence. Trey wasn't looking at him for a statement. He was deep in thought. When he did speak, he was gazing off into the distance, into a future that only he could see.

"I think I need to just do it. Make it a *fait accompli* and then as things get more back to normal, that will just be part of the normal. We're already accepting a hell of a lot of radically different things as normal now."

He looked back at Eric then and chuckled.

"I need to learn from you. Take a page from your book. Isn't that what you do, Eric? You and Dani? Just do it. Go out there and do something and make it happen. Make it yours. Don't ask for permission. Hell, you don't even ask for forgiveness afterwards!"

He laughed at that, and at Eric's expression. Eric had come close to getting a guilty look on his face, since he had kept the soldiers and plundered Dallas for far longer than they had originally agreed.

"One way I could go would be to run for President. The problem with that is the current President is in for the duration of the emergency. How long is that? Nobody knows. It could be two years. It could be twenty. And no one has any idea how we would hold an election. Sure, they did it before television and the Internet and all of that, but we never have. We don't know how to run a campaign like that. At the minimum we'd need reliable communications across the country, newspapers, a clear road network or open tracks for trains to run so that the candidates could hold rallies in various places. All of which means it's not going to happen any time soon. And the outcome would be uncertain.

"But even the Presidency is something that is kind of out of touch with what I feel I need to do. My heart is in Texas and I need to stay here and help Texans. It would be great to help the country but I have an emergency right here at home. It's kind of like if everyone's house is on fire, then what do you do? Personally, I'm going to fight the fire at my house first."

He looked intently at Eric.

"I agree. I'm with you," he replied to Trey's unspoken question. "I want Texas to have more of a say in matters. As long as we're not shooting at other Americans, let's do it."

The Governor smiled, then his eyes got a faraway look again.

"I'm glad to have you on board. But don't say anything about this yet. We're still talking. We've been talking for months but there are still months to go.

"I know you're eager to go back to your ranch. Why don't you take a week and then come back? And bring Dani with you. I hear that the banking and the oilfield operations are going well but we need to push both of those out some more. I have three other groups that are working on getting the O&G operations back up. Three viable groups, that is. There are a lot of smaller ones but these are going to be the big players. I am going to send them to you for their security needs.

"I know that will stretch you out some, because they can't pay you right now except in company stock. You'll have to keep people fed and watered out of your own pocket, but believe me, this will pay off in the long run. That's why I'm steering the big players towards you and keeping the small fry away.

"You'll be okay. I hear the Marshall bank is a gold mine and I understand Dani is already working to get the bank in Wichita Falls set up. And she's been wheeling and dealing with Louisiana."

"You probably know more than me about all of that," Eric replied. "Dani and I exchange letters but she keeps it kind of light on the details in case the information gets into the wrong hands." He smiled broadly. "She did mention that she has some big new toys for me, though."

Trey laughed. "Oh, that list! Mr. Lee told me all about that. That was just... I stand in awe of that move. I've heard that Dani is kind of a magician. She performs a little sleight of hand. She gets someone to focus on one thing and ignore the other, when the other is the thing that she's going to benefit from the most.

"And I want her to do it again with Oklahoma and Arkansas. Maybe Colorado, too. We've had feelers from all of those states. I have some other people setting up banks in the west and the south so one of them will get Mexico and New Mexico but I think you're probably in a better financial position to handle Colorado. How many more truckloads of valuables do you have?"

Eric looked thoughtful. One of the thoughts was that he didn't need to let Trey know the full and complete truth of how much they had. On the other hand, he wanted to assure him that they were financially capable.

"As far as I know, Dani hasn't brought any more gold to the mint. We still have the Rolexes, then. We give those out as rewards but maybe we could sell off some portion of them. We could sell some of the jewelry if you have a guy that could give us a better price."

"Ah, you're never going to get anything near what the price tags show. Especially now that people can pick that stuff up if they're willing to risk getting shot. The thing that gives you the best price over small-time scavengers is that the jewelers can buy in bulk from you, and in complete safety. If they're smart, they'll steer clear of a couple of sketchy guys coming in with a small bag full of stuff."

Eric shrugged.

"Okay, if we're coming back next week, we'll bring a load in to sell if you can have your guy available. Make it all one trip instead of multiple."

"Good deal. Talk to your people once you get back. See what you can do to increase your oilfield guard force. You probably need to look at tripling it. And I understand that you're getting some locomotives from Louisiana. I might want to borrow one of those. That would make it a lot easier for me to travel around the state. I already have some guys building out some boxcars into passenger cars."

Well, that's why we asked for six. Eric thought. *We thought we'd get three or four, and might end up with two running ones because of other reasons. This one will be used in a good cause. We'll probably never get it back. But we wouldn't have any if it weren't for him, more than likely.*

Aloud he said "Of course. We'll even give you one of the ones that almost runs." They both laughed at his little joke.

Chapter 32

Eric had planned to go to Fort Cavazos to visit with Major Batista and, if nothing else, thank him for the use of the soldiers in Dallas the past few months. After meeting with the governor, he had another item on his agenda. Eric had wanted to see about taking some of the soldiers on at MCC. More than a few soldiers had asked if he was hiring and he would be happy to have them. Now, with the governor giving him the head's up on the increased oilfield security role, he had a more pressing need.

At Fort Cavazos, Eric made arrangements to sit down one-on-one with Major Batista over beers at what was currently functioning as the Officers Club. The Major was looking a little haggard. After Eric had pushed for the eradication of the *Pistoleros* in Dallas, the governor had thought that a few artillery strikes on gangs in other cities would be a good idea.

Criminal gangs had a much freer hand now with the reduction in police forces and the crippling effect that the lack of radio and 911 call centers had on their operations. At the same time, the gangs were under assault from rivals, so they had to fort up, bunch up all in one area and defend their territory. That made them easy targets for artillery strikes.

Following the model that they had taken in Dallas, the Army surrounded the area with armored vehicles, called for the women and children to come out, and then pulverized the area with high explosive 155mm shells. Anyone attempting to flee was shot by the gunners in the Bradleys and Striker vehicles. One such strike in a city usually made all of the other gangs sit up and take notice. So far, there had been strikes in Houston, San Antonio, and Brownsville.

The secondary effect of the strikes was that the remaining gangs dispersed, so they didn't offer a nice, big juicy target for artillery. That made them less fortified and therefore easier targets for their rivals. Either way, it reduced the size of all of the gangs and made recruiting more difficult. It was attractive to join a gang that had a fortress and lots of troops. It was much less appealing if they were hiding like rats in small groups and being shot at by other gangs.

On top of missions like that, the soldiers had to maintain as much of the post as they could and work to feed themselves and the surviving dependents. This involved doing the same thing everyone else was doing: farming and ranching.

After some general discussion, Eric got down to business.

"I want to see what we can do to avoid what may be a conflict coming up," he began. "It's a conflict between you and me, not from anything that either one of us did, but because of our positions. There are a number of your soldiers that have expressed a desire to come onboard my operation, Marten Oilfield Security. Now, I told you at the beginning that I did not want to pirate any of your people, and there is the conflict. I still don't want to pirate them, but what is the status of their enlistment? In general terms, of course."

The Major made a sour face.

"That question has come up and I regret to say that it is not resolved. If a soldier has time left on his or her enlistment, then they need to serve that out, in my opinion. The question comes in after that point. The last word we got was a declaration of emergency, which placed all separations from service on hold."

"And you have no update on that? Is there any communication between you and higher headquarters?"

"Not really. We have no long-distance communications, and we've only had the one messenger. For all I know, one could arrive in ten minutes from now, or it may be six months. And remember that we sent out a team every month for several months, trying to make their way to D.C., and we never heard anything back from any of them. Whether they were ambushed on the way or just took off and went home or what, I have no idea."

"Okay, I understand you can't release them. No problem. How about putting them on TDY to assist the Texas Army

National Guard? I'll feed them. That takes that worry off of your back. I'll even take the dependents that are associated with those soldiers."

TDY was temporary duty, an assignment to go somewhere away from one's normal duty station for some period of time.

"What are you going to do with them? They can't work for you, technically. That would be illegal. I have men working on local ranches in exchange for food but that's to feed the personnel and dependents on post. Allowing others to use soldiers to work for their profit is something very different."

"No, no, this would be perfectly legal. They're going to be training state militia and running security operations for vital industries essential to our country, namely food and oil production." Eric smiled broadly.

Batista thought: *In other words, work for you.* But he didn't say that, because then that would be part of the record, even if the only record would be in their memories. If no one said it out loud, then no one could prove that the thought ever occurred to either one of them.

Aloud, he asked "How many are we talking about?"

"I don't know how many want to come, but I'll take two hundred plus dependents. Wait, let me clarify that. Up to two hundred dependents. Four hundred people maximum, of which a minimum of two hundred are soldiers."

The Major's eyebrows went up and he sat back in his chair. That was a bit more than ten percent of his men, which was a large portion. The dependents, though, that was worth something. The problem he had was that Fort Cavazos was a big clump of people in a land that didn't currently need, and had trouble feeding, a big clump of people. He almost took the offer right off the bat.

"Let me talk to my people tomorrow morning. Obviously, I can't let you have all of my mechanics, for example. There would have to be limits." *And there* will *be one dependent per soldier*, the Major thought. *I'll order dependents to go if there aren't enough volunteers.*

"Sure. I want this to be a good thing for both of us."

Business out of the way, they did a few twelve-ounce curls and swapped war stories.

***

The next morning, Major Batista agreed to the two hundred soldiers, with some additional caveats that gave him control over who went and who stayed. Eric was fine with all of that because he also had a say-so in who was even considered a candidate to go. He could weed out any shitbirds that he knew of, and he hoped to grab a few good NCOs and have them weigh in on who should and shouldn't be considered.

When everything was nailed down, Eric said "Great! The governor wants me back in Austin in a week, so I can be here in about ten days. How about we make the decisions then? Put the word out today, let people sign up, and then that gives you time to evaluate them. And get the equipment ready."

"You mean their personal gear?"

"No, no, their equipment. If they're going to be training people, they have to have equipment to train them on. M109s, Bradleys, Strykers, all of that. Plus, maintenance parts and ammunition. Lots and lots of ammunition. I can provide the fuel and oil. And transportation for them and their trainees to get around. We can load up on a train and run it to my ramp."

Batista sat for a minute, thinking that he did have a surplus of equipment, way more than he could man or even reasonably maintain in accordance with the Army's preventative maintenance schedules. He could get in trouble for failing to maintain equipment. But if he signed the equipment over to someone else, namely the Texas Army National Guard in the person of Eric, then that headache was no longer his. He almost smiled at that.

"Deal," he replied. The more he thought about it, the faster he wanted to get the supply officer to start making up the hand receipts.

***

Eric spent a couple of hours visiting the men he had just been working with in Dallas. He had seen them last week but he had an ulterior motive. He put the word out to a number of good NCOs, sergeants and staff sergeants, about the TDY. He wanted them to filter the volunteers so that he got good people.

Frequently, when a command has to send someone TDY, they don't exactly send their best people. In fact, they almost always consider it to be a house-cleaning that allows them to take out the trash and send the people that they would love to get rid of. That means the idiots, the incompetents, and the troublemakers. Eric didn't want those.

The same went for equipment. If a command transferred equipment, they started at the bottom of the barrel. They sent the lemons, the equipment that never ran right, that always had problems the mechanics could never fix. Eric wanted the NCOs to filter out that junk, too. He knew he'd have to put up with some problem children, both human and mechanical, but he was going to try to minimize the percentage.

"Also think about setting up an NCO academy," he told the little group of sergeants he was chatting with. "Or maybe 'academy' is too grand a word for it. Call this one a leadership course. Maybe a week. Might be less. I just want people, civilians, to get an idea of what is required of them in a leadership position. I don't want to run them around and make them do pushups or march in formation. Figure that we are not really a military organization. I guess the main thing that I want to teach is a sense of responsibility. You have to do your job and also take care of your people, that sort of thing.

"Then I want a tougher NCO course for the Security people. These guys and gals are going to be guarding oil refineries and pipelines and stuff like that. I don't care about marching but they should be able to line up in a formation, dress-right-dress and all of that. Push-ups are good. As a matter of fact, we can set up an obstacle course. The Security organization is going to be a lot more military than the civilian leadership course."

He paused to think for a moment before he sighed and gave his head a half-shake.

"Y'all realize all of this is what I think is the right way to do things. I don't know. No one has been in this situation before. But all y'all have brains and good experience. Use them. Give me suggestions. I would love it if you came to me with a plan and all I had to say was 'excellent, now go do it'."

Chapter 33

Finally back home, Eric and Dani did take a couple of days off, but then it was back to work with a vengeance. Once they started talking business, Dani was all ears.

"Damn! Are they going to issue a common currency if there is a coalition of Texas and surrounding states? If so, that kicks us out of exchanging money and making a profit on it."

"I doubt it," Eric mused. "That would just cut Trey's funds, too. Every time they buy Louisiana paper from us, they're making a thirteen percent profit. He's not going to give that up willingly. Besides, he's going to direct at least two and maybe three states to come to us for some of those high-dollar promissory notes like you're doing with Louisiana."

Dani smiled with an expression that was almost predatory.

"We're not doing too badly with that. They still owe us some of the items on our list. Maybe ten percent. They're reluctant to give up some of the running eighteen-wheelers and some other stuff but not much, really. They jumped on it with both feet and started shipping trainloads of stuff to us within a week, so I went ahead and gave them the fifteen percent rate. Then they got a twenty million dollar block at twenty-two percent, so that was a two point three million dollar profit right there."

"Wow! That's fantastic! If they've sent us ninety percent of the list, I'm amazed. We wrote down what we wanted and then doubled it, even tripled it in some cases, so we actually wanted only half or less of what we asked for. I'm almost speechless that they agreed to give us that much."

He paused for a moment.

"The bad news is that you did such a good job you are going to have to do it some more. You are now the chief financial negotiator."

"I was hoping you were going to do that, since you're back from Dallas." She looked like he had pulled the rug out from under her feet.

"Not a chance, *chica*. You do it too well. You have the experience."

She sat back, crossed her arms, pouted, and looked at him to make sure he saw her pouting.

He sat back, crossed his arms, and stared at her with his head slightly cocked to one side. She was pointedly ignoring him now, looking off in another direction. They sat like that for a minute.

"The Governor of the State of Texas told me he was impressed with how well you did."

No reply.

"Very impressed."

No reply.

"He said you were a magician."

No reply, but he could see her dip her head a little and he knew she was trying to not smile.

"And he said he wants you to talk to these other states and cheat them just as badly as —"

"He did *not* say that!" Dani spun around quickly enough to induce whiplash in a normal human being and was staring at him in shocked disbelief. Which quickly turned to irritation as Eric cracked up laughing.

"Oh, you bastard! He was saying nice things about me! You just lied about that last one! He never said that!"

Her outrage just made him laugh harder.

She jumped up, snatched a pillow from the couch, and started hitting him with it.

He covered his head with his arms and laughed harder.

Chapter 34

The Gold Runs were kept secret as much as possible. As the banks exchanged money, they had to be resupplied with Texas gold and silver and the Louisiana paper had to be moved out. This was less of an issue with the Austin bank, as it was in the city, the Texas mint was in the area, and there was less money exchanged there anyway.

The Marshall bank was the busy one in terms of cash exchanges. The schedule, trucks, personnel, and makeup of the Gold Runs between Austin and the ranch and from there to Marshall were varied. Sometimes decoys were sent out. They tried every trick in the book, but there was still a possibility of determined individuals getting lucky.

Mixed luck, as it turned out in this case.

No one was going to crack The Vault without major effort. The Vault was in the middle of the HQ complex. It was concrete block filled with rebar and concrete, inside a building, inside double fencing. There was a guard inside along with guard dogs outside. At the second fence there was a guard shack with guards that controlled access. All fences had barbed wire at the top, concertina razor wire when they could find it.

Out from the fence and surrounding the HQ was a village of sorts, housing for the people, all of whom had access to weapons. Anyone trying to shoot their way in would have to contend with angry residents shooting at them from all directions, besides the guards and the duty NCO and people up front, plus the Security people that would come running at the radio call. And the roadblocks on the main routes.

The bank in Marshall had beefed up security after the attempted robbery and then again with the number of people and the amount of gold they had to have on hand now. One thing was that they had configured the parking lot with concrete barricades in front of the building so that a vehicle could pull up only when the outside guards allowed it to do so.

There weren't going to be any getaway vehicles waiting right outside now.

The guards had semi-automatic shotguns with full-auto military M4 rifles available nearby and there were fenced pedestrian pathways into and out of the bank. There were armed guards inside and the tellers were protected behind bulletproof Plexiglas. In other words, the bank was about as secure as any place could be.

So, the way to get gold, seemingly the weakest link, was to hit a Gold Run.

Brennan sent this Gold Run off as normal and it got a few miles, less than ten, out on a county road. It was going through a low area with a creek and a small bridge, heading uphill when the firing began. Bandits had been on the right road at the right time to hit the convoy. That was about all of their good luck.

The first shot slammed into the windshield of the lead vehicle — and stopped. This vehicle was an up-armored Humvee and was intended to withstand any rounds smaller than .50 BMG. It cracked the glass and scared the driver, who took his foot off of the gas and ducked for a moment, until his co-driver yelling for him to get up and punch it made him sit back up and accelerate out of there.

That first shot was followed by a volley of more shots, six men unloading as fast as they could fire. The gunner in the turret of the lead vehicle fell down inside the vehicle, silent and gushing blood.

The next vehicle was the Gold Truck, also an armored Humvee that accelerated through the gunfire, hit but unharmed.

The third vehicle, also a Humvee, was slower to accelerate. The driver had slammed on the brakes when the first ones slowed abruptly, and now punched the accelerator, but the Humvee is not known for quick maneuvers. This actually worked in favor of the convoy since it gave the gunner time to shoot from a more stationary platform.

And he had a nice weapon. It was a Mark 19 grenade launcher, basically a machine gun that shoots 40mm high explosive grenades. He could see from the smoke and the movement where the ambushers were, and they were close! Too close for a military ambush. He spun his weapon around and laid a string of grenades right along their firing line. Dirt and fallen leaves and pine needles mushroomed into the air with the blasts and then he swung around to the front where he had also seen gunsmoke.

There were two men at the top of the hill and the gunner started walking his rounds up to them, seeing where one shot hits and adjusting his aim for the next. One of the men fired a round that passed frighteningly close to the gunner but he was charged with adrenaline and ignored it. The man jumped up and ran off, leaving his rifle on the ground. The gunner thought his next shot would be right on the last man and pressed the trigger, only to have the vehicle under him suddenly lurch forward. His barrel swung up and the grenade sailed uselessly up into the air. He tried to pivot around but they were moving now and then they were in thick trees and he couldn't see any targets.

The last vehicle in line was a gun truck, just a standard Dodge Ram pickup truck. It accelerated after the others with two men in the bed, clipped onto the rollbar and shooting back at the ambushers. In frustration, one of the attackers unloaded twelve or fifteen rounds at the truck before it went over the ridge and out of sight.

The whole thing only took a few seconds. Then all was quiet there for a moment except for the cries of the wounded.

"Son of a bitch!" one man spat with a vengeance. "Let's go."

"What about — what about them? The wounded?"

"Just leave them. We can't care for them." He surveyed the wounded and saw one holding his thigh, blood seeping through his fingers. "Except Dillon. He knows where the place is. Just him."

They walked away, helping Dillon hop along on one leg between them. One man lay still in the dirt and the leaves, one thrashed around weakly and called to them for help, while one tried to crawl away. His legs were mostly gone below the knees. He didn't make a sound. He just crawled, the stumps of his legs digging into the ground, obviously not causing him any pain although they squirted blood as his heart pulsed.

There was a shot and the three men walking ducked as one. Shots are not a single event. There is the blast at the muzzle of the rifle and then there is the sonic boom going on as the bullet travels through the distance. Someone standing to the side of a shot can hear it as two distinct sounds. If the bullet comes near to the hearer, then there will be a whiplash crack. There was just the one shot and booming away from them, so the men started moving towards the trucks again.

There should have been two of them parked in a little clearing by the side of the creek that probably flooded every time it rained hard. There was one, and a hundred yards down there was the other, nosed down into the creek bed and almost tipped over. One rear wheel hung in the air. The back window was shattered and the windshield was splashed in red.

One of the men that had been on the hill was standing there. He gestured at the truck in the creek. 'That bastard got scared and tried to take off. Take off and leave us!" He paused and looked behind the three men. "Where's the rest?"

"They ain't coming. Ever. Get in the Goddamn truck."

Chapter 35

The Gold Run convoy got a couple of miles down the road and pulled up into a defensive position for a quick status check. The convoy commander, a twenty-six-year-old former insurance salesman, tried not to hyperventilate as he saw the blood. Lots of blood.

The gunner in the front vehicle looked dead after seemingly pouring a couple of gallons of blood out everywhere. The guys in the gun truck were worse. The two in the back were bad. One of them had a major piece of his skull missing and was all the more gruesome for the fact that he hung from the strap he had used to secure himself to the rollbar. The other was twitching and bleeding a lot. The bed of the truck seemed to be awash in blood.

The driver, a female, was hit in the right elbow. She had driven with a flat tire using her left arm against the steering wheel while putting pressure on the wound and crying. The passenger was bleeding in three places but not seriously injured.

They abandoned the shot-up truck and the obviously-dead headshot casualty, manhandled the others into the Humvees, and took off for a hospital in Henderson. That was one thing that was in every truck, a set of detailed maps and locations of things like hospitals. The assistant drivers had already gotten on the radios and reported in. MCC HQ knew what was going on. A response was coming.

***

Brennan was onsite at the ambush point within twenty minutes. She had grabbed ten troops and three trucks and taken off. The first truck rounded up some of their medics and went straight to the hospital to help out if needed. The others went to the ambush site.

Taylor had jumped in with Brennan. Dani had stayed at HQ by the radio. Her first instinct had been to go but Brennan convinced her to stay to coordinate any efforts that they needed. Brennan was the experienced investigator and Dani obviously could authorize any action on the spot, so she was the logical choice to hold down the fort. The thought occurred to her that Eric had mentioned this exact same thing. She wanted to be out there on the front line where the action was, but her current rank dictated that she stay back from the front line to coordinate the bigger plan. As Eric put it, you don't pay generals to be riflemen.

***

Brennan and Taylor stood over the wounded man, just behind the medic they had brought with them. He was the one living person they found here and he probably wouldn't be among the living for much longer. His right side was mangled by a grenade blast, but he spoke calmly. He was in shock and well beyond pain at this point.

"Those bastards left me. Left me! Damn them. I hope they rot in hell!"

"If you want to get back at them, tell me who they are," Brennan offered in a soft, soothing voice.

The man started rattling off names, seven of them. Brennan scribbled them in a little notebook. Taylor's head snapped up at one of them.

"Dillon? That bastard! He likes to hang around HQ whenever he can. Tries to chat me up all the time. He's been with us from the start! That motherfucker!"

Brennan listened to her, nodded, and then turned back to the wounded man. "What's their plan now? Once you got the gold, where were you going?"

"I dunno. There was a place one of them knew. They were keeping that secret." A lightbulb went off in his head. "Dillon.

It must have been Dillon. He was wounded and they left the wounded like me, but they took him."

"So, it was some place Dillon knew, but no one else knew it?"

"Yeah. He knew it. Maybe he used to live there. I don't know. I don't know where the place is."

"How badly was he wounded?"

"Not bad. He was... he was walking. I mean, they had to help him. I didn't see any blood on him. I just saw him from the back as those bastards were walking away. He was hopping on one leg and they were supporting him."

"You think he was hit in the leg, then? And maybe a minor wound?"

"I'm gonna die here, aren't I? I was just a God damned restaurant manager and all this happened." He put the one hand that still functioned over his mouth and tried not to cry.

Brennan looked at Taylor and bobbed her head for her to come along. They looked at the two dead men and recognized one but didn't know his name. He had crawled away a bit until he bled to death, leaving his feet and lower legs behind. The other had caught a grenade more or less in the teeth and there was nothing left to recognize. A body, but no features.

Then they followed a whistle from one of their people who had found the truck in the creek. The driver had taken a head shot and it hadn't done his face any good. They dragged his body out of the truck and Brennan used a twig to push a flap of skin and skull back into place to make him look a little more like he did before he got shot in the back of the head with a deer rifle.

Taylor shook her head. "I've seen him, too, but I can't think of his name. He's one of the new guys. From the 750 Group. All these guys are 750 except Dillon."

They turned to walk back.

"You need that wounded guy anymore?" Taylor asked. She ran her tongue over her suddenly-dry lips. Her heart rate had stepped up, too.

"No. He might be dead by the time we walk back. Are you going to help him along if he's not?"

Taylor pulled her pistol and looked Brennan in the eye. Brennan met her eyes briefly and then looked away.

"If I leave five or six guys here with you, can you get that truck out of the creek? And there's supposed to be another one with a flat tire up the road a couple of miles. And we need all of the bodies back for identification."

Taylor took the change of subject as permission. "Absolutely. You want us at the hospital? To help secure the gold truck?"

"Oh, yeah, the gold. Yes. Let's get some more guns on that. As a matter of fact, how about I only leave four guys with you? Is that enough?"

"We'll handle it."

***

The medic was still kneeling beside the wounded man but had stopped even holding pressure on any of the wounds. Nothing she could do was going to save the man and obviously no one was at all interested in rushing him to a hospital. He had a blanket on to treat for shock, one of those Mylar emergency blankets, but that was it.

Taylor pulled the blanket off and handed it to the medic.

"Go back to the truck," she ordered.

The medic, a young Asian girl named Susan who wanted to be a doctor, looked up at her, uncomprehending. But the man knew.

He started babbling "Oh, God, oh, God, oh, God." He turned his head and closed his eyes and started sobbing again.

"Go on. You're done here," Taylor prompted. Susan slowly rose to her feet, staring at the pistol in her hand with dawning horror.

"Susan, please come over here," Brennan called out. The girl turned and walked over to her, almost in a daze, clutching the EMT bag and the blanket to her. Brennan put an arm around her shoulders and walked towards the truck, carrying the girl along with her. She almost had to run to keep up.

There was a shot, loud in the crisp, cool air, and Susan hunched her shoulders down at the sound. She tried to stop and turn to look but Brennan wasn't stopping and she was easily twice as big as the girl. They didn't even slow down. She got her footing back and tried to look over Brennan's shoulder but she was too short.

Brennan spoke to the troops and pointed and four of them broke off and walked in Taylor's direction.

She was staring down at the body of the man she'd just executed but she wasn't seeing him at all. She was thinking *Dillon. The Boggy Creek Monster, like Bigfoot, somewhere around Texarkana but not in Texas. That means Southwest Arkansas or Northwest Louisiana. You're going to die, you motherfucker. Real soon, you are going to die.*

Chapter 36

Taylor cleaned the interior of the truck out as best she could with what she had on hand, and then they got it hauled out of the creek and loaded with bodies. The guy who lost the rock-paper-scissors World Championship, held moments ago right there in the remote woods, drove it back to the ranch. Next, they found the truck with the flat tire and got it changed after unstrapping the dead body from the rollbar and wrapping him in a blanket in the bed. And cleaning the blood out of that interior.

They were all pretty grim by the time they arrived at the hospital. Things got worse.

The Humvee gunner was dead and the guy from the back of the gun truck had died, so that made three. The driver had a bad wound in her right elbow and was going to have to have surgery. She might never regain full use of the arm. The passenger was patched up and on his feet and ready to kick someone's ass for ambushing them.

"I'm going to go ahead with the Gold Run," Brennan said to Taylor when they arrived. "Let's rearrange personnel a little bit and you can take a truck and the shot-up truck back. And the bodies."

***

On the ride back, a furious, seething anger grew in Taylor. She had been betrayed. All of them had been. Dillon hadn't been her boyfriend or even a potential candidate. He had talked to her and mildly flirted, but that was a lot of guys. He was just some guy to her, personally, but he had been there from the early days and now he had betrayed them all. He had taken the food and shelter and security that Eric and Dani had freely offered him and this is how he had repaid them.

She was outraged. And she was going to do something about it. She was going to hunt the bastard down and kill him.

Her. Alone. She wasn't going to lead a SWAT team in. She was going to do it. She didn't know why it was so important that she do it alone, but it was.

It just was.

***

There was an investigation of sorts when Brennan got back from the Gold Run but there weren't any mysteries or revelations. It was pretty simple. Some scumbags from the 750 Group and Dillon had decided to murder their fellow MCC people in order to rob MCC of gold. There was no way to sugarcoat that, and no reason to.

As a matter of fact, the bodies were put on display and people were invited to view them, and the call went out for any information. That didn't really produce any actionable material. Apparently, the men had gotten word of a Gold Run, bailed out of their work details, and set up a poorly thought-out ambush.

There were some serious discussions with the influential 750 Group people and seven or eight men disappeared over the next few days. Not disappeared like into a shallow grave but decided that the best action for their continued existence on this earth was to go somewhere else.

Supposedly a couple of them had prison tattoos and weren't going to wait for the hot weather to come around and have someone see them when they wore short sleeves. Without the Internet and television, people talked. One of the favorite topics was Taylor the Ice Princess casually pulling her pistol and popping the guy with the prison tattoo in the head. Of course, all of the details were wrong but the basic fact was true. Actually, the rumor was less brutal than the truth. That was just backed up, if anyone needed proof, by her more recent execution of the wounded man in front of plenty of witnesses. If that scared off some bad seeds that was a good thing.

But there was no real information on where the killers had gone.

***

Effective immediately the Gold Runs were now exclusively done with armored Humvees, lots of them. The cost per convoy rose considerably but Eric and Dani weren't going to cheap out and lose people. Blood always weighs more than gold. They had the Humvees from the Louisiana National Guard now, equipped with grenade launchers and M2 .50 caliber machine guns, and they didn't let them sit idle.

And they started shipping the much bulkier Louisiana paper to Austin on the trains. Eric had three of them now, which sped up the transportation considerably. People didn't have to just sit and wait for the next train to come in. One was always in Dallas being loaded and one at the ranch dock being unloaded. The third might be on a run to Austin or Fort Cavazos or in transit. Supplies and equipment were coming in by the trainload, literally. They were short trains, admittedly. They didn't have enough engines to run long, heavy strings of cars that required multiple engines. But it made more sense to run shorter trains more often since the ability to load and unload them was limited.

Chapter 37

Sunday was a day of less work for Taylor. Not a day off. Days off really didn't happen very much. Dani went to church and Taylor usually went with her, although she wasn't Catholic. She really wasn't anything religious, although there had been some vague relationship to some Protestant church in her family history somewhere.

But this morning she begged off. As soon as Dani was out the door, she grabbed her gear and lit out. She had three stops to make, to check out a truck, grab a bit of ordnance, load up some food and water, and then she was on the road.

She had the keys to anything that was locked up. She'd unloaded all of her gear the previous night, made sure there were no markings on anything that could tie them to the ranch, and then repacked everything.

She left a note where Dani would see it as soon as she came in:

Dani,
I have something I have to do. Hopefully I'll be successful and be back in a few days. If not, then don't worry about it. I truly cannot express how much I appreciate everything you and Eric have done for me. I love you both more than I have ever loved anyone in the world. I wish both of you a long and happy life. Continue to save the world!
All my love!
Taylor

When she had written it the night before, she'd cried quietly.

***

Taylor's first stop was Atlanta, Texas, south of Texarkana. If the Boggy Creek place was around Texarkana somewhere, then she planned to make a ring around that city. If this didn't pan out, her next stop was Bradley, Arkansas and then north from there to Lewisville, Hope, and then maybe Mineral Springs.

Not quite to Atlanta, she spotted a place that looked like an inhabited public business, a convenience store. It was a no-name and included gas pumps, snacks and soft drinks, and a restaurant, fairly common for the area. She parked heading out and slung her rifle in the Professional Hunter mode. This is on the non-dominant side, muzzle down, and was developed by African hunters who want to walk with their rifle slung but ready to bring up to firing position in case they run up on dangerous game.

It is the fastest possible position to go from slung to ready. Assuming a right-handed person, the rifle will be on the left side. The left hand will hang naturally right beside and likely touch the handguard. To bring it into position, the hunter just grabs the stock, pulls it forward while rotating it, and drives it into the shoulder. Meanwhile, the right hand is going for the proper position on the buttstock or the pistol grip, depending on the rifle. That's all there is to it. Each hand only touches the rifle once and doesn't move or switch position again. It's surprisingly fast, especially for someone who's never seen it in action.

She opened the door and looked in, sweeping the room with her eyes, ready to bolt if needed. Five men, two at a table to the left, two at a table in the middle, including a policeman, and a guy in once-white cook's attire leaning on a counter. They all stopped talking and looked at her but it didn't look threatening. She took one step inside and looked at the cook.

"Do you have gasoline?" she asked.

"How are you paying?" he replied.

"I have Louisiana paper and a little bit of Texas metal."

"It's thirty dollars a gallon paper, twenty-six dollars coin."

She thought that was outrageous but she didn't have a lot of experience with buying gas. She was actually too young to have had a driver's license in the pre-Hexen world. Eric had been collecting tanker trucks full of gasoline and diesel for months and she'd never bought it before. She didn't really need it now, either, so she decided to pass.

"On another subject, I'm looking for a place where there was the Boggy Creek monster."

While she was talking, the policeman and his companion had stood and she saw that the cop just had the shirt, not the whole uniform. He had blue jeans on. Plus, he had long hair and a beard and just didn't look very clean or cop-ish. But she hesitated, and that almost ruined her. She let the cop get close enough to grab her arm.

"Now you just hold still, girl," he ordered. "Marc, get her other arm."

Oh, Hell, no! If he really was a cop he should have talked to her first and not just gone immediately to laying hands on her. This was wrong!

With her right arm in his grasp there was no reason to go to the rifle. Fortunately, she had her Glock in the five o'clock position, around behind her back. That meant that she could also reach it left-handed, and she was experienced in left-handed shooting.

She twisted to get her hand on the pistol. The rifle was in the way but she could get to it. The other guy, Marc, was one step away from trapping her left so she had to move now!

She swept her arm around, in tight to her body to keep the guy from making a grab for it, jammed it into the 'cop's' stomach, and pulled the trigger twice as fast as she could. He half-grunted-half-yelled "Oh, Jesus!", stepped back a couple of paces and fell, taking some chairs down with him when he went.

The other guy stopped, undecided if he should jump her or surrender or run. It didn't matter, although he didn't know that. Taylor was going to shoot him regardless of what he did. That decision had already been made by the time she drew her pistol. It just remained to be done, which she did before the fake cop had hit the floor. He was so close she didn't bother to aim, just swung the muzzle on him and started pulling the trigger.

She put six bullets into him as he tried to turn away, not really an effective tactic when you're getting shot. The sides and back are not much more bulletproof than the chest, maybe less so. He went down in a heap and Taylor sidestepped while she checked out the other men.

Eric had drilled into her "shoot, move, communicate, reload, seek cover, but never just stand there" so she did. The two men at the other table were up, one turning and running as fast as he could into the kitchen and presumably out the back door. The cook was also standing, looking openmouthed at the scene but not moving. He had been chatting with the patrons when she came in and so was on the dining room side of the counter and not behind it.

"FREEZE!" she yelled at them. "Don't fucking move if you don't want to get shot!"

They both raised their hands. While she had a second, she slapped the Glock down on the table in front of her and transitioned to her rifle, a much more powerful weapon.

That's when the other guy made his last mistake.

He had never seen someone bring a rifle up from the Professional Hunter position, so he had no idea how fast it was. When he saw her put her pistol down, he thought he had time to drop his arms and draw his own pistol.

Technically, he was correct.

He did manage to get it out of the holster but it was a long way from being on target and ready to fire when Taylor put a pair of three-round bursts into him. The good thing about the AR series of weapons is that the thumb naturally rests on or near the selector switch, depending on hand size. Taylor could go from Safe past Fire and on to Auto with no pause or hesitation.

She saw the guy go for his gun and she had plenty of time to sweep her rifle up and fire before she was in any real danger.

She was going to point the rifle at him anyway, but had had no intention of shooting him. If he was going to threaten her, though, then she was going to put him down.

She started shooting at his crotch, another recommendation from Eric, and let the recoil raise the muzzle so that the following shots stitched through his stomach and chest. He bent abruptly at the waist when the first bullets hit him and his face slammed into the table in front of him. The second burst of fire went over his head but he was done for. His knees bent and he hit the floor hard on his back, his pistol sliding across the linoleum tiles.

The cook dropped to his knees, wringing his hands, begging "Please, cher, please, cher, please, cher." That's pronounced 'sha', not like the singer Cher, and means 'dear' or 'sweetheart' in Cajun French.

She used her left to reholster her pistol and moved again, closer to the cook and the fake cop. That one was thrashing around slowly on the floor and moaning softly. She covered him with the muzzle but looked at the cook.

"Is he a cop?" she asked.

"No, no, he's my cousin, on my mother's side. He's just wearing the shirt to make things safer here."

"Safer? He was trying to fucking kidnap me! You call that safer?"

A spike of rage surged up in her and she saw red, thinking about this bastard kidnapping her. She pulled the trigger a couple of times, riddling the fake cop's body with nine or ten bullets. He immediately went still and limp. The cook crouched lower, almost going into a fetal position, and lost control of his bowels and bladder when she swung the rifle up to point at him.

"Now I'm going to ask you one more fucking time. Where is the Boggy Creek monster supposed to be?"

"Fouke, Arkansas. It's a half-hour east of here, maybe forty-five minutes. Up to Atlanta and then east on 249."

"Okay, second question. Did you see four men in a truck come by headed that way? Olive drab green, like the military. Had a rollbar all around the bed and lights on top."

"I didn't see them, no."

"Okay. I'm going to leave now. If anyone takes a shot at me as I drive away, I'm going to come back here and kill you and everyone else I find. Sometime. I'm not going to come back immediately. You'll never know when. You'll never see me coming."

"No, no, no one. No shooting."

She checked out the parking lot, took a quick look around the side of the building, then jumped in her truck and hauled ass, weaving down the road to make a harder target. If someone shot at her, they missed and she didn't hear the shot. She got the shakes, coming down from the adrenaline rush, but she drove okay. Eric had insisted that she learn to drive, and drive a stick shift, too, although this was an automatic.

***

She found 249 and then stopped to look at her map. That route was going to go into Interstate 49, which came out of Shreveport and may be clogged with a Jam. She figured out an alternate path on back roads which took her up north past Fouke and then south into it.

She hated that the cook knew where she was headed, but she wasn't going to shoot him just to keep him quiet. She would just have to watch her back and try to be quick about it. And never go through that place again. While she had the map out, she traced out a return route through McLeod, Kildare, Lodi, and Jefferson down to Marshall and she was good from there.

That was just stupid, she thought as she drove. *Pure, one hundred percent stupid. Why did they try to grab me? Because I was armed? Everybody's armed these days! Especially a female travelling alone! I wasn't doing anything wrong. If that dumb ass thought he could just lay hands on me... But he's not going to try to pull that shit again, now, is he?*

And that half-wit trying to draw on me. What did he think I was doing, surrendering? The only reason I was putting down my pistol was to transition to my rifle. Fuck him, too. Like an innocent girl can't walk into a restaurant without being attacked.

Chapter 38

That was the only place she had trouble. She had good experiences at other places, especially when they saw she wasn't begging and had actual Texas coin to spend. It took no time to tour the entire city of Fouke, current population about seventy, down from eight hundred sixty-seven pre-Hexen.

The big attraction was the Monster Mart, a convenience store which obviously played off of the Boggy Creek monster legend the same way there were tourist traps around Loch Ness and Roswell, New Mexico. A huge bigfoot-type head and arms surrounded the sign on the roof and there were smaller sculptures and paintings inside and outside, plus display cases with what were allegedly plaster casts of his footprints.

Taylor talked to people there and a couple of other places and said she was looking for a local boy, Dillon Bartow. At the first place, the woman asked her what the gun was for.

"Protection. It seems people keep trying to kidnap me."

"Well, you certainly are a pretty one, honey. Did this Dillon try to kidnap you?"

Taylor had a sudden thought and put on a sad face, looking down.

"No, he —" she hesitated and stroked her stomach once. "— left me." If she hadn't been wearing a hoodie and jacket, she could never have lied about being pregnant. Her stomach was way too flat to pull that off otherwise.

"Oh, honey!" the woman exclaimed. She blew out a breath. "Men!"

"He took off in a truck with some friends." Taylor described the truck and the men and the woman promised to ask around. Taylor flashed a handful of gold coins at her, $100 pieces, and said "I really need to find him."

"I'll get right on that. How can I let you know if I find anything?"

Taylor walked the aisles of the store until she found something that would work, a couple of rolls of red duct tape. She handed one to the woman. "Put a strip of this on the outside of the window. That way I can drive by and look. If I see tape, I'll come in and talk to you."

She paid for the other roll of tape and went on to the next person she could ask. The act about the pregnant young girl looking for the runaway father seemed to work like a charm. It gave her a legitimate excuse for asking about him and engendered sympathy and outrage that he would leave her. Plus, there was that reward in gold to think about.

After exhausting Fouke, there wasn't a lot more around. It was kind of in the middle of nowhere. She headed south, looking for any stores or churches or any inhabitants to ask and also for a place to spend the night. She found an abandoned house, pulled the truck in behind it, and slept curled up in the cab, in her clothes. She felt safer there than breaking into the house and sleeping in one of those musty beds.

The next day she headed north of Fouke until she got to a traffic jam, then backtracked and went east. Next it was south on 29, crossing over into Louisiana into the town of Plain Dealing, named after a plantation whose owner fancied himself to be a fair trader. Considering how much she had to pay for gas, she doubted that the tradition had continued.

The third day saw her back in Fouke and wondering if this was an idiotic quest when she saw the red tape.

The woman's eye lit up when she saw Taylor.

"I've got something for you, but how do I know you're going to give me my money?" Taylor gave her the big, innocent puppy eyes that usually worked so well. She pulled out a stack of Louisiana paper money and said "Hold onto this. If I find him based on your info, then I'll come back and take this back and give you the gold."

The woman looked at the cash, looked into the puppy dog eyes, sighed, and took the money. "Okay. Dillon's mother has an aunt. The aunt and her husband live here. That is, used to

231

live here. You know, Hexen. But Dillon and the family used to come here to the aunt and uncle's place for holidays and summer vacation and all, so that's how he's familiar with this place. They're from Little Rock or somewhere up around there. That's why I didn't recognize the last name."

"What's the aunt's name? Where is their place?"

"I happen to have a map." She held up a piece of paper, but wasn't offering it to Taylor. Taylor could take a hint. She came up with two $100 gold coins and placed them on the counter, with a finger on each, and slid them to the middle of the table. She kept her fingers on the coins. The woman put the paper down beside the coins and they made the exchange.

As Taylor drove off her heart was thumping.

Am I crazy? Should I just go back and let Eric know that I found them? Or would that give time for word to filter back to them, and then they'll bail out? People talk. That woman had to ask around to find out the information. That's going to get back to them, and soon.

Then she noticed a state trooper coming down the street and decided to turn at the first street and see what he did. She breathed a sigh of relief when he went straight, but she figured she might want to at least change the license plates. It might help to hide her if someone was looking for her to discuss that little disagreement a few days ago. There was no sense in not doing it. It's not like the plates meant anything now. The cops weren't going to call them in and find out she was running fake tags. There was no place to call in to, and no way to verify a tag.

***

She drove past the place on the map once and couldn't see much. There was a mailbox with the right number, a gate, and an overgrown driveway that disappeared into the trees. But those ruts through the weeds in the driveway told the story: there had been traffic through here. The next driveway, a quarter mile down the road, was overgrown and undisturbed. The one after that, even further down, had an open gate and cut grass. Someone was living there openly and aboveboard. She kept going a couple of miles and pulled into an overgrown dirt road, got off the road a ways, and stopped to eat lunch and plan.

She knew exactly what Eric would do: gather intelligence. Do a reconnaissance of the site, find out who's there and when, and evaluate the strengths and weaknesses of the place. She thought about everything she could and ended up taking a little nap. The sun coming in through the windows warmed up the cab and make things snug and comfortable. After a couple of hours had passed, she drove by the place again. If she had turned around and immediately gone by it again, that would have looked suspicious. With a two-hour gap, no one should notice and if they did, she had gone somewhere, done something, and was now returning. Innocent, innocent, innocent.

She figured the driveway wouldn't tell her anything she hadn't seen the first time so she checked out the driveways on the other side of the road. She would have really liked Google Earth about now to get an easy overhead view of things!

She went another couple of miles in the other direction, took a left, and went down there a ways until she found what looked like an abandoned house near the road. She called out and knocked on the door, standard procedure. Her truck had a small tool kit and she swapped license plates out with a pickup in the driveway. Since Arkansas only requires a plate on the back, she just pulled the front one off of her truck and discarded it. Then she sat and thought some more while she waited.

Four of them. One of me. What can I do to even those odds? I either need a force multiplier or I need to divide and conquer. She took inventory: *pistol, knife, AR rifle, the short barrel one with the suppressor, and the 6.5 Creedmoor Ruger American Predator bolt gun with suppressor. Also, four hand grenades and four flash bangs, although the grenades scare me. I can't throw them as far away from me as I want them to be when they go off. Camo gear and camo paint, so I can hide in the woods and surveil them. Binoculars. Tactical vest with a dozen magazines, full up except for the half mag I burned off shooting those assholes a few days ago. Two boxes of Creedmoor hundred and forty grain Hornady Black boat-tailed hollow points, forty rounds.*

She was up before dawn the next day and in the woods at the side of the road, right in a curve, all camoed up and face painted in greens and browns. She didn't know if the men she hunted were staying at the house or moving around. If they were moving, there were only two directions they could go and she was sitting on one of them. If she didn't see them, then she'd be on the other route this afternoon to try to catch them coming back.

She had a fifty-fifty chance and she guessed right, but the circumstances were against her. Headlights came down the road in the dark, too early for her to see who was in the truck. She had to put her head down and close her eyes to remain hidden and preserve her night vision. As soon as the truck went past, she popped her head up but she couldn't tell much about the occupants other than there appeared to be three of them. One was riding in the bed, head down and trying to grab a little bit more sleep. Where was the fourth?

But it was the MCC truck. No doubt about that, even though she couldn't really tell the color in the dark. The rollbar and the lights made a distinctive silhouette.

I'm all dressed up. Where can I go? She thought.

She walked back to her truck and drove past the driveway again, down to the next. The gate was padlocked and she didn't have bolt cutters. She debated crashing the gate and ended up leaving the truck where it was and jumping the gate. If anyone asked, she'd claim she was hunting to feed her starving kids.

God, I'm going to turn into such a liar! crossed her mind.

She slung the Ruger across her back, wanting it to be secure and not minding if it would be slow to bring into action. The AR was in her hands, and the tac vest was filled with magazines and grenades. The grenades were M67 fragmentation types, six and a half ounces of explosive Composition B, with a casualty radius of sixteen feet in every direction. The flash bangs were M84s. She was loaded for bear.

She made her way down the driveway for a while before she turned into the woods, jumped the fence, and was in Dillon's relative's property. She had no idea where to go but figured she would see something as big as a house before anyone saw her, and she did.

It was a nice house, a big white two story, almost an antebellum style but not that lavish. She smelled the smoke and edged around the house, keeping back in the woods until she could see the back yard and the figure working there. She watched through her binoculars as Dillon, with a lame leg, threw wood on a fire in a little makeshift smokehouse and boiled water to purify it on a grill. He could apparently only walk with the aid of a crutch but he could sit and feed both fires from a camp chair. The pots of water he boiled were small enough that he could handle them one-handed when he propped himself against a table.

He was wounded. Not badly, apparently, but enough that he was on maid duty.

He's smoking meat and purifying water while the others go off and what? Work normal jobs?

She wanted to draw down on him and get some answers but she held off her impatience. Instead, she pulled back, found her way back to her truck, and drove quietly off. She went back to the house where she'd swapped the license plates and thought about things.

Taking Dillon was no issue. She could have shot him earlier and he'd have never known what hit him. It was the others that were the problem. There were any number of points where she could ambush them but that was a risk. Not to her own safety so much, but risky that one or more would escape.

In the truck, they were in a steel and glass obstacle, which could deflect or even stop a bullet, and the truck was a quickly moving target. Obviously, she would aim for the driver first, but even if she scored and he crashed the truck, there was no guarantee that the others wouldn't bail out and escape. Suppose the truck veered off the road and went up into the woods? The two others could run in two different directions and she'd never track both down.

A close-up ambush was almost as bad. She could lock the gate with her own padlock and they would be stationary targets while they fumbled with it. But they would more than likely be on both sides of the truck, meaning that one or two of them would have cover from her fire. There was no guarantee that she'd win that gunfight.

She could take Dillon out and ambush them as they walked in the door. Unless they didn't all walk in the door at the same time. What if they all spread out and only one came into the house? That would leave two outside to run or attack her, now trapped in the house. Her AR was suppressed but it still made noise. It wasn't Hollywood-fake quiet.

How about in their sleep? She didn't even consider that one any further. Sneaking around in a dark, unfamiliar house was unappealing, plus it just came back to the same issue of not being able to quietly kill them one by one. Even the grenades tossed into bedrooms wouldn't guarantee kills. It could just leave armed, wounded and pissed-off men waiting for her to show her face in the door.

The other possibilities involved asking for help, either from the local authorities or from MCC. The ranch seemed a long way off and these guys might decide to bolt any minute, so she didn't really like that idea. And would the local authorities believe a fifteen-year-old girl who had been lying to people around town? And was carrying grenades and a suppressed automatic weapon? She'd probably be taken straight to jail.

And if she asked for help that meant that *she* hadn't fixed the problem.

Chapter 39

That afternoon she rode past the house and pulled into an overgrown driveway without a gate, a different one than before. She knocked on the door and stepped back, waited a while, and tried it again. Abandoned, just like she thought. She put the truck behind the house, geared up, and cautiously approached the road. She listened carefully and didn't hear any trucks coming, so she went for it. A quick sprint across the road, over the fence, and she was into the woods and hidden.

She was in the woods beside the house, watching through binoculars from a couple of hundred yards off when they got back that afternoon. They parked in front, got out, got their rifles out from behind the seat, and walked in the front door.

She started thinking about those hand grenades and a diversion.

She was in the other woods and watched the truck go by again with three guys in it the next morning, pretty much right on schedule. She lay there and ran through the plan in her mind one more time and decided to go with it. She walked back to her truck and started her operation.

With her truck hidden behind the house she'd used the previous afternoon; she walked out to the road. She'd left the bolt-action rifle but had everything else with her. It was still dark enough that she could see headlights coming long before they would spot her. The coast looked clear so she sprinted across the road, over the fence, and into the woods. She took a compass heading, just to be on the safe side. She intended to keep to deep woods and didn't want to get turned around. People tend to curve their paths towards their dominant hand if they lack landmarks.

Behind the house, she didn't see Dillon.

Damn it! The day I want him to hang out in the yard he's not in the yard!

She settled down to wait, making sure that her background did not silhouette her. If she tried to find him in the house that just gave him the opportunity to ambush her. She had to assume that he had a rifle and potentially a pistol. So, she waited.

It took a couple of hours but eventually he started making trips back and forth from the house to the yard, setting up to do laundry. Taylor briefly wondered where he got the water from. MCC had some guys that were manufacturing the old hand-pumps to retrofit on existing wells with dead electric pumps. But she needed to act so she dismissed it from her mind.

Dillon was involved in the washing now and making some amount of noise that should cover her approach. She moved slowly through the woods, shuffling her feet rather than stomping them down to keep from cracking any sticks. Once she was in the yard her movement was much faster and easier. She closed to about twenty feet and stopped. She thought about saying something but she was mad at him and didn't feel like thinking of anything clever. She used her left hand to tap on the handguard of her rifle. He idly looked over in her direction, then saw her and jumped back.

"Shit!" he cried in surprise, then lost his crutch and fell. "Shit!" he said again, in pain this time, grabbing his leg near the wound.

Instantly she was closer to him, but not so close he could grab her, rifle aimed at his chest.

"Don't move!"

He showed empty hands.

"Now slowly raise your shirt."

She saw no weapons.

"Taylor? I almost didn't recognize you with the camouflage paint."

"Shut up. Lie on your stomach and raise your shirt." Once he did that she knelt, put the muzzle of the suppressor against the back of his head, and frisked him. When she got near his crotch he said "I've always wanted you to do that."

"Shut. Up."

She checked around the other side and he said "I've always loved you."

She straightened up, took a step back, and then stepped forward with her combat boot swinging hard. It caught him in the side just below the ribs and he grunted and clutched his hands to the area, grimacing in pain.

"How many times do I have to tell you to shut up? Are you wounded in the leg there? Want me to kick that a few times?"

He looked disappointed and paled a bit at the thought of her kicking the wound.

"No. I'd rather you didn't."

"Do what I tell you, then. Now, is there anyone else in the house?"

"No. I imagine you saw the other guys leave."

"We've been watching you assholes for days."

"We? Where is we? I only see you."

"You don't need to know. How about guns? What guns are in the house?"

"My rifle is downstairs, near the back door."

"How about pistols?"

"There aren't any pistols in the house."

"Okay, here's how this is going to go. You are going to do what I tell you to do. You move any way that I don't like, I'm going to shoot you. Any way at all. I don't need an excuse. I don't need to justify my actions."

"That's the story of your life, isn't it, Little Miss Princess Taylor? You can do any damn thing you want to do. The rules don't apply to you. They never have in your life. Princess Taylor. You know that's what people call you behind your back, don't you?"

"Fuck you. I wouldn't be here at all if you bastards hadn't murdered good men and tried to rob us."

He looked down, seemingly ashamed.

"I got caught up in that. I didn't want to do it and then all of a sudden, I was in too deep. And it wasn't supposed to be like that. It wasn't my fault."

"You lying piece of shit! That wasn't a robbery. That was an ambush. You motherfuckers just started shooting people right off the bat! Just shut up. Just shut up. I'm not going to discuss it. Today is going to be real simple. I tell you to do something. You do it. Got that? Because I am going to hurt you, badly, if you try anything. If I'm feeling merciful. Otherwise, I'll just light you up. You feel like me shooting you a few times?"

She had moved around behind him and fired off another kick, this time to a kidney.

He grunted and rolled out of her kicking range.

"Get up. We're going to go into the house slowly so I can look around. Don't try to run. You won't make it. Hell, if you ran off and hid in a closet somewhere I could just burn the house down and shoot you when you come out. Don't try anything."

Taylor tossed the crutch to Dillon and watched him as he struggled to get up.

If she had looked up, she may have seen the face looking down on her from the upstairs window.

Chapter 40

Dillon walked into the kitchen and stopped. Taylor stood in the doorway with her foot against the door so no one could slam it into her. She moved cautiously, scanning 360 degrees, and saw the rifle leaning against the door trim.

"Put your crutch on the table and lean against that wall," she ordered.

That should slow him down if he tried to come after her. She used her left hand to put the rifle on the table and drop the magazine. The next part was harder. She set her rifle down, muzzle still pointed at Dillon, worked the bolt of the other rifle to eject any round in the chamber, and then pushed the pin to hinge the upper receiver away from the lower. Then she pulled the bolt out and dropped it into one of her cargo pockets. The rifle couldn't fire without that bolt. She did it all by feel while keeping an eye on Dillon.

The other thing she did was to adjust her sling so that she could drape it over her shoulder and have the rifle hang in firing position. She realized that she was going to have to hold the rifle on him all day long, and that was going to get tiring. Or maybe she could find somewhere to lock him up.

They went through the rest of the downstairs slowly and carefully and then started on the upstairs. Dillon walked into the first bedroom and moved across the room to a corner. Taylor followed, giving him credit for staying in front of her far enough that she didn't have to tell him to move. She didn't want him close enough to make a grab for her.

She stopped partway into the room and told him to open the closet. Then she heard and felt it behind her, a slap of bare feet on the wood flooring and a rush of air and movement as a big body hurtled towards her.

She got halfway turned around, swinging the muzzle up, when it slammed into her, carrying her inexorably the rest of the way across the room, to crash into the wall. If the initial collision hadn't knocked the breath out of her, then the impact with the wall completed the job. Her rifle was trapped between their bodies so she went for the Glock. A strong hand clamped down on her wrist and pushed down from a greater height, preventing her from drawing her pistol. She could have gone for it with her left but her back was pressed too tightly into the wall for her arm to fit.

Then the punches began. The first was the worst. It hit her directly in her left eye, and she took the full force of it. There was only a little sideways movement possible that would lessen the blow. Taylor felt like stars had exploded off of her from that hit. Two more followed while she reeled from that one. The one saving grace was that the guy was so close to her that he could only deliver short hooks without a lot of weight behind them.

She tucked her head tight in to the chest of her attacker, offering up the top of her head as a target to protect her more delicate face. She was just thankful that this person didn't have a knife.

Like she did, come to think of it.

The problem was, it was on her right side, right beside her pistol. She couldn't get to it.

Shit! The pocketknife is going to have to do.

Her knife, the one she couldn't get to, was a nice Fallkniven S1 with a five-inch blade. That was more of a fighting knife, and she carried a smaller lock blade for general utility use, a Kershaw Vapor II. This only had a three-and-a-half-inch blade, but half of it was serrated. She had this one clipped inside her left pocket and it had a thumb stud that allowed her to open it one-handed.

Except that you had to hold it in your right hand to use the thumb stud.

Shit! Shit! Shit!

She managed to get enough of a grip on the blade itself to get it partially swiveled out into position, enough that she could flick her wrist hard a couple of times and get the blade to snap open the rest of the way and lock in place. Now she could fight back.

Her main fear was that she was going to stab herself, so she brought the knife up to what she thought was the attacker's ribcage, did a small test stab and didn't feel any pain, and gave the knife a hard shove. It slipped between the ribs and into the body easily, surprisingly easily. But there was absolutely no reaction. The punches continued, one after another.

What the fuck? Taylor thought. *A knife between his ribs and he doesn't even twitch? Is he just stoned out of his mind?*

That's when she got scared, feeling like a glass of freezing cold water was being poured down her spine. And next she got mad. Her hand started running like a sewing machine on high speed, stabbing in again and again and again, all to no effect. She varied her target, still being careful not to plunge the knife into her own body.

It was a legitimate concern. Their bodies were crushed together and pushing against each other, trembling with the effort, jerking and twisting and moving as each sought a small advantage over the other. Targeting her attacker's body meant stabbing within inches of her own.

She jammed the knife into his kidney and twisted, the knife starting to slip in her grasp from blood on the smooth stainless steel handle. She righted her grip and drew long slashes down the man's back, from high on the left shoulder to low on the right hip, thinking that maybe surface slashes would hurt more than stabs and cause some reaction, cause him to back off some. She stabbed him in the buttocks.

But no. Nothing worked.

The punches continued to rain in on her head and she feared that she was going to lose this fight. None of the current punches were that bad but the cumulative effect would put her down if they didn't stop. She was starved for air with all of the effort she was expending and with the close conditions. And the guy stank. Not body odor, although there was that, but some harsh, acrid smell that she didn't recognize. The single word *drugs* darted through Taylor's consciousness.

She pushed off from the wall, using it for leverage to shove the man, and got him to back off a few inches. That gave her the opportunity to get a head butt in, but it was a weak one, and the guy was back on her in a second, pushing her back into the wall. At the last moment, she tried to slide off to the left. To the right was a corner and she really didn't want to be trapped there. The punches continued, one after another.

She slid the knife into his belly and pushed it, sawing through cloth and flesh and muscle and whatever was in the way. The something jerked her arm. She felt the strap of her rifle slip off of her shoulder and mentally shouted a loud NO!

Dillon had joined the fight and was trying to pull her rifle away from her. That would mean her death, probably after a gang-rape. More likely after a long series of gang rapes.

She stabbed the knife out blindly at Dillon, her head still tucked into the guy's chest for protection. She slashed a zigzag in the air blindly, just wanting him to back off more than anything. She did feel her knuckles brush his arm but didn't think the blade bit.

The sling was now just barely above her elbow. If she let go of her pistol to grab for the rifle, then the other guy could get her pistol. If she didn't, she could lose the rifle. Either way she'd die.

Desperate, she slid her left arm along the handguard and then down, trying to get the strap wrapped around it without slicing the strap. Success! Kind of. The sling now went from one elbow to the other, limiting her movement. But she was able to slash the knife around a bit and prevent Dillon from getting a hand on the rifle.

The punches continued, one after another, like clockwork. *Okay, one thing at a time.*

She shoved herself towards the corner deliberately. For one thing, that would put the man's body between her and

Dillon, shielding her from him. For another, it may be an unexpected move and may buy her some time.

It did. The guy managed to keep his hand clamped on her wrist so her pistol was still immobilized but he slipped in his own blood on the floor and one knee buckled. Taylor bent her own knee enough to stab the man's thigh like a maniac, five or six times in what seemed like a second, the razor-sharp blade plunging through denim and skin and muscle like it was all just air. She couldn't move her arm too much with the sling binding her, and that slowed her down but didn't affect whether the knife cut deeply or not.

It did, but the blood on the handle was making her fingers slide down towards the blade. She'd cut herself previously on the needlelike serrations and knew that they would lay her hand open to the bone if she allowed it to slide across them. Unless she could shift her grip and risk dropping the knife, she was going to have to stop using her one weapon.

Then Dillon was back, desperately jerking the rifle and shouting something. He could only use one hand and couldn't plant both feet and pull with all his weight and strength because he had to balance on the crutch. That was Taylor's salvation. She couldn't see out of her left eye, her head and face hurt, and those stars seemed to be spinning crazily around her head, making her dizzy. She was hot and panting for air. It was all just part of the chaos and madness of the moment.

Her attacker tried to take a shuffling step back, maybe feeling the knife for the first time, and Taylor finally had some room. Mere inches, but some room. She head-butted him once, then again, pain exploding in her own head each time. She felt her own knees wobble, almost spent, and would have fallen if she hadn't had the wall holding her up. She slid towards the other wall in the corner, but Dillon jerked the rifle again and pulled her back.

But the blows were hurting the man, too, and he drew back.

His hand came off of her wrist.

Off, and only a couple of inches away, and then he realized what that meant and tried to reverse direction, tried to get his hand back onto hers to prevent her from drawing her pistol.

Too late, motherfucker! flashed through Taylor's mind.

She brought the Glock up out of the holster, barely clearing it before she started firing. The barrel was aimed low, but the man's hand and legs were right in front of her and she kept pulling the trigger as fast as she could. Dillon got one last jerk in on the rifle, throwing a shot off to the side somewhere, but she wasn't aiming anyway at this point. This was just launching bullets in the general direction of the threat.

The big man turned and tried to run, his left hand shattered by a bullet and holes in his thigh and hip. That gave Taylor room to bring her pistol up in the usual two-handed grip, with the rifle dangling by its strap from her elbows, and get some more accurate fire in. As he turned, he sideswiped Dillon, knocking him off balance and sending him crashing to the floor. The big man only took a couple of steps further before he hit the floor too, slipping in his own blood. Taylor pumped bullets into his back as fast as she could pull the trigger until the slide locked back.

She had already dropped the knife when she put both hands on the pistol. Now she dropped the pistol, just opened her hands and let it fall, as she transitioned to her rifle. It took a second to get unwound from the strap, and then she had it up and firing, ripping bursts off into the big guy's back. He had stopped moving before she got the rifle into action but she was not going to take any chances at this point. She dumped half a magazine, twelve or fifteen rounds, into him before she made herself stop.

She swung the muzzle to cover Dillon, hesitated a second, then felt her knees give way. She fought it only enough to be graceful, to slide down the wall in a controlled manner rather than a crash to the floor. She sat there, gasping for air, but she couldn't rest just yet. She pulled a fresh magazine from a pouch and put it in her lap, then fired the rest of her current mag in an arc around her. She included the stairwell and the general direction of the other two or three bedrooms on this floor, shooting through the wall, then reloaded. White dust blossomed from the perforated drywall and drifted in the air.

Anyone else in the house should have gotten the message that she was still fighting and deadly and pissed off. Now she could rest a little. And breathe.

She looked over at Dillon, who was lying flat on the floor to stay out of the line of fire and watching her intently. She had to swivel her head around because she couldn't see out of her left eye now. She just sat there and took in deep breaths for a minute or two.

One thing she did was take a long look at the guy that had attacked her. He seemed a lot different now, crumpled on the floor with that rag-doll slump that the dead have. A few seconds ago, he'd seemed as big as a grizzly bear. Now, he was so much smaller and less intimidating. And that long hair...

"Who's this asshole?" she finally asked.

"Some girl that Mike picked up."

"*Girl?*" She almost choked on the word.

"And you just killed her. But then, that's what you do, isn't it?"

"Fuck you. That bitch jumped me. And you led me into that trap so you're on thin fucking ice, asshole."

"You're going to kill me anyway, aren't you?"

"Actually, I was thinking about taking you back to the ranch."

"Why? So Dani can shoot me? Or Brennan can hang me? All you women are psychos."

"What time do those assholes get back? What, are they working regular jobs somewhere?"

"Yeah. I couldn't get a job until my leg heals. They come back about four o'clock."

That fit in with what she had seen yesterday.

"I'm going to ask you one more time: is there anyone else in the house?"

"No."

"Let me tell you what's going to happen here. If you don't cooperate with me or if you lie to me again, then I've got a good six hours to play with you before I have to deal with your friends. When I say play, that means I'm going to think of ways to inflict pain on you. Did you hear the story about Dani running a cheese grater over the guy's dick? And then she cut the whole works off? Do they have a cheese grater in the kitchen here?"

Dillon turned pale.

"You want to talk about me being psycho? You haven't seen psycho yet, motherfucker. There are two hundred and six bones in the human body. How many of yours do you think I can break before you faint from the pain? How much of your skin can I strip off of your body — I'm talking about skinning you alive here — before you die from shock? You want to be a blind man? All that takes is two little stabs, but I would twist it for good measure." She scooped up her bloody knife and wiggled the tip around a little.

He swallowed hard.

Taylor realized she was sitting in a puddle of blood when her butt felt wet but thought the point was kind of moot since she had blood all over her anyway. She had put an awful lot of holes in the woman's body while they were right up against each other, and now gravity was draining the rest of the blood out onto the floor.

It didn't matter. She just sat there in the blood and rested for a good ten minutes before she forced herself up.

Chapter 41

The first stop was the back yard, the laundry, to get Dillon's clothes changed. He had been lying in the puddle — the *lake* — of blood, too, and Taylor had plans. She didn't need him in bloody clothes.

Once in clean clothing, she herded him around the house until he found some tools and a few other items. She had him nail two by fours across all of the doors upstairs, in case there was anyone still hiding up there. That may have been just paranoia on her part, but it's not really paranoia if people genuinely are out to get you. She also had him nail the front door shut from the inside, with two by fours at the top, bottom, and a couple in the middle. If there was only one board, someone could possibly crash into it hard enough to break it and get the thing to swing at least partially open.

The next project was to find a couple of cans that had held beans or peas or something and screw them to the porch bannisters. The house had a nice big front porch with steps leading up to it. At the top of the steps were two bannisters which anchored the railing around the porch. Anyone walking up the steps walked between the bannisters. She would load that trap later.

The last project was to string barbed wire on one side of the house. She wanted to close that side off as an escape route, so she had Dillon nail barbed wire that was in the barn to the side of the house and then across to tent stakes and chunks of firewood and whatever they could find. It didn't have to be taut. As a matter of fact, it would be a more effective trap if it was loose. That way, anyone running into it would tend to get tangled up in it. She also had him screw a can to that side of the house.

***

All the projects done, she walked Dillon into a bathroom and indicated the linen closet. "Get in. And don't bitch. It's just for fifteen minutes."

She closed the door on him and nailed a board across it. That gave her a little time for herself. She sat on the bed and cried quietly for a few minutes. Her face hurt and she had a headache and her butt was wet and itchy with blood and she hadn't showered in days and she wanted to go home.

When she felt better, she cleaned herself up as much as she could. There wasn't a whole lot she could do. She didn't have a change of clothes with her, and the left side of her face hurt so much she couldn't touch it to wash the camo paint off.

Dillon had been locked up for more like thirty minutes, but he kept his mouth shut about it. A lot of the fight had gone out of him, seeing her kill that girl.

They ate lunch in the back yard, her sitting on the steps and him on the ground out in the grass with his crutch out of reach. If he tried anything, either fleeing or coming at her, she would have plenty of time to shoot him at her leisure.

"I figured out how you knew where to find me," he said.

She didn't reply.

"I was talking to you and I mentioned the Boggy Creek monster."

Silence.

"I guess, looking at it now, that was a stupid thing to do."

"Yes. You were stupid. You were trying to chat me up and you told me about this place and then you committed murder and attempted theft and came right here to 'hide out'." She made air quotes when she said the last two words.

"I guess I should be flattered you remembered that. It was a couple months ago. I should be flattered you remember me at all. I mean, you're so beautiful and —"

"Oh, shut up! Just shut the fuck up! You're finished eating. Get in that little tool shed. Now!"

Dillon spent the next few hours in the toolshed, a little steel building with a low roof and no windows. Taylor put a screwdriver through the holes provided for a padlock to keep him in. That way she didn't have to stay on constant alert.

A little after two o'clock she let him out. She approached the shed quietly from the side, reached around to pull the screwdriver out, and then backed off quickly. If he had heard her movements and tried to jump her, he'd have been heading in the wrong direction. But there was no resistance, and he limped out on command and raised his shirt to prove he didn't have any weapons tucking into his pants.

She walked him around to the front of the house, where she had set out some items she had found inside: a bottle of Jack Daniel's and a variety of cold and headache medicine.

"You want me to overdose?" he asked. "That's how you're going to kill me?"

"Seriously? Do you really think I have a problem with shooting you? All I want to do is to knock you out for a few hours. If you overdose, then that's a risk I'm willing for you to take. The other option is for me to beat you on the head with that hammer until you're unconscious. Which one do you think you have a better chance of waking up from? Your choice."

He gave her a poor-little-me look and started in on the medications and Jack.

Chapter 42

The three men drove up in their stolen truck and saw Dillon sprawled in the yard, facedown at the bottom of the stairs. It looked like he had taken a tumble down them while drunk. The smell of alcohol and the bottle of Jack on its side may have made that impression.

"Look at this asshole spilling good whiskey!" The driver picked up the bottle and swigged from it.

"We going to carry him in?" came from one of the others.

"Fuck him. Let him sleep right where he is."

He walked up the steps and almost to the door, but turned when he heard some odd noises behind him — two thumps, two pops, and a rattle of something. There were two green balls rolling around on the porch towards him. When he had walked between the bannisters, he had pulled the fishing lines that had slid the M67 hand grenades out of the cans screwed to the bannisters.

The grenades already had the pins pulled, which actually takes a fair amount of effort, but the cans prevented the spoons from flying off to fire the fuses. When he hit the fishing lines, the grenades slid out onto the porch, the spoons flew off, and he had five seconds left. It took two of those to recognize the danger and start to react.

He leaped towards the door. It was such a tempting refuge, right there in front of him. His hand was already on the knob. All he had to do was turn it, jump inside, and slam the door. It might not protect him completely from the grenades, but it was better armor than his skin.

The knob turned and... the door didn't budge. His face banged into it and he wasted a second looking at it, as if that would tell him something. He twisted the knob as far over as it would go and rammed his shoulder into the wood.

Nothing.

He started to hit the door with his shoulder again but abandoned the effort halfway through, dropped the Jack Daniel's bottle, and turned to run.

Too late.

The two blasts went off almost simultaneously, riddling the guy on the porch with hot steel moving at high velocity, to say nothing of the effects of being within a couple of feet of most of a pound of high explosive. He was actually stepping over one grenade when it went off.

Then a flash-bang grenade came sailing out from the side of the house, followed quickly by a second at a different angle. These explode with an intensely bright flash, as bright as a million candles, and a hundred and seventy-five decibel or more boom. This is a sound that is way off of the charts. A loud rock concert may go a hundred and twenty decibels. Pain begins at about one twenty-five. Besides those two effects, the concussion leaves a person feeling as if they have been punched.

Taylor came out from around the side of the house, moving quickly but not running, rifle at the low ready position, scanning for targets. With her left eye swollen shut she had to turn her head more than usual to get the full picture and she had hearing protection on so her senses were limited.

The second guy had been on the steps when the blasts went off and the bannisters blocked the majority of the grenade fragments from him but not the concussion, and not the flash-bangs. As a matter of fact, the first flash-bang had almost hit him in the chest.

He was sitting on the ground, dazed. Except for the expression on his face, he looked like a guy at the beach, sitting with legs splayed out, leaning back with his arms out behind him to support his torso. Taylor stopped walking long enough to hammer two rounds into his chest. The bullets slammed their way through the man's body and then threw up gouts of dirt and grass when they plowed into the yard behind him. His elbows bent and he just laid back, the dazed expression on his face never changing a bit.

Taylor stepped forward and swung to the side to view the guy on the porch. He was face down, motionless, and leaking blood from multiple wounds. That would probably hold him for now.

Where's the third guy?! Is he on the other side of the truck, sneaking up on me?!

A flash of fear went through her body, like pouring a cold iced tea on her neck, enough so that it sloshed down both her front and back. She hated being blind in one eye and having her hearing dulled. She scanned all around her wildly for what seemed like a long time, but was really only a couple of seconds.

She almost reached up to dig the foam earplugs out when there was another explosion.

The third guy had run as soon as the first grenades went off, rounding the house and piling straight into the barbed wire. He had tripped on the ankle-height wire and gone down but bounced right back up and reversed course, seeing the barbed wire tangle blocking that route. He ripped his clothes and skin in multiple places but that didn't slow him at all.

The grenade he dislodged went off behind him just as he rounded the corner and caused him to duck but didn't do any damage that slowed him down.

When he saw Taylor, his eyes went wide and he tried to put on the brakes, slipping on the tall grass and going into a crouch to keep from falling down entirely. He had lost his rifle somewhere, probably tangled up in the barbed wire, and he threw both arms up in front of his face, palms out.

"Wait! Wait!"

Too late for that. He got the same double-tap in the chest that his friend had received. One of the bullets pretty much took off a thumb before impacting his chest. He went over on his side and curled up in a fetal position.

Taylor scanned all around, just paranoid that there may be someone else, but didn't see anyone. She put two bullets into the guy on the porch even though it was probably unnecessary.

Just to be on the safe side, she pulled out the hearing protection and moved into the woods at the side of the yard where she had a wide field of view. She could see almost all the way to the gate and both the front and side of the house. She reloaded and lay there for a while, not completely camouflaged but difficult to spot. Anyone coming to see what the noise was about would probably head straight to the front of the house and then focus on the bodies.

She would be able to engage them or fade back into the woods, whichever was appropriate, but no one seemed interested. She figured that the grenades and flash-bangs just sounded like some random gunshots at a distance. People in the country tended to ignore gunshots, even before the end of civilization. Maybe they'd text a neighbor to chat about what they were shooting at, but no one was very enthusiastic about investigating shots nowadays. It was much more likely that they would head to the house, put a rifle in their hands, sit behind some cover, like maybe a sandbagged position around a window, and scan the perimeter in case trouble was coming for them.

Her main problem was staying still. With an adrenaline dump like that, she could run around the yard in circles, like a dog having the zoomies, but she needed to stay still. Then the adrenaline faded out and she felt exhausted. She wanted to take a nap, but her face ached enough to keep her awake — unfortunately.

Chapter 43

With no one else to deal with, it was time to get back to work. She wished she could magically wake Dillon up and put him to work, but he might never regain consciousness up for all she knew. She also understood that some overdoses caused brain damage or made the kidneys shut down and bad things like that.

Well, he was going to die one way or the other, and soon. He had been correct when he said MCC would shoot or hang him if they got their hands on him. That meant there was no reason to bring him back alive. And there was no way she was going to try to tie him up and drive by herself. It was too risky and there was nothing to be gained from it.

She could just imagine him getting loose and jumping out, or worse, finding something like a tire tool to smash through the back window and into her head. Then she'd have to fight the truck to a stop while he was free to whale away on her head. Nope.

Not going to happen.

She looped a rope around his chest and then to the bumper of the truck and dragged him across the yard to a nearly tree with a convenient horizontal branch at the right height. She untied the rope from the bumper, threw it over the branch, tied it back to the bumper, and drove forward a few feet, hauling him up into the air.

I bet this exact limb had a kid's swing on it at one time, she thought. *Fifteen years ago, when Dillon was about five or six, he might have swung from this tree. But my face and head hurt way too much to think about the irony right now.*

She shouldered her rifle, switched it to single shot, and paused. She didn't want to consider the irony but she did have other thoughts flooding through her mind. And emotions. She thought it was like when you walked into the cosmetic department in Neimann Marcus, where the ladies were standing there with their perfumes, ready to spritz your wrist so you could smell the scent and buy, buy, buy. It seemed like each one was standing in her own little cloud of perfume. Only instead of perfumes, they were feelings, carried on a strong breeze that rushed up and engulfed her and then blew on past, making way for the next.

Anger: *You bastard, you murdered our people just for your own greed!*

Betrayal: *We took you in with open arms and this is how you repay us?*

Dread: *God, are all men like this? You lying bastard. And trying to make me feel guilty! That's just low.*

Disappointment: *I'm never going to have a boyfriend if they're all like that.*

Deeper disappointment: *As if anyone will have me anyway. They probably all* do *think I'm a psycho.*

Pride: *But I'm not! I'm defending our people and our way of life! I'm not killing people at random.*

Honesty: *But I do...* She paused. Paused for what seemed to be a long time, stopping the thought before she could complete it. And then she did complete it.

...enjoy it.

She heard the words as if whispered and carried on that same breeze that blew in the emotions. She turned her head fractionally, as if starting to scan the area for the person that had whispered the words, but stopped. She knew the words had come from inside her.

She realized she was breathing hard and her heart was racing.

I have to get back to business. She used that as an excuse to push that little voice back into its dark corner.

Business.

She placed a steadying hand on Dillon's leg for a moment to stop him from twisting in the wind and gazed up at him.

Alive, she thought. *Young. Healthy male, unless he'd overdosed. Strong. Proven dangerous. Right this second, I have the power of life and death over him. I can end his life with a press of my finger.*

…enjoy it.

She didn't realize it but her heart rate had gone up even from a few seconds ago and she was almost panting.

…enjoy it.

She licked her lips.

…enjoy it.

She gave a low moan as if a lover was working on just the right spot, doing just the right thing.

…enjoy it.

…enjoy it.

…enjoy it.

…enjoy it …enjoy it …enjoy it …enjoy it …enjoy it …enjoy it …enjoy it …enjoy it, enjoy it, enjoy it, enjoy, enjoy, enjoy, enjoy, enjoy, enjoy, enjoy, enjoy, joy, joy, joy, joy, joy, joy, joy.

Abruptly she swung the rifle up the rest of the way into position and fired a round into his temple. The bullet went all the way through his skull, carrying something with it that dropped off to the side. Something else hit her in the head, a drop of something wet. She didn't notice.

Blood poured out of the wrecked skull, a lot of blood. Taylor stepped back to get away from any splash, breathing heavily. She shivered and looked all around her, hoping that no one had seen her. She wasn't sure what had just happened but she didn't want any witnesses. Specifically, no witnesses to what she had felt, but that was silly, wasn't it? No one could witness that, could they?

She didn't even know what she had felt. It wasn't an orgasm. She had experienced those; self-induced ones, anyway. She shook her head to snap out of it. She still had work to do.

Business.

There would be plenty of time to think on the drive back. Maybe she could ask Dani about it.

She walked down the driveway, left the gate open, and walked to her truck hidden behind the house a half mile down the road. She drove back and got the truck under Dillon where she could lower him into the bed. She untied the rope from the bumper of the other truck and it got away from her, slipping through her fingers. Dillon's body fell down into the truck bed and his head hit the side with a loud bang that rattled the whole truck.

Oh, shit, I'll bet that hurt! she thought, then almost laughed at herself. *No. It didn't. It didn't hurt him a bit.*

She loaded the three other bodies into the truck the same laborious way. It was slow work jockeying the two trucks back and forth but she wasn't strong enough to just toss them up into the bed and she wanted to bring back proof. She wanted to bring back the truck they stole, too, but thought that towing it might be too much for her. She could just imagine the tow strap failing and the truck going out of control and rolling, spilling dead bodies all across the highway. She almost laughed at that, too.

Yeah, let's not do that. I have the directions how to get here if they want the truck back.

She didn't even think about how she had almost laughed. She really didn't even realize just how much she had changed from that innocent little girl less than a year ago.

Finished loading, she laid out a full set of clothing for herself on the passenger seat. It wasn't fresh, exactly. She'd worn it a couple of days ago, but it was dry. She made sure her rifle was easily accessible and set a couple of bottles of water and a bandanna nearby. Standing there in the yard, she stripped completely naked, grimaced at how freezing cold the water seemed to be when she wiped down with it, and then dressed. It wasn't a good bath but at least she was out of those pants and panties that were damp with that woman's blood. Truthfully, everything she had been wearing was damp and crusting up with her blood.

The truck had gas in it, she had a water bottle and beef jerky near at hand, she had a map, and she was ready to go home. Without really thinking about it, she stopped at the store in Fouke and walked in.

The woman that ran the place looked at her swollen and bruised and camo-streaked face and her jaw dropped.

"Oh, honey!" she cried. "Did he hit you?"

"We're good. Don't worry about it." She placed a stack of gold coins on the counter. "Keep that Louisiana paper money, too." She turned and walked out.

The woman followed Taylor out to the truck, offering to help, offering her a place to spend the night, trying to assist a young girl in need, until she glanced into the bed of the truck. Her mouth dropped open again and her expression froze as she started to back away.

Taylor waved and drove off. She didn't see it but a little tsunami of blood and other bodily fluids washed through the truck bed and spilled out the back, splashing onto the parking lot as the truck accelerated. The woman gagged at the sight and smell and turned her back on the vile mess. It didn't help. She started throwing up.

That was probably a mistake. If a cop happens along and she flags him down then he could theoretically catch up to me before I cross the state line. And some of them have CB radios working now. Taylor was heading south but now she made a loop to go north without passing by the woman's store again. *Now I just have to avoid that place in Texas.*

***

She had a couple of hours during the drive to think, and she did. The ranch was running and they were feeding people. That wasn't solely her responsibility, but she was a part of it, and she felt good about it. She was helping to rebuild civilization. How cool was that?

The banks were also up and running, and making money. Money was always good. As a former rich girl, she knew that instinctively. Even with the troubles, the attempted bank robbery and the ambush, they were a good thing. And maybe the fact that all of the bad guys in both of those incidents were dead would send the right message; that it was a bad idea for anyone to try that again.

The message that she had sent. Her. Alone. Maybe not entirely alone at the bank, but certainly in this case.

Don't mess with us. Don't mess with me. *Call me a princess, that's fine. This princess will kill you. I've written that in blood, in big, uppercase letters.*

Chapter 44

The security at the MCC roadblock spotted the truck's headlights from way off and went on alert. Sad to say, but every encounter with people in this post-Hexen world was potentially life-threatening.

The truck switched lights from bright to dim and then to parking lights and slowed as it drew closer, which was normal MCC courtesy to not blind the guys on guard duty. It wasn't one of their standard trucks but could be one of their stealths. The stealths looked just like they did whenever they acquired them. Their normal trucks were equipped with quiet mufflers, extra lights, roll bars, winches, and brush-buster bumpers.

One of the guards walked up to the driver's side and shined a flashlight in her face, an old Maglite that used an incandescent bulb and survived the EMP that fried all of the LED flashlights.

"Jesus, what happened to you?" he exclaimed when he saw her bruised and swollen face.

"Wow, you're a real charmer, aren't you? That's how you make a girl feel good about herself? I'm Taylor. You're one of the new guys that just came in, aren't you? I don't remember your name."

The guy stared at her, more surprised by her appearance that anything. And what in God's name was that smell?

"Tell them it's Taylor." She pointed at the other guards, tired of the guy just standing there, shining the flashlight in her face.

He turned and parroted "It's Taylor!" Then he swept his light across the bed, stepped in for a closer look, and jumped back.

"Aw, Jesus! Jesus!"

The other two guards ran up at full speed.

"Oh, my God, Taylor! Oh, my God! What happened? Are you okay? Where have you been?"

Tears suddenly came to her eyes. Actually, the injured one had been weeping all day. Tears came to the good one and she choked, trying not to break down all of the way into body-shaking boo-hoos.

She took a moment to calm herself.

"I just want to go home," she said softly.

Then one of them took a look in the bed of her truck.

"What the f-f-f...?" His voice trailed off and he looked at Taylor, wide eyed.

"Those are the guys that ambushed our gold convoy," she explained simply.

The guy looked at the passenger side of the cab, found it empty, and then looked down the road to see if there was another truck. There was nothing but empty road.

"And you hunted them down all by yourself?"

"You know, it probably wouldn't be the most courteous thing to drive this truck onto the ranch like this," Taylor mused. "Let me pull it over and one of you can give me a ride in. I'm sure Eric will want to come and see this."

The guards all helped her move her gear and the robbers' rifles into their truck.

"Be careful with that chest rig. There are hand grenades in it," she had advised. "I guess I should have taped the spoons when I headed back."

They treated her gear a lot more delicately after that. Like fine china. Fine china that could potentially kill you.

As the guard's truck drove off with Taylor and one of the guys, the new guy looked incredulously at the other, more experienced guard.

"What the hell, man? Who the hell is that girl? Who the *fuck* drives around with a truckload of dead bodies like this?"

He knew who Taylor was and he had heard stories about her but wrote them off as absolute bullshit told to the new guys. At the time, he had thought *Seriously, she's a hot young secretary. That's all. What does she do, spin around in a circle and — Shazam! — she's a Navy SEAL cold blooded killer ninja all of a sudden? Who dreams up these stupid stories?* He certainly didn't believe a word of them.

And then she drives up right in front of him, alone, wounded, streaks of camouflage paint still on her face, carrying hand grenades and a God damned arsenal, dried blood in her hair, with four shot-to-shit dead bodies in a puddle of congealed blood in the bed of her truck.

It didn't help that dragging the bodies to the tree had pulled their clothing off so they were all naked from the waist down.

The new guy was speechless. He couldn't process it. In his experience, even with his horizons expanded since Hexen, teenaged girls just didn't turn into lethal killers. Dani, yeah, but she was Hispanic. Not beautiful, long-legged blondes with big, innocent eyes. He could easily fantasize about Taylor, in a few years, in front of a camera with her clothes off. What he couldn't possibly imagine was her now, just as he had seen her minutes ago with his own eyes.

The veteran guard looked at the bodies one more time, then tapped on the side of the truck, deep in thought.

"On the one hand, when she's old enough I'd love to have a long session between the sheets with her, but the truth is I'd probably turn her down if she offered it to me. Any girl that does this to people — and this is not her first time… Man, what if you piss her off and you're asleep in her bed, next thing you know she's got you all tied up and she's cutting important parts of your anatomy off or something. Yeah, I don't think so. She scares the shit out of me. Her and Dani both. I don't mind admitting it."

He shook his head and moved away from the truck, away from the smell of blood and shit and unwashed bodies and punctured internal organs.

Chapter 45

That night when I got back from my little adventure, Dani and I sat and drank and cried for a long time. Mainly I was just so relieved to get back home, Taylor wrote.

Home.

That word means so much more to me now. I guess this is really the first place that I have ever appreciated as a home. It's strange to think that it took losing my parents and everything else and running for my life in order for me to find home. Eric says that sometimes blood isn't family and family isn't blood. I knew what he meant but I never really appreciated it until now.

Apparently, there were a lot of things I never appreciated until now. I've grown up a lot. Probably more than I ever would have if Hexen hadn't come.

Dani alternated between crying with me and bitching at me, which I fully deserved. I still can't explain why I just had to go on that little adventure all by myself. It was stupid. They were worried as hell about me and that is the part that I regret the most.

Actually, that's the only regret I have about that whole deal.

Eric wisely left us alone to cry and drink, other than getting Ms. Mitchell to look at my wounds. Really it all just amounted to a black eye and some bumps and bruises. Add 'holding an ice pack to my face' while all of that crying and drinking was going on. But the first thing I did was take a long, hot shower and try to get the matted blood out of my hair and the camo paint off of my face. After seeing my face in the mirror the first time, I tried to not look in the mirror again.

Yeah, I'm a real beauty queen now!

Oh, and Eric also drove out to the roadblock to look in the bed of the truck. He believed me but I asked him to go look. He showed some people the bodies that night. I don't know what happened to them after that. I'm sure Eric and the guys dumped them somewhere for the scavengers to have. There's no respect for criminals here, and there shouldn't be.

Twenty-two.

I'm fifteen years old and I've killed twenty-two people. Two women. Twenty men.

I don't know if that makes me good.

I don't know if that makes me bad.

I guess it means I've adapted to this world. But that doesn't answer the questions.

Maybe the fact that I'm asking the questions proves that I'm still sane.

Maybe it doesn't.

Epilogue

The next morning, Eric got a moment alone with Dani in a truck. He stopped short of their destination, just pulled over to the side of the road, and looked at her. He didn't need to say anything.

"Yeah, I've been thinking about it, too," she said, reading his mind.

"She did a hell of a job," he replied. "Tracked those guys down and took them all out."

After staring at him for a couple of seconds, she blurted out "You're proud of her."

He shrugged. "We trained her. We created her. Look, what would have happened at the bank, or if the bikers had caught us with our pants down? And this--"

"Yeah, what about this?"

"I would have preferred that she come to us if she had a clue where they were, and then we could have gone in there with a team. But she did it. She was successful."

"She's fifteen! She shouldn't be out hunting men down!"

"I know. You're right. Maybe she's done her thing, you know, scratched that itch. Had her high adventure."

Dani turned, stared out the windshield, and sighed loudly.

He figured that was the end of the discussion. As he pulled the truck back onto the road, he thought *Honestly, I think it's much more likely that she just got a taste. She's not done. That may be an itch that never goes away. And I don't know if there's anything we can do about it.*

To be continued ...

Hexen

When nine out of ten people in the world have died in a brutal plague, what do those who remain do to pick up the pieces? Does the creed, "Duty, Honor, Country" have a place any more if there's no country left?

On his way across the devastated remains of Texas, Marine Corps veteran and survivor Eric Marten rescues a young woman from a vicious attack by men who have turned into savages. As Dani slowly learns to trust him, they try to stay alive in the deathlands that America has become, using all their wits to survive a post-apocalyptic nightmare.

90% Death Rate: A Post Apocalyptic Thriller

Angel of Death: A Post Apocalyptic Thriller

<u>Join the Crew!</u>
Sign up for our newsletter for the latest news on new releases and more.

Follow our authors at their Amazon Pages!

J.F. Holmes (2 x Dragon Finalist)
Shane Gries (Dragon Finalist)
Lucas Marcum
Al Hagan
James Copley
Jason Kyle
G. Scott Huggins
Michael Morton
Charles Hackney
Jon LaForce
Jason Weiser
Kal Spriggs

More Books from Cannon Publishing

The Fae Wars

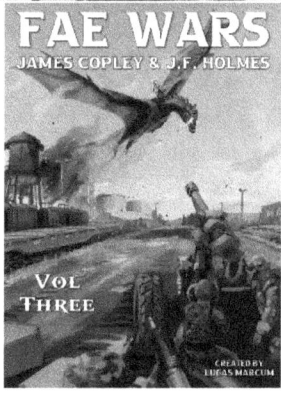

An ancient enemy invades Earth, returning to claim their home world. The men and women of the US Military find themselves matching technology against magic as cities burn and armies clash.

Onslaught
The Fall
Futures Past
Tales from the Occupation: A Fae Wars Anthology
Insurgent
Ghost

Irregular Scout Team One

In July of 2016 a plague swept the world, and the civilization collapsed and fell. For a lone National Guard sergeant, a veteran of the wars overseas who had settled down to a new life, the nightmare began on a hot summer evening at the barricades. Orders and chaos, gunfire and being overrun, his unit dwindles away in the face of the infected.

Months later, living in the ruins, the thud of helicopter rotors followed by a crash and the rescue of a downed pilot leads Sergeant First Class Nick Agostine back into the arms of the

US military. From his experience comes the idea of teams, military and civilians experienced in dealing with the undead and barbarism of the wilds. The first Irregular Scout Team leads the way for Task Force Liberty to advance down the Mohawk Valley in Upstate NY, making contact with survivors and clearing out the infected with stealth and firepower.

Volume 1
Volume 2
Volume 3: Civil War
Volume 4: Bad Company

The Line

When the world descends into chaos and anarchy with an unbelievably swift plague, turning victims into ravenous maniacs, the soldiers of America's storied 1st Infantry are asked to hold the line. From the brutal streets of urban combat to the bloodied, desperate defense on the plains of Kansas, they fight a war against an unrelenting enemy who used to be their fellow citizens.

As civilization falls, can they hold the line?

The Thin Dead Line

Dead Storm Rising
The Big Dead One

Fallen Empire

What's a soldier to do when the war is over? When he's only known conflict his whole life? Since time immemorial the solution has been to find another war, this time for pay. Whoever has the credits and wins the high bid gets the experienced fighter. Sometimes, though, the credits aren't enough to cover the price.

Empires rise, but Empires also fall. The Terran Union has spent five centuries under the control of the alien Grausians, like a barbarian tribe under the thumb of Rome. Now, after almost two decades of civil war and succession struggles, the formerly subject races have settled back in their ancient territories to lick their wounds and re-arm, leaving hundreds of settled planets to exist in a political vacuum.

Into that space steps the free companies, mercenary units that fight for gold, honor, power and glory. Veterans who can't get the wars out of their souls, new recruits looking for adventure, corporations with their own agenda.

Join us in a 27th Century that echoes history.

The Irish Brigade
Overrun
Silent Violence

Athenaeum, Inc

The Professor has problems, and not just what decades of soldiering did to his back and his knees. His boss just died, leaving him as CEO of the extremely discreet intelligence contractor Athenaeum, Incorporated. His old buddy the Operations Director is a highly skilled Army Ranger veteran but his finance chief is slightly unhinged and spends her money on highly inappropriate work outfits. The surviving old men on the Board of Directors are stuck in the 1970s. Running Athenaeum out of an old Cold War bunker and keeping their roster of experts together is expensive, but the government contracts are drying up or going to bigger, flashier corporate players.

Door Number Three
Doubling Down

Offworld

When nuclear war erupts on Earth, the American colony in the Alpha Centauri system is left stranded. As the new day dawns, a furious attack by the native inhabitants threatens to overwhelm the colony's defenses. It's left to the thin red line of the US Army's 9th Regiment to stem the tide and ensure humanity's survival in this harsh new world.

From two time Dragon Finalist and author of the best selling series "Irregular Scout Team One" and "Invasion" comes a new tale that tells of the struggle for survival on a brutal planet.

Offworld: Ragnarok
Offworld: Expeditions

Humanity engages in a desperate struggle with an alien species for this side of the Orion Arm. Space ships die in instantaneous bursts of light and turn into vapor, but on the ground Marines scream and lie wounded in the mud and blood, praying for the Valkyries to come save them.

They aren't wishing for death and a Nordic goddess to take them to Valhalla, the wounded are praying for the men and women of the '348th Field Hospital MEDEVAC to dive through fire and hell to come save them. Because they know that ...

Valkyries never die!

Valkyrie
Valkyrie: Rebellion
Valkyrie: Attrition

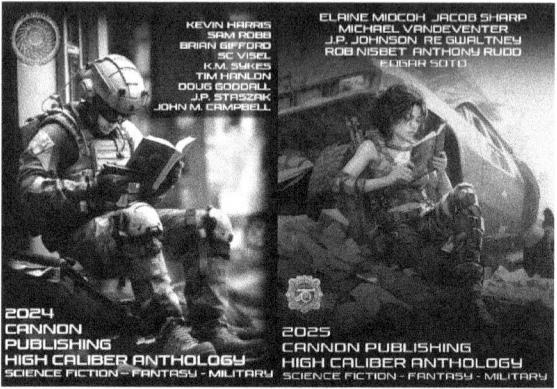

The Cannon High Caliber Awards are an annual contest for new writers. In it we ask them to submit a novella length story of Science Fiction, Military or Fantasy genre to challenge their skills.

2024
2025

The Wishkiller Saga

While on patrol Captain Aethal Paaling discovers evidence that an ancient terror has reached the rich soil of his home: the Lotus, a prolific growth whose addictive leaves devour their victims from within turning their hosts into horrible, terrifyingly violent mockeries of humanity. Created at the dawn of history by the twisted power of a godly relic called the Well, the return of the Lotus may be a harbinger of even more horrors to come.

Carrying the fatal news to the capital, Aethal discovers that even in the face of death itself, the Lords Paramount of Verlaen will fight to keep their secrets and their power. With only the guidance of his legendary Greater Rifle and the aid of the Pheonix Lancers, the soldier must find his way through the halls of a forgotten holy order and into deep dens of crime seeking answers.

He must find the truth as quickly as he can, because the Lotus may have already taken root among those he loves... and fighting it may cost him everything, including his soul.

A Cold and Mortal Spring

Hexen

When nine out of ten people in the world have died in a brutal plague, what do those who remain do to pick up the pieces? Does the creed, "Duty, Honor, Country" have a place any more if there's no country left?

On his way across the devastated remains of Texas, Marine Corps veteran and survivor Eric Marten rescues a young woman from a vicious attack by men who have turned into savages. As Dani slowly learns to trust him, they try to stay alive in the deathlands that America has become, using all their wits to survive a post-apocalyptic nightmare.

90% Death Rate: A Post Apocalyptic Thriller
Angel of Death: A Post Apocalyptic Thriller

Hell Train

A single train carries what might be the last vestige of civilization through a hellish nightmare.
A few hundred alive out of millions, lights going out all across what was once America as the possessed arose from the dead and murdered the living. A few hundred survivors travel across the country in an armored train, seeking some place to shelter in a fallen world. All that remains is a dystopian nightmare marked by rains of blood, impossible horrors, and portals to Hell opening in the skies.

US Army Captain Jack Zamora is responsible for their safety, a self-imposed burden that wears on him every day. Fighting off undead, protecting the survivors, keeping the train running and supplied as his team desperately plans their next moves. Starvation and disease threaten. but it gets worse, because the ancient gods have sent their emissaries, horrific beings of myth and legend that walk the Earth. Things that can drain a man's very life essence or even that of an entire city.

Hell Train: All Aboard

The Path

Sometimes a hero isn't what you expect, and the one you need comes from the castaways of society.

Nearly broken and at the end of his rope, former decorated scout pilot and prisoner of war, Red has finally accepted the inevitable. He and his kin have no future in the Human Confederation of Worlds, being gene mods and barely human themselves. With the help of his friend he flees Terra for adventure and fortune out in the reaches of the galaxy. Along the way he's dragged back into conflict that calls on all his piloting skills and he learns the deeper meaning of Kin, as his crew becomes his family.

Path to Freedom: The Path, Book One

Invasion

More than a decade after the Confederated Earth Forces were defeated, their commanding general, a boyhood protegee, lives in exile and disgrace. His life on an isolated farm is forever changed when two strangers show up at his homestead, and the war comes crashing back down on him. The problem though, remains the same. How do you fight an enemy that is technologically superior and holds the high ground?

Invasion: Resistance
Invasion: Day of Battle

Invasion: Total War

The military experience is timeless, and echoes down from our past and into our future. Along the way, not everything is as it seems. Thirteen stories from established and new writers in the field of Military Science Fiction and Military Fantasy bring you tales of the terrors of combat and the even greater fear of the unknown in Cannon Publishing's first Bi-Annual Military Anthology.

Fifteen classic Science Fiction stories from both masters of the craft and up and coming new writers!

A tyrannical United Nations pulls the strings of its colony worlds, ruling with an iron fist. Corporate interests take precedence, and brushfire rebellions smolder on the edges. One system, home to the only alien species yet discovered, with human allies throws off the yoke and calls itself Independence.

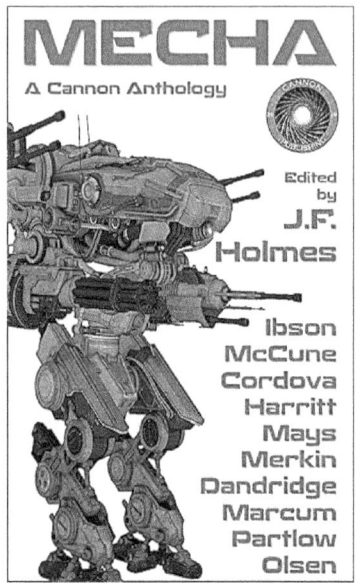

Feedback from the slight pressure of a hand closing sends a powerful mechanical arm smashing into an opponent. A neural link hurls blustering plasma fire from your suit's shoulder mounted cannon. Your reactor levels scream with overload as return fire smashes into your armor, and damage alarms wail while you hurl your twenty ton body sideways for cover.

You're a Mecha, a mechanical fighting machine with a human pilot. The guy that the infantry curse at in training and pray for in combat. The machine that the last hopes of your people ride on. The construct that strikes fear deep into alien hearts as they hear your turbines power up. The one able to pass through hell and come out the other side victorious, or die trying.

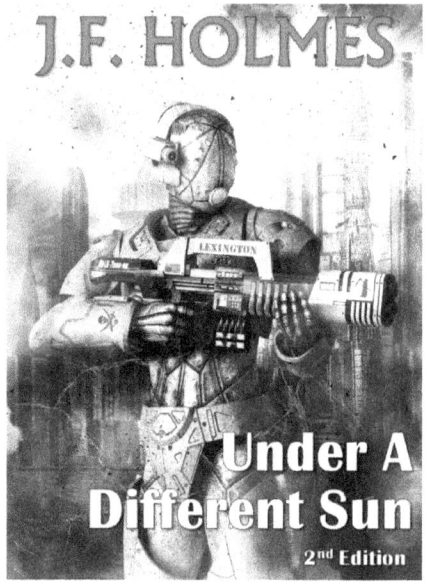

In the near future, massive empires rule the stars, and west of the Reach, they are battling for control of new systems. In the no-mans land between the front lines, Captain Nate Meric and the crew of the privateer Lexington fight for prize money, and loyalty to their ship and their friends. Beneath it all, though, runs a hidden dream. To see America restored, and take her rightful place among the stars.

Brian Corel, former slave, gladiator, ex-fiance to an Empress, exiled Captain of the Taland Royal Guard and now owner of the frigate *Widowmaker,* does the best he can to balance the lives of his crew with his own desire to live life as a free man.

Skirting the border between being a privateer and an outright pirate, Corel stumbles into a war with a religious cult intent on corrupting the kingdom of an old friend and has to set things right while grieving over his lost love. Along the way he signs a dragon into his crew and has to risk everything to rescue his brother from the grasp of a demon that has destroyed an entire continent.

There are some things a PhD doesn't prepare you for, like running two feet of steel through the guts of a flesh-eating monster straight out of a nightmare, while ducking razor sharp claws. Or having the sword critique your fighting style while you do it.

Dave Howard had a problem. Last week, he was out looking for a teaching job in the middle of a wrecked job market. This week he was neck deep in green blood and hellfire. Dragged into it by the very sword, his grandfathers' mysterious possessed blade, that was now walking him through hacking up a ghoul without getting his own head cut off. This wasn't exactly what he had gone to school for, and the University he had just taken a job with seemed to be anything BUT an academic institution. More like some kind of monster hunting bunch of weirdo nerds. Maybe his degree in Personality Psychology might be useful there, at least. The fighting though ... as he dodged another swipe of claws and awkwardly tried to follow the instructions the sword was screaming at him, he shot back at it, "Hell, I'm Canadian! Swordplay isn't in my cultural DNA!"

The legions are but a memory, the glory of Rome only a shadow of crumbling ruins and broken walls.

A darkening tide of barbarism was washing across Britain's shores and the lights of civilization were slowly flickering out into darkness, only kept burning by the legendary Red Dragons cavalry unit. Led by their Tribune, Arthur, who serves no kingdom but goes where the fight is hardest and most crucial, they wage desperate battles to keep back the tide. The Red Dragons ride the length of Britannia to fight the invading Saxons, Scoti and Picts, wherever they show, from across the seas or down from the Highlands.

At sixteen years old Peredur of Gwynedd has listened all his life to the stories of his father Pelinor fighting with Ambrosius Aurelianus. When word comes that his older brother has been slain in battle with the Saxons, his desire for revenge leads him to follow in his father's footsteps as a warrior, becoming a cavalryman with the Red Dragons. Along the way he may either find himself a warrior and leader worthy of Arthur or be left lying forgotten in the dust of history.

Two souls collide in the middle of a deadly war.

Sergeant Sylvie Lyons of Her Majesty's Royal Engineers wishes she'd listened to her grandda's advice and stayed away from the military.

USMC Sergeant Hondo Cassidy wants nothing more in life than being a Marine and fighting.

Hondo and Sylvie find themselves thrown together when his artillerymen are assigned to provide security for her engineers deep in the desert of Afghanistan.. Amidst death, destruction, cultural misunderstanding and the inevitable that happens when you mix an all male unit of Marines with an engineer unit that is mostly female, Sylvie and Hondo find in each other a reason to live.

That is, if they can survive.

www.ingramcontent.com/pod-product-compliance
Lightning Source LLC
Chambersburg PA
CBHW070919260626
47162CB00007B/2727